SHADOWS OF THE SKY

AN URBAN FANTASY MYSTERY

CECILIA DOMINIC

To everyone who made it through, especially those who are still struggling. May we all find our wings again.

Editing services by Evil Eye Editing

Cover by Best Page Forward

Ebook ISBN: 978-1-945074-67-7

Paperback ISBN: 978-1-945074-68-4

LOOK FOR THESE OTHER TITLES BY CECILIA DOMINIC:

Urban Fantasy Series:

The Lycanthropy Files
The Wolf's Shadow
Long Shadows
Blood's Shadow
A Million Shadows

The Fae Files
The Shadow Project
Shadows of the Heart
The Shadowed Path
Shadows of the Sky
Rising Shadows (autumn 2022)
Shadows of the Past (early 2023)

Dream Weavers & Truth Seekers
Perchance to Dream
Truth Seeker
Tangled Dreams

Web of Truth

Steampunk Series:

The Aether Psychics
Noble Secrets
Eros Element
Clockwork Phantom
Aether Spirit
Aether Rising

The Inspector Davidson Mysteries
The Art of Piracy
Mission: Nutcracker

$$1$$

REINE

"Incoming!"

The blackness that had replaced the gray stone walls of Lawrence's room at the Institute for Lycanthropic Reversal gradually brightened to a more traditional hospital setting. Lawrence's hand lay limp in my left hand, and Agent Micah held my right. Lawrence's head lolled to one side, and his skin had gone gray, but not the strong, vibrant gray of his gargoyle form.

Then his hand was yanked from me, and Agent Micah pulled me aside as a medical team in green scrubs pushed his hospital bed away.

The connection between me and Lawrence stretched to a tenuous thread, and had it not been for the agent's strong grip, I would have toppled to the ground. Maybe Agent Minerva had been right. Maybe if Lawrence died, I would, too, since we'd accidentally gone ahead and bonded ourselves. That's how it felt. Or maybe the giant, hollow ache in my chest reflected grief, despair, fear of impending death...

I had never feared death before, at least not my own. Nor of someone I loved.

Love. That was a word I hadn't expected to make myself susceptible to. I shook my head and silently scolded myself.

Pull it together, Reine. You are a Fae. You are a queen. And queens did what needed to be done. Like figure out...

"Where in Hades am I?" I asked Micah out loud. We stood in a windowless room, so I lacked external visual cues. I straightened my spine while seeking a connection with the earth for strength. And Fae, did I find it. A nice magical power source in the form of a crossing of at least two, if not three, ley lines lay under the hospital. The words of a powerful witch came back to me, of a web tightening around me, and I suppressed a shiver. I'd evaded the trap my mother set for me. While I had no doubt she'd come after me again to challenge my rule, I thought I'd weakened her enough she'd have to go recharge somewhere else for a while.

But I'd made the mistake of underestimating an enemy before.

Micah stepped back but held on to my upper arms. "We're in Aerie Hospital."

That made sense, but more questions popped into my head. This close, I could see his resemblance to Lawrence. Was it because they were both gargoyles...or could Micah and Minerva be related to him? But he didn't think he had any family aside from his mother, who'd retreated to The Aerie, the gargoyle enclave that sounded more like a village than a modern medical center.

Apparently satisfied that I wouldn't end up on the floor, Micah nodded and released me. Then he gestured for me to follow him. We walked out of an empty room with cream-colored walls and into an ICU with a large nurse's station in the middle and glassed-in rooms with medical equipment. Only a few of the beds had occupants.

"We don't get sick much," Micah explained. In spite of his hushed tones, a nurse at the station glared at him and put a finger to her lips. He shrugged, mouthing, "Sorry." She blushed and smiled, then made shooing motions with her hands.

We walked out of the ward and into a corridor. Large windows showed me the curves of mountains with a mix of pine and hardwood trees. I continued to accompany Micah, although I wanted to follow the quivering, invisible thread that tied me to Lawrence. I pressed a hand to my chest, sending him whatever strength I could, which wasn't much. My ears rang, and I had to concentrate on not wobbling as I walked, like I had mild vertigo. It wasn't normal for a Fae to be yanked from one place to another...and I still didn't know how far I'd come.

Micah stopped in front of an elevator and pressed the down button. Good, I'd be closer to the earth and better able to recover...and help Lawrence.

"And where is Aerie Hospital? Is it attached to The Aerie?"

Micah jerked a thumb toward the left. "Yes, the town is just a couple of miles away."

"Great. I'm a medical doctor, by the way. Maybe I can help."

Minerva joined us, and her scowl deepened, if that was possible. "Because you were doing a bang-up job back in Scotland. Doctor Gordon almost died."

Hope lifted my heart above responding to her insult. "Almost? You mean he's okay?"

She snorted. "I wouldn't say okay, but he's improving. Doctor Lucia is treating him personally."

"And Doctor Lucia has experience with—?" I gestured to the two of them.

"Yes, he does," Minerva snapped. "And things are complicated here, so don't say anything else. We need to debrief you before you can ask anything that will get us—or you—in trouble."

Intriguing. I nodded, and the elevator doors opened with a ding. Micah mashed the button for the lowest floor, charmingly labeled, *T-Terrace*.

When the doors opened, the heavenly scents of butter, cinnamon, and coffee assaulted my nose, and I almost fainted from hunger right there. That's not an exaggeration—I stumbled, and Micah caught me.

"Get it some food." Minerva took my arm from him and led me to a small office. I sensed we'd gone underground, to a level of the hospital surrounded by granite and—to my surprise—obsidian. Where were we?

"I'm not an *it*," I complained, but I sank into the chair she led me to. At least she hadn't referred to me as a creature. "And how did we get here? I'm not used to traveling like that. Wait." My brain began to catch up with my circumstances. "You shouldn't be able to do that, to bring four supernatural beings plus hospital equipment to a different place...how far away?" Now that we sat underground, I sensed a nearness to a place I'd been recently, which meant somewhere in the Southeastern United States. All right, that fit the trees. They'd taken us to somewhere in the Appalachians, then. I hoped Sir Raleigh would follow soon.

"A few thousand miles." Minerva sat behind the desk and regarded me with her stony, cold, gray eyes. Her dark hair, dusky skin, and the shape of her face definitely showed her resemblance to the other gargoyles I'd met, except in her, their chiseled features translated to high cheekbones and strong shape. Not beautiful, exactly, but striking if she didn't look like she hated me and everything I stood for. Which, from what I knew of gargoyle and Fae history, was likely.

"Are you part of the Truth Seekers?" I hated bringing up Merlin's vigilante "law-enforcement" agency, but I could see him lending them the transportation spell.

Another snort. "No. We don't deal with them."

Micah pushed through the door, paper coffee cup held in each hand and the folded top of a paper bag in his teeth. He handed Minerva one cup and me the other. I sniffed—black tea. He gave me the bag, and I opened it to find a chocolate croissant.

"Thank you." I tore into the pastry. Perfectly buttery and flaky, and not at all what I expected for hospital food. "Where did you get this?" I asked, and I am not ashamed to say I licked my fingers so I didn't miss a single crumb.

Micah smiled. "The hospital has a coffee shop and bakery. They treat their staff well."

"All right, thank you. Could you please tell me how I just traveled from Scotland to the US and what in Hades is going on?"

Micah and Minerva exchanged glances, and I sensed rather than heard the whisper of the silent communication between close siblings, possibly even twins. They didn't know how much to tell me. While they had taken care of me, they had no reason to trust me. I decided to try again.

"Really, I want to help. Yes, I'm bonded to Law—Doctor Gordon. I'm also a medical doctor, and while I admit I don't have much experience in gargoyle medicine, I have treated all kinds of magical creatures at this point. I'm sure I could learn quickly, and I can monitor him through our bond."

They both regarded me with an almost condescending amusement for a moment longer than was necessary, and then Minerva informed me, "And I'm in command of the security forces of the Aerie, which means I outrank you, Fae. We haven't decided how much to trust you. You'll have to talk to Mum for that." Her phone buzzed, and she picked it up. "Ah, she's here now."

MICAH AND MINERVA brought me out of the office and to a conference room, where two striking people stood embroiled in an intense conversation about Lawrence and the best options.

The woman appeared to be in her fifties, but I sensed she had more like five or so centuries behind her. She stood with hands on hips and chin up—a pose of authority. She wanted him moved to her house. I both liked her and immediately distrusted her, and the conflicting instincts intrigued me. Her energy said gargoyle, and the passion with which she argued, plus her features and magical signature, told me who she was —Lawrence's mother.

Wait—Minerva had referred to her as "mother." Lawrence had siblings he didn't know about? But how? Why hadn't his mother told him?

I could figure that out later. I needed to attend to what was happening.

The other person, a handsome man in a white lab coat, argued against allowing Lawrence to leave the hospital, citing the uniqueness of the case. He fiddled with his badge pull around his neck that displayed his hospital ID—scowling picture and all. His short, dark-brown hair curled at his temples with sweat, and a dark fringe of lashes ringed his eyes. Stubble stood out against his jaw, and he spoke with a lilting accent. Italian. In him, I sensed stubbornness, the need for justice and fairness, and the same desire I had—to heal the world, no matter the creature. Again, conflicting impulses—to like him and be wary of him—hit me. He didn't have a shifter aura. In fact, his aura was so skillfully hidden, I couldn't tell what he was. A powerful wizard, perhaps?

The Aerie was to be a place of contradictions, mysteries, and powerful beings, it seemed.

It was too late to hide who I was from Micah and Minerva, but I quickly glamoured myself so I'd appear to be a young woman, late twenties to early thirties with white blonde hair and totally normal ears. The ID in my wallet, which thankfully had come with me in my handbag along with my phone and keys, said I was named Renee River, and if someone searched for me, they'd find I had an appointment as a physician specializing in rare disorders at a small hospital in Scotland.

When my glamour took hold, the man stopped and turned toward me with a frown. He rubbed his left ear. Definitely some talent there, and it was time to turn on the charm.

The woman followed his gaze, and her scowl mirrored Minerva's. Yes, relation confirmed.

"Is this *her*?" she asked in the same tone one would inquire about a turd found in the refrigerator.

"Yes, ma'am." Minerva sounded meeker than I thought possible.

Lawrence's mum studied me for a full minute. I refused to be intimidated, and so I regarded her in turn. Finally, she told me, "I am Agnes Gordon, Regent of the Gargoyle Clan."

I attempted to keep my surprise from showing. Lawrence was a prince, or at least the equivalent? Whereas in many cases, it could have made our situation easier, this bit of knowledge introduced a whole new set of complications.

The man cleared his throat and smiled at me. I felt his charm switch on, and I grinned back, relieved that at least someone would be friendly. Maybe. Or maybe it would be better to face open hostility than hidden enmity. I decided I'd enjoy his deceptive warmth, but I wouldn't fall for it.

"I am Doctor Barton Lucia." He didn't extend his hand. Ah, he *was* accustomed to dealing with magical beings.

"Doctor Renee River." Then, because the question kept burning in my mind, I added, "Is Lawrence all right?"

The Regent answered. "You don't have to tell her anything. She's not family. She doesn't have any right to know about his condition."

He spoke patiently, but an edge of exasperation came through. "No, but perhaps she can enlighten me as to how it developed, which will help me treat him."

Touché. In spite of myself, I liked Doctor Barton Lucia more with every second.

Agnes returned to speaking around me. "What do you know of her, Minerva? Is she trustworthy?"

"I am still gathering data. She's a legit doctor. Max Fortuna vouches for her, as does the former Lycanthrope Council Investigator, Gabriel McCord."

Agnes didn't soften, but she did regard me with a little more respect in spite of saying, "Friends in low places, I see. Fine, you can help with Lawrence's case, but you are not to reveal who—or what—you are to anyone outside this room."

Barton Lucia looked between the two of us. "And who, or what, is she?"

Agnes wrinkled her nose. "She's a Fae. Can't you tell?"

He crossed his arms and cocked his head. "Her glamour is compelling. She shouldn't have any trouble hiding who she is."

I sensed a partial truth in his words, but I smiled. "Thank you, Regent Gordon." I declined to tell her about my own royal lineage or title. There was no point getting into a pissing contest with her, and I could always invoke my Fae queen rank later if needed.

"Come, let's grab some coffee, and you can tell me how Doctor Gordon ended up in his current condition." Barton spread his hands. "Within what you're able, of course. I won't pry into your personal business."

At least someone here had some respect.

"Good." Agnes nodded like she'd arranged everything, not him. "I'm going to go see my son. You said that will be all right, Doctor Lucia?"

"Yes, just don't try to wake him. He'll come out of it when he's ready. I'm going to discuss the next steps with Doctor River."

Agnes swept out of the room with Micah and Minerva, leaving me with Doctor Lucia.

"I'll have my assistant bring some coffee. How do you take yours?"

I recognized the old dance, and I almost sagged with gratitude for someone following protocol. I held up my cup. "That's not necessary, but thank you. I'm fine with my tea, and I acknowledge your keeping with the accords of hospitality toward Fae." An old-fashioned gentleman would be more difficult to keep my guard up around, and I sensed I'd enjoy the challenge until he got comfortable, crossed one ankle over his other knee, and asked his first question.

"You're welcome. All right, then. Please tell me how a gargoyle ended up with Fae Fire poisoning."

2

LAWRENCE

My hospital bed rocked like it had been tossed by waves. The darkness that had enveloped me in its crushing grip and clogged my lungs loosened, and pure air flowed into my nostrils. I attempted to open my mouth, seeking more, but something held it closed. I sucked in oxygen through pursed lips, and a hand rested on my chest, guiding the pace of my respiration.

A soft male voice, Italian in lilt, said, "There you go. Slow and easy. This medicine's going to save you, but you can't have it all at once. It'll freeze your lungs."

Freeze my lungs? How did that work? I didn't know of anything that would cause the chilly sensation that outlined each of the branches in my lungs in icy blue. But as painful as it was, it helped each breath come easier until blackness closed over me.

The next time I woke, I found myself in a different hospital room from the one I'd gone to sleep in. Whereas the healing ward of the Institute for Lycanthropic Reversal had a medieval castle vibe, this one shone clean and modern. My window overlooked a cloudy sky with the tops of old mountains in the near distance. A lump that pinned the sheets down between my legs stirred, and I found the strength to lift my head and look into the green eyes of Sir Raleigh, Reine's grimalkin guardian and guide. A smile made the cracks in my parched lips sting, but I couldn't resist saying, "Raleigh, I don't think we're in Kansas anymore. Or Scotland, for that matter."

He stretched and arched his back like he was a normal cat, but he didn't deign to say anything to me. He spoke to me rarely, and only in the most important of circumstances. Right, no help from the cat, then.

I recalled the person who had spoken to me during my treatment. Italian, maybe? I knew I'd been out of it, but I thought I'd remember an hours-long journey by plane or boat or train or...

"How the hell did we get here?" I opened my eyes. Huh, I guess I'd fallen asleep again. This time there was no sign of the cat. The next hour—my best guess of the amount of time passing—involved me struggling to stay awake. Every time I thought I had achieved a consciousness that would last more than a minute, the rhythmic beeping of the heart monitor would put me to sleep. At one point, I dreamed of a voice, old like rock worn down to its essence, saying something like, "I have done what you wish. Now I want her."

"Apparently they're bonded," another voice, one from my past replied. "I cannot promise anything that will hurt my son."

"Leave that to me. In fact, I can take care of two problems at once." Cackling laughter.

Could Reine be in danger? Although I couldn't leave the bed, much less change, my inner gargoyle stirred and lashed his tail, and I finally found the strength to force my eyes open.

No sign of Sir Raleigh, the cat-shaped grimalkin, but he could be hiding. And only one person stood in the room, at least that I could see from my limited range of vision.

"Mother?"

She walked to the side of the bed and squeezed my hand. "Yes, Lawrence. How are you feeling?" Her northern English accent had faded to a trace, but her voice sounded the same. She definitely looked older than the last time I'd seen her, and she'd cut her long hair so it framed her face in dark parentheses threaded with white. A jeweled pin sat at the throat of her white blouse, and her dark suit had obviously been tailored. Most odd of all, since my father had never given her one—she now wore a wedding ring.

"Confused," I answered honestly. "Where am I?"

"You're in the hospital in The Aerie. We have world-class care here now so no one has to be hurt for longer than necessary."

"The Aerie... So I'm in Georgia?" I recalled the legends that the gargoyles had fled with the Scottish and Irish migration to the States and settled in the Southeast.

"Yes, dear. You didn't realize you were so close to home, did you?" Her question conveyed hope. Did she think I'd stay?

Whereas Reine had been desperate to join her kind, I hadn't been as enthused to find mine, not until I'd figured out and taken my revenge on the Fae who had killed my father. And when the trail had gone cold, I'd settled into my existence in Atlanta. I had faith that Fate would bring me face-to-face with his killer, and while that had happened, it hadn't gone the way I expected.

Plus, my mother hadn't exactly reached out to me, either.

"Lawrence?" My mother's voice brought me back to the situation at hand.

"Sorry, whatever drugs they gave me are making my mind slippy. What happened? How did I get here?"

"I have someone I want you to meet. Two someones. That will help clarify things."

She turned and gestured to whoever waited outside the room. Two gargoyles in human form walked in. One, a young man about my height, grinned at me. The other, a young woman who looked like my mother had in her youth, regarded me warily.

"Lawrence, meet Micah and Minerva, your younger brother and sister."

"Half-brother and sister," Minerva clarified. "Obviously."

"Right, obviously. They didn't have sperm-saving technology when my father was killed." I looked to my mother for explanation. Was this why she'd never contacted me to let me know where she was? She had started a new family with a new man? But then, where was he?

"I know it's a shock, but I couldn't keep them from you. They're the ones who brought you here. Brought you home."

There was that word again, home. I wanted to quote a movie line about it not meaning what she thought it meant, but did they have movies in The Aerie? They must.

"And your husband, their father?" My anger surprised me. She'd been—still was—an attractive woman. Why shouldn't she have sought out and found love again?

Minerva answered. "He died about twenty years ago. Before we built this." She motioned to our surroundings.

"He was half-human," my mother explained. "The doctors didn't know how to treat his injuries, so now we have a place for gargoyles with doctors who specialize in what can go wrong with us."

"So we're out, then? People know about us?" That didn't sit right, either. What sort of authority did she wield to go around the fundamental rule of paranormal creatures? And how had I not heard anything? It seemed that someone at the CPDC would have been alerted.

"Oh, no," Micah finally spoke. "They're gargoyle doctors, except for Barton Lucia, who is descended from the Benandanti and didn't find the legends weird."

"It's a way to keep them here," my mother explained. "Rather than running off and starting lives elsewhere."

I was starting to get an idea where Minerva's sour attitude came from. I'd chafe under the pressure to remain close to home. In fact, I did resent it, and the hospital felt more like a prison with each moment.

I yawned, and my eyelids grew heavy. "I'm tired. Can we talk later?" Why wasn't a nurse chasing them out?

In fact, one did come in and gently told them that the doctors didn't want me talking to anyone for more than ten minutes, at least not now. She treated my mother with deference, and said, "You can come back this afternoon, Regent."

"What?" That woke me up. "You're the gargoyle regent?"

She kissed me on my forehead. "We can talk more later. Get some sleep. Now, Minerva, where did you leave that Fae?"

That Fae could only mean Reine, but sleep overtook me before I could ask.

3

REINE

"Excuse me?" I asked. "Fae Fire poisoning? That's not possible. At least, that's not what happened."

"And what did happen?" Barton raised an eyebrow.

Drat, rookie mistake. He knew a Fae couldn't lie, and fatigue kept me from making the effort to twist the truth, so I gave him the basics. "He spent too long in Faerie, and then he got caught in the middle of a Fae battle. There was no Fae fire, though."

"His lungs were in poor shape. I had to use a *cryo fidelis* spell to start repairing them."

I recoiled internally. "You did *what*? What were you thinking? You could have killed him." A movement in the corner of my eye caught my attention—a gray tail disappearing under the table. Good, Sir Raleigh had found us.

"Please, Doctor River, calm down." He used the tone men have employed on hysterical women from time immemorial. It worked as well as it usually does, too.

I barely kept myself from giving *him* a dose of Fae fire. "Did he consent to it?"

"No, he was unconscious. Please believe it was a last-ditch

effort." He stood, and, placing a hand on my shoulder, looked deep into my eyes with his thickly lashed hazel ones. "We were losing him, Renee."

That threw cold water on my ire, and I took a deep, shuddering breath. "I see. How did it work?"

He had the grace not to gloat, but he did allow some smugness through. "He's now off oxygen, but he's exhausted and deconditioned. What was he doing in Faerie?"

I sank back in the chair, the weight of almost losing Lawrence a numbing heaviness in my chest. "Walking the Shadowed Path to protect his friend and his friend's daughter." I shook my head. "It's way too complicated to go into now."

Sir Raleigh jumped onto my lap, and I rubbed his soft ears. His purr rumbled through me.

Now Lucia leaned back, his face a mask of disgust. "Is that a...cat? How did it get in here? Wait." He narrowed his eyes at Sir Raleigh. "That's not a normal feline, is it?"

Barton Lucia seemed to have some knowledge of paranormal things, and the longer I spent with him, the more of a sense I got of his heritage. Not just wizard, but Benandanti, the cursed order of monks. Interesting. He must have been a descendant or something.

"It's a grimalkin. He only looks like a cat."

"You're just full of surprises, aren't you?" He held out a hand, and Raleigh sniffed it, then hesitated and turned his back on Barton. "I don't think he likes me."

"After that welcome, I wouldn't be surprised. But no...he would have hissed or growled. He just doesn't find you worthy of notice."

"He's definitely cat-like."

Then Raleigh's ears perked up, and he jumped off my lap, but he disappeared before he landed on the floor.

"What? Where did he go?"

I stood. "I believe your patient has woken up. Perhaps we should go talk to him."

He rose as well and gestured for me to precede him from the room. "After you. By the way, please call me Barton."

I sighed, but I replied, "And you may address me as Reine. While we walk, you can tell me where, exactly, I am."

BY THIS POINT, I'd figured out I was somewhere in the Appalachian Mountains, and the longer I stayed, the more precise my sense of location became. Consequently, I'd landed somewhere in the north Georgia mountains.

How did I feel about being back in Georgia? Decidedly mixed. Prior to being given the mission to uncover the traitor at the Center for Paranormal Disease Control, my life had been an easy combination of managing my little crystal shop from afar, communing with the animals around my small house in the woods, and tweaking the Lycanthrope Council and Wizard Tribunal. Oh, and longing to return to Faerie. Now that I'd been back to Faerie, had been crowned its queen, and been snatched away with Lawrence—all in the span of a month or so —I had to figure out what to do next. I needed to return...but I also needed to sort out loose ends, including Lawrence and his goddaughter Kestrel.

I followed Barton back into the elevator and up to the third floor, where we met Agnes again, along with her two children and an entourage. Seriously, she had two nurses, a medical aide, and another physician trotting to keep up with her as she strode toward us. She'd be magnificent in her gargoyle form.

"...the moment he wakes up, improves, gets worse, or—oh, Doctor Lucia, there you are!"

"Regent Gordon." He inclined his head. I made a mental note to ask him if he knew why she'd kept her surname after her second marriage, and then another note on top of it that I didn't need to be any more involved with Barton Lucia than necessary.

"I was just telling your crew here that I want hourly updates on my son. And that she"—she narrowed her eyes at me—"isn't to be allowed anywhere near him since it's obvious that his involvement with the Fae have landed him in this predicament."

My head spun with how *out* they were about paranormal things here, as opposed to, oh, everywhere else. What would they think about it at the PBI—Paranormal Bureau of Investigations? I'd definitely have to get word to them.

No, it wasn't my problem. I needed to get Lawrence sorted, figure out where we stood and what kind of future, if any, we could have, and then get back to Faerie before the Great Rising. As queen, it would be my responsibility to handle the horde of those who had been killed in the largest war in history and some of whom would be reincarnating as hungry revenants.

Barton spoke deferentially, but firmly. "Actually, Doctor River has just the expertise we need in Doctor Gordon's case, so I'd like to extend temporary privileges to her and make her part of the treatment team."

Props to him for mansplaining and asking a favor in the same breath, and extra props to Agnes for seeming to listen.

With a sigh, she said, "Doctor River, a word?"

We walked into an empty room, and the view of the forest-covered mountains, their leaves deepening from spring to summer green, lifted my heart. I turned to face the dragon, er, gargoyle.

"Yes, Regent?" To be fair, unlike my mother, she hadn't engaged in any plots to kill me yet. But then, we'd only just met.

Her expression softened, and she touched my hair. I clenched my hands so I wouldn't bat hers away. I invoked a protective spell so she couldn't steal any of the individual strands.

"You're a pretty thing, aren't you?"

Bitchy me wanted to say, "Your son seems to think so." Instead, I remained quiet.

"And you're the first Fae we've had in the Aerie in, well, a while. I'd like to give you the chance to help us out, and in doing so, repay the debt that the Fae who murdered my husband incurred with his foul deed."

Her words, albeit old-fashioned, rang with power. I didn't tell her that said murderous Fae was my brother, and that it had been a case of mistaken identity. Since I was related, the request stuck to me.

Yes, there I was, cleaning up Rhys' mess yet again. Still, I wouldn't agree without knowing exactly what she wanted. I'd relearned that the hard way with my last request from a paranormal.

"What do you want me to do?"

"We haven't had a child born in the Aerie to gargoyle parents in almost two decades. Our community is dying without children, and I want to know why."

Well, that wasn't exactly a simple task. At least I knew that up front. "Have you looked into environmental toxins? Water contamination?" *Regent bitchiness?*

"We've eliminated all the obvious culprits. I've also had a witch come in and sweep for magic."

"That would have to be one powerful spell, or group of them, to suppress the natural reproductive process. Especially of an endangered group of paranormals."

She narrowed her eyes. "What would you know of our status?"

Oooh, touchy subject. I shrugged. "Only that your son was the first I'd met..." Since the one who maimed Rhys. But I hadn't met that one, only heard about him.

She didn't seem to catch the incompletion. "There are pockets of us, only a few of them, across the world. We're the only one with this problem. I want you to find out why. If you do, I will count the debt between my kind and yours to be satisfied."

Again, I felt the power behind her words, but also the imbalance. In truth, no one knew the roots of the ancient rift between Fae and gargoyle, who had once been our allies and protectors. The records as to why the atmosphere of Faerie had become poisonous to them and exactly when that happened were lost. I'd recently found out that Fae historians kept the organizational scheme of the records in their heads—not even a card catalog—so it wasn't surprising. Solving this task might cancel our family debt, at least most of it, but there was still the long-ago rift to address. Could this get me one step closer? Having the gargoyles as allies again would help in the conflict that approached.

Sir Raleigh appeared and twined around my legs. I picked him up and took comfort in his solid, purring warmth.

"What is that cat doing in here?"

"He's my guardian. He keeps me from making stupid mistakes sometimes. What do you think, Sir Raleigh?" I didn't expect him to answer, but he did.

"*There is more here than I can see right now. Be careful in your agreements.*"

"By the way, if you don't agree, I will ban you from seeing my son ever again."

All righty, then. I doubted she could keep me away from Lawrence forever, but my curiosity had been piqued.

I decided to go for a patented vague Fae answer. "I will do the best I can in the time I have."

She gave me a look both measured and sad. "That's reasonable. Come on, let's see Lawrence."

4

REINE

I followed Agnes into Lawrence's room, where a slender redheaded nurse wearing green scrubs turned from adjusting an IV. Lawrence looked better—definitely less gray, and I don't mean gargoyle gray—and his eyes twitched under their lids in his sleep. The nurse put a finger to her lips, and Agnes nodded. She grabbed my arm in a firm grip and dragged me out of there.

"But I wanted to touch him." I recognized the irrational need to make sure he was real, not some illusion.

Agnes spoke in a mom tone. "He needs his rest. You can come back this evening."

I sighed, but I didn't argue. As much as I hated to admit it, she was in charge here, and I was just some silly Fae who had happened to wander in.

No, I wasn't a silly Fae, but I might as well have had human-level powers for all the good I could do. I'd already tried and failed to heal Lawrence, which meant I needed to stand aside. I'd heard that the presence of family could be healing. Whoever had said that had obviously not met my family, but I'd let Lawrence have his chance with his. I suspected there would be some interesting conversations when he had the opportunity—and breath—to have them.

"Can I do anything?" I asked Barton, who had appeared with a scowl on his face.

"You can go away and let him get some sleep."

I started to argue that I'd like to stay close in case he woke, but Sir Raleigh rubbed my leg so hard I nearly lost my balance. "*Message received,*" I told the grimalkin via secret conversation. "*We can go.*" He didn't respond, so I guessed I was correct. If he wanted us to leave, that must mean there was something else to discover.

"When can I come back?"

Barton checked his watch. "Come around six." He sighed and looked at Agnes. "Only one of you at a time, please. I'd like Doctor River to come this evening. She can fill in some holes in my case history."

"Fine." With a huff, Agnes pulled out her cell phone and walked away, effectively leaving me on my own with Barton. I arched an eyebrow at him, inviting him to say more. He gave me a long look of the, *I'm trying to decide how much to trust you* variety. He nodded, but not in a way that satisfied any of the elements of my curiosity, and stalked off in the opposite direction from where Agnes had gone, effectively leaving me alone. There was also no sign of the M twins, so after a lingering look at Lawrence, I blew him a kiss and left the hospital through the entrance lobby, which was decorated in bright colors, not the shades of stone I'd come to associate with the gargoyles.

Once outside, I took a deep breath to clear the combination odor of antiseptic and anxiety unique to hospitals. The mountain air had the warmth of late spring, and a cool breeze rustled the leaves in the trees surrounding the small parking lot. Heavy gray clouds covered the sky, but I couldn't sense any impending rain. The rounded mountains murmured to me, their language so subtle it took me a second to hear it. I couldn't tell whether they greeted me or warned me.

Either would be appropriate since something in the atmosphere felt wrong. Nothing looked amiss, and I doubted anyone but a Fae or other powerful paranormal would be able to tell. The best analogy I could come up with was when the milk goes sour, and you get just a whiff when you open the fridge door, but then you question yourself when you sniff harder and don't smell anything off.

"Prrrowl?" Sir Raleigh asked.

"You feel it, too, huh?" I looked down into his bright green eyes and couldn't resist picking him up and kissing him on that extra soft spot between his ears. He wriggled and shot me an indignant glare, so I put him back down.

Then I remembered I wasn't the only one concerned about a certain gargoyle. I took out my phone and dialed Kestrel, Lawrence's godchild and recently orphaned trickster witch, who was staying at my place in Scotland.

She picked up on the first ring. "Reine! Where are you? Where's Uncle Lawrence? Is he okay?"

I held the phone away from my ear at her panicked tone. "In The Aerie. And he's, well, not fine, but doing better. They got him here just in time."

A long exhale. "Good. Where is it?"

"Georgia, in the mountains. It was here all along. Do you know anything about it?"

She snorted. "No. Mom always said gargoyles are an intensely private bunch, and they didn't like to answer questions about themselves, so don't bother."

I paused, feeling the note of grief in her statement about her late mother. "They're intensely something. Are you all right? Do you want to join me?" I couldn't believe I was asking, but she'd proved herself to be a capable young woman.

"No, I need to get back to Atlanta. I have...things...to take care of."

Like her father's funeral arrangements. Lawrence being in the hospital at the Institute for Lycanthropic Reversal had kept her in Scotland.

"Do you need help?"

"No," she snapped. "This is witches' business. Aria is going to help me with the double funeral."

Her harsh tone didn't surprise me. She still hadn't forgiven me for keeping her from trying to resurrect her father. "Gods, Kestrel, I can't imagine what you must be going through."

"No, you can't but thanks for your sympathy. Look, I need to go."

"Go where? You're stuck at my cottage." Which felt very far away right now.

"No, Max and Lonna invited me for dinner. He said he'd help me get home when it's time, and someone will be by to pick me up any minute."

Good old Max. I couldn't count on many humans or wizards, but he always came through. I once again thanked whatever goddess of fortune had been smiling on me when we'd met, even if our relationship had been rocky at times.

"Tell Max and Lonna hello for me."

She clicked off, and an unexpected pang of homesickness stabbed through me, more bewildering because I had no idea where I felt homesick for. Faerie had changed since I'd left. Plus, it had turned out to be problematic and hostile in every sense to Lawrence. But now my cottage in Scotland didn't fit the definition of *home,* either.

I needed to figure out my next move. As a self-reliant Fae, a Fae queen for goddess' sake, I could act decisively and with authority. Or...

"Where to now, kitty?"

With tail held high, Sir Raleigh stalked through the parking lot, but not to the main road. He jumped from the asphalt to a dirt path, and I followed him. The woods covered us in dappled shadows. The air temperature dropped a few degrees, and I shivered, not from the mild coolness, but from the sour and still elusive note in the air. Could this be what Agnes referred to, the force that kept the gargoyles from reproducing? It grew stronger as we moved away from the hospital.

A full body shiver overtook me when I crossed a magical barrier, which tingled like the wall of static that used to cover the surface of old televisions. Sir Raleigh's fur stood on end, and he whirled around in circles like he searched for an attacker. I knelt and ran my hand over his soft coat to soothe him, and I'm sure the confusion in his eyes mirrored my own. Whereas the sky over the hospital and surrounding area had an ominous, impending storm appearance, inside the wall of power, it shone a perfect autumn blue with a few fluffy white clouds.

"Well, this certainly isn't what I was expecting."

We stepped out of the woods and followed the path into a town that looked like it had been modeled on an Alpine village. A wooden sign proclaimed in curly blue font over a white background, "Welcome to The Aerie, A Magical Mountain Town."

"Indeed, but not the kind of magic I anticipated."

We crossed a bridge over a merrily bubbling stream, and I sent out a silent call for whatever dryad may be present, if any. Most of them had been chased into other dimensions by pollution, so I wasn't surprised when no one answered me. That gave me an idea, though. If I could find the place's mirror in the Collective Unconscious, the parallel dimension closest to our own where some dreamers could travel, maybe I could figure out what warped it here. For that was the sense I had, that this place felt bent around the edges, like I looked through subtly imperfect glass. That explained the wrongness, but still not its origin or purpose.

The path turned to asphalt as we walked toward the town. Sir Raleigh trotted along beside me and looked around. About twenty feet away from the stream—the border of its flood zone? —we stopped beside a life-sized statue of a gargoyle. A gray square in front of it that resembled a tombstone proclaimed, *"Rest your soul, Augie. You guarded us well in life, may you do so in death."*

I cocked my head and studied it. The statue seemed to look back at me, and I shivered under its intense gaze, which appeared to follow me no matter which way I stepped. "This is interesting, Sir Raleigh. What do you make of it?"

He didn't respond. Just my luck, I had a grimalkin who didn't want to talk to me. He resembled Ellerin, the gray Fae who'd sent him to me, in temperament, or at least his determined inscrutability. Ellerin also happened to be my father. Sir Raleigh twitched his tail and walked away, and I followed, but I glanced one more time over my shoulder at the statue. Who was Augie? What had happened to him?

Luckily the first building we came to was a visitor's center, which had been constructed to resemble a barn, but with windows. In fact, all the buildings had a newness that belied their deliberately weathered appearance. It made sense that the gargoyles, an ancient race, would want a village that looked like it, too, was ancient, at least according to the standards of the country they were in. That had always amused me about the United States, how their "old" buildings dated back a few hundred years, like they counted as ancient if they had to have their wiring and plumbing updated. I'd quickly found, though, that Americans didn't like being told that I lived in a cottage that was older than their country.

A cheerful bell chimed as we entered under a sign proclaiming, "The Aerie Visitor's Center - Come on in, Y'all!"

A young woman looked up from the list she was making at the main desk. She held a telephone to her ear and gave me a "one minute" finger point. Her energy said gargoyle, but she didn't look like any gargoyle I'd ever seen or heard about. Not that I had that much experience with them, but I'd never seen one more curvy than strong. Instead of stony and angular like Lawrence's family's, her face had a soft roundness to it that immediately put me at ease. Was that intentional, some sort of welcoming role?

She regarded me with a frank openness and curiosity, and too late, I remembered to fluff my hair over my pointed ears. How could I have forgotten? I nodded and looked around while listening to her.

"Yes, that's right. To the Beltane Field... Uh huh. There's a path up there. You'll need to carry it..." She waved me over and handed me a flyer for The Aerie Beltane Festival and Fireworks.

"Thanks," I mouthed and blinked to clear the disorienting sense that I'd lost track of time in Faerie, but we were close to Beltane, a pagan fertility feast. I couldn't decide if it was ironic or sad that the gargoyles, who couldn't reproduce, had to celebrate it.

I searched the place for clues into this community's history and attitudes. Black and white photographs on the walls documented the building of the Aerie for "a band of exiles from Scotland come to Appalachia to settle in and bring their values to a brand new world." As per usual, there was no mention of the native tribes who must have been there beforehand.

"Can I help you, miss?" the clerk asked in a cheery tone after hanging up the phone.

"Yes, actually." I smiled at her and cloaked myself in a glamour so she'd think that, while I may have a striking appearance, she just imagined the ears. "I just wandered into town and was wondering if you could recommend a place to stay."

"Just wandered in, huh?" She laughed, the sound bright and

a touch too eager. "Oh! What a cute cat. Someplace pet-friendly, then?"

Sir Raleigh jumped up on her desk and submitted to an enthusiastic ear rubbing, all the while giving me a look that said: *See what I put up with for you?*

"Yes. He's well-behaved, as you can see."

That earned me a true glare from my grimalkin companion, who returned to the floor and proceeded to clean himself.

"He's a doll. I recommend the Stone River Inn. It's just across the public parking area and has a lovely view of the water."

Sir Raleigh paused and shook his head. He had a good point—an inn, or traditional hotel, would have plenty of eyes to spy on us. If I was going to help Agnes with her mission, I'd need to be able to come and go without someone monitoring me.

"Do you have any suggestions for someplace more private, and perhaps budget friendly? My partner is in the hospital, and I'm not sure how long I'll be here." Both of which were true statements, although I didn't know how I felt about Lawrence being my partner.

She pursed her lips. "Oh, you poor dear." She pulled out a paper map and circled one of the buildings in town before handing it to me. "Here, go see Astrid at the fudge shop. She has a cottage she manages and sometimes rents out to people with family in the hospital. It's a little outside of town, but it should do the trick."

"Thank you."

"You're welcome. The Aerie is a sweet little town, and we do what we can to support our residents and visitors."

"So you've been here a while?"

She puffed her chest out. "I'm from here. Grew up here and attended the community college in Westfield, the next town over. I just couldn't bring myself to go too far away."

Before I could figure out how to broach the uncomfortable subject of the town's lack of children, the bell jingled again, this time with a sharp, angry, "Ding!" Minerva stalked in.

The clerk jumped to her feet and smoothed her skirt. "Oh! Agent Gordon. What a p-pleasant surprise. What brings you in?"

"Looking for her." Minerva jerked a thumb in my direction, then glared at me. "Did you get what you came for?"

I put my hands on my hips, unwilling to let her intimidate me. "If you mean a place to stay, then yes. It's not like anyone at the hospital was helpful."

"You could have asked me." Her tone indicated she didn't consider Karen Lovejoy, as the woman's nametag said, a reliable source of useful information.

"Oh, I'm sure she didn't want to bother you, Agent," Karen chirped. "You have so many more important things to do."

The anxiety in her voice pitched it higher and grated in my ears. I turned to her with the friendliest grin I could muster. "You're absolutely right. I know you must be dealing with a lot, Agent Minerva, like...?"

The gargoyle in question narrowed her eyes. "Like being the head of the town's security force. Come on." She scooped her hand toward her in a "come on, then" gesture she probably was accustomed to people obeying.

Well, not this queen. "I didn't say I was finished here."

"You said you got what you came for. Do you know where you're staying?"

Damn, she had me there, and while I was on a mission for her mother, I didn't know how much Agnes had shared with Minerva. I definitely didn't want to have the discussion in front of Karen.

"No. Apparently, I'm supposed to talk to an Astrid at the fudge shop." Which sounded delightful. I had the notorious

Fae sweet tooth, and the stress of the morning made me crave something chocolate.

"I'll take you to her. Karen." She dipped her head, and Karen's cheeks pinked as she fluttered her fingers. Her energy showed equal parts anxiety and interest, and I guessed that she might be the town gossip on the hunt for a new tidbit.

"Bye, and thanks again for your help." I tried to keep the resignation out of my tone.

I knew Fae politics could be difficult, but nothing compared to small-town human ones. That's why I'd stayed out of Lycan Village as much as possible and ran my business through a human/witch proxy. It seemed like I wouldn't have the same luxury of anonymity in The Aerie.

Indeed, after I followed Minerva out, I glanced over my shoulder to see Karen bent over her cell phone, her thumbs tapping furiously away.

5

REINE

Minerva turned left, and Sir Raleigh and I followed her along a wooded path that opened out to a public parking lot. Cars and SUVs occupied only about an eighth of the parking spots. As Karen had said, the Stone River Inn, a three-story hotel with a Tudor-style exterior, sat across the lot and behind a park with well-maintained grass and a playground.

A playground? In a place with no children? That piqued my curiosity enough to ask Minerva, "If your town is having a kid shortage, why is there a place for them to play?"

She didn't seem shocked by my question. Had Agnes told her what she'd asked me to do? Was that why Minerva had followed me—to see if I was taking my mission seriously?

When she answered, her tone lacked the sorrow her mother's had. "It's for the tourists. We have a winter festival here, and then hikers, white water rafters, and tubers like to come here in the summer. They say it's quieter than Helen."

"Right. And you have the big medical center. Is that the main one for the area?"

"Yep, biggest one until you go over the border to North Carolina and Tennessee."

We walked along the park by a covered picnic area. It would be a nice place to visit, aside from the weird energy barrier. I wanted to talk to Agnes about that before I mentioned it to Minerva. Something about the dour agent made me suspect she looked for reasons to dismiss me, and I needed to make sure Lawrence was sorted out before she found a reason to do so. I thanked the gods that Rhys wasn't with me. He'd put his foot in his mouth and get us run out of town.

I thought I walked fast, but she covered the ground in strides so long and purposeful that I almost had to trot to keep up with her. "I'm sure if you give me directions, I can find the fudge shop."

She snorted. "It's quicker to bring you there."

We reached Main Street—indicated by a wooden street sign at the corner of the park. It had the cutesy arrows pointing in different directions with the number of miles to different places. Westfield, which Karen had mentioned, was about ten miles away. Atlanta, Chattanooga, Murphy... All place names I recognized, but they didn't feel like they belonged to the same world as this place, which gave me another clue. Could the energy field be holding it in a different dimension, or at the border of one?

It seemed like whatever answer I came up with increased my questions. Like, who would do that, and why? Someone with a big secret, most likely.

From what I could tell, The Aerie was similar to a lot of other small, Southern towns. Perhaps there had been a railroad going through it at one point, or maybe their commerce had come over the mountain pathways or through the river. The main street could be described as quaint, cute, or any other number of adjectives that people from the city liked to apply to a collection of buildings shorter than four stories and with a minimum of stoplights.

Although it was midafternoon on a weekday, a fair number of people walked along the streets. Their energy told me that they were mostly gargoyles with a few witches and wizards. No plain humans. I burned with curiosity to know how *out* the magical creatures were here as compared to the hospital. If humans came here, would they suspect they were actually in the minority? That would be different. What would they do? How would they react?

"Is something wrong?" Minerva glared at me from under her bangs.

I couldn't tell her the whole truth, that my instinctive fear of humans finding out that Fae could manipulate all five elements and change one to the other, was extremely high at the moment. So I simply said, "Yes, it's a lot to take in."

"Why, haven't you ever seen a small town before?"

It was my turn to glare at her. "Of course I've been to small towns. Villages, hamlets, Shires, I've seen them all."

She scowled, obviously not getting my hobbit joke. "Then what's wrong with this one?"

We paused before crossing the street. Not a lot of cars were parked along it, or driving on it, but I got the sense that she and I stood in a vortex of challenge. How had I offended her? Or, had Agnes infected her children and the other gargoyles with her hatred for the Fae? Or had the prejudice already been there?

"Nothing. It's quaint, and the shops look very cute. I'll definitely have to check them out, especially since you brought me here before I could even grab a change of clothes or other basics. Look, I know time was of the essence, but I'm in a predicament here."

No sympathy. When traffic paused, we moved to the other

side of the road. "You mean, you can shop when you're not taking care of my big brother."

"I can't go back to the hospital for a few hours." I was just about to tell her where *she* could go when she stopped, and I almost bumped into her. Sir Raleigh sniffed the air. A heavenly smell of sugar, chocolate, and butter wafted out to us. It promised comfort, at least for a little while. I imagined it tempted the visitors in the park across the street to come over for, "Fudge, Cookies, Ice Cream, & Other Delightful Treats." But when Minerva tried the door, it was locked.

"WELL, I guess you're on your own." Minerva shrugged and stalked away from me. She had her cell phone to her ear before she crossed the street again, and I wondered who she was talking to. Micah? Agnes?

What had been the point of her following me, other than to annoy me? Perhaps she was evaluating the level of threat I posed since she apparently led her mother's security force. Noted—the gargoyles firmly believed in nepotism. All right, I couldn't fault them for that considering I'd left my father and brother along with a flirty dark Fae to watch over Faerie in my absence.

The click of a lock drew my attention back to the sweet shop. A friendly face with red hair and freckles peered from the gloom inside.

"Is she gone?" Her voice, the first soft and comforting one I'd heard in The Aerie, floated out to me.

"Yes, thankfully."

The lights inside the shop came on, illuminating the pastel-decorated shop and the woman, whom I presumed to be Astrid, which meant "beauty." It fit. Her wide blue eyes sparkled with the light blue of glaciers, and her hair, tied back, shone like copper. She grinned with an openness I'd not yet encountered in the strange little town, and she stepped back and gestured for me to come inside.

"I am sorry, but not the cat. Health codes."

"Sorry, Raleigh."

He gave her a long look, then sat outside the door with a huff. I followed her inside.

"Thank you. Don't mistake me," she said with an accent I couldn't quite define, but something Scandinavian. "I don't mind Agent Minerva, but my wares are so sensitive, her presence sours them. You, on the other hand, bring a certain sweetness with you. Fae, *jah*?"

So she saw through my glamour. Interesting. I decided to play along. "Yes, although not of any importance here."

"Ah, but you're always important. You know of the enmity between the Regent's family and your kind?"

I couldn't suppress my scoff. "All too well."

She cocked her head. "I sense a story, but I shall let you tell it in your own time. Come in. How can I comfort you?"

Her question hit me in the center of my chest, and the stress of the morning nearly welled up in a sob. Gods, I needed comfort. I'd been wrenched from my Earth realm home to this strange place with beings who would banish me or worse if they knew of my associations, all for a gargoyle I had shared passion with but still couldn't admit my feelings for.

Not inclined to reveal my vulnerability to this stranger, I turned my attention to the wares of the shop. I practically drooled over her case of goodies. Of course there were the requisite trays of fudge, all different shades of brown and tan and cream, some studded with flavorings and extends like Oreo bits, caramel, and even peppermint pieces. Then, on the middle shelf, cookies, brownies, and cupcakes tempted those who might want an alternative fix for their sweet tooth. Finally, the lowest shelf held small cakes, all decorated whimsically in bright colors, except for one tempting midnight chocolate confection. That's the one that drew my gaze.

Astrid, who had walked around to the back of the counter, grinned at me. "Ah, that's the specialty here. It's a dark chocolate cake with fudge icing and a layer of dark cherry jam in the middle. Those in the know come specifically for that cake. I serve it with whipped cream. That makes it reminiscent of Black Forest cake, but I don't have to make the whipped icing."

Judging from the looks of the cakes, it didn't seem like she had an issue with any kind of icing, but every cook had their foibles.

"Is it possible to get by the slice?"

"Of course. Just one?" She stopped just shy of winking at me, and I sensed she was a fellow dessert addict.

"That will do for now, thank you."

When I thanked her, she raised her eyebrows. Her surprise reminded me that people considered Fae to be rude and haughty, but I wasn't feeling like a Fae, much less a royal Fae. All I wanted to do was curl up somewhere and take a nap, then go see Lawrence and figure out what the heck I was going to do with the situation.

Right, I had come here for a purpose other than dessert. "The lady at the visitor center told me that you have a cabin for rent."

"That's right."

"Is it currently available?"

She put my piece of cake into a white box, and then she took out a canister of freshly whipped cream and added a generous dollop. She finished it off with a compostable fork, which she laid across the top of the cake.

"It is, but I'll warn you, I haven't had it cleaned in a while. I did after the last guests, but that was a month ago, and I'm sure it needs to be aired out."

"How much do you charge?"

"It's two hundred a night for tourists, seventy-five for hospital-related stays. Which are you?" She raised her eyebrows again, this time in challenge.

"You know I can't lie to you, so I'm being honest when I tell you that it's for however long my...friend...is in the hospital. We arrived this morning."

"I won't invade your privacy any further, then. If you give me a credit card to run, I'll go ahead and get the key and give you directions."

"I appreciate it."

"If you like, I can have someone come by and give it a quick dusting and airing out. Actually, it's a slow afternoon, so I can."

"No thank you. I can take care of it as long as you don't mind a little magic helping."

Disappointment flickered across her beautiful features, but she smiled. "Not at all. Once you get in there, you'll probably be able to sense that's how I do it."

I handed over my credit card, and she swiped it, both for the cake and for three nights, which was her minimum. Then she frowned.

"It's not going through. Do you have another I could try?"

Dread poured through me. My card had never failed to work before. I had the entire treasury of Faerie backing it.

"No, that's the only one I have. I can give you enough cash for the cake and a night. You'll have to do an exchange, though. It's in pounds."

She leaned forward, her elbows on top of the display case, and gave me a long look. "I can tell this upsets you. How about this? I'll give you one night as a favor since we haven't had a Fae here before, and I'll give you a second night in exchange for cleaning the place. The cake is on me."

Although her offer was reasonable and generous, it made my jaw clench. Here I was, the Queen of Faerie, and I was going to exchange cleaning, of all things, for a night in a cottage I hadn't even seen. Plus, I would be in her debt—never a good thing, especially with a relative stranger.

I looked through my wallet and found a twenty-dollar bill that had apparently stayed in there from my time in Atlanta. "At least let me pay for the cake. I'll give my bank a call and see what's going on, and then I'll get back to you about the cabin."

Again, she seemed disappointed. Perhaps she was one of those witches who got off on doing things for people. No, I was annoyed, and it wasn't fair to take it out on her, or at least my impression of her. She had been nothing but nice to me.

I paid for the cake, and then Sir Raleigh and I went across the street to the park and sat on a bench to eat my snack. The rich, dark chocolate soothed my hunger, but not my anxiety. What was going on? If anything, as Queen of Faerie, I should be more financially secure, and I hated the vulnerable feeling. Was this a sign I should find a place where I could open a portal and return home?

A shadow fell across my lap, and I looked up to see Minerva standing over me, her arms crossed. "Problem?"

Gods, why couldn't she leave me alone? But could she help? I wasn't going to ask directly. That would make me look too weak. But I couldn't lie.

"Yes, actually. My credit card was declined at Astrid's, so I can't pay for a place to stay."

"You're a Fae. Can't you sleep in the woods or something?"

She had a point. "Yes, I could, but I've become accustomed to modern amenities." I looked through my bag to see if I could find more cash and came up with a couple more twenties. "All right, I have enough for food."

She shifted her weight from one foot to the other. "Have you tried the card anywhere else?"

"No." One decline was embarrassing enough.

"Come on." With her characteristic sharp *follow me* hand

motion, she stalked off. I shrugged and followed her. She had a point. Maybe it was a fluke, something about Astrid's system.

She led me across the street again to a coffee shop, which had a lovely little courtyard seating area.

"Do you drink coffee?"

"No, tea."

For the first time, something like amusement softened her hard expression for a moment. "Pretty sure they have that here, too."

With Sir Raleigh once again waiting patiently outside, I ordered a large English breakfast tea at the counter and added a scone to make the credit card minimum. With shaking hands, I gave over my card, which worked. Relief flooded through me.

Minerva watched the entire transaction, and when I had my tea and scone in hand, we walked back up to Astrid's.

"Tell her if your card doesn't work again, the town will cover it, and you can pay us back."

"Thank you. I owe you."

"No, we're even. I'm helping you because you tried to take care of my brother."

I chose not to comment on her choice of words—*tried.* "Got it."

She nodded. "Just stay out of trouble. We've worked hard to make things safe for paranormals here, and we've succeeded to the point we haven't had a murder in twenty years and nothing more violent than a rare bar brawl. Don't screw it up." With that, she stalked off again.

My card worked this time, although Astrid seemed less friendly than previously. Was she grumpy I'd gotten tea from elsewhere? I'd stashed the scone in my bag, but the paper bag it was in crinkled when I put my wallet back in after paying her. And what was up with my unlikely rescuer Minerva?

The Aerie might be safe for paranormals, but the sense of vague threat lingered even as I crossed the barrier, which didn't extend as far as Astrid's cabin. Did that have something to do with the *safety* Minerva had described? Or the infertility issues?

With that in mind, I opted not to go to the cabin right away. Instead, I decided to continue to test my credit card at the boutiques in town. As much as I typically enjoyed shopping in small, local places, I couldn't focus on it. Questions thrummed through my head in a constant beat.

Who knew gargoyles had so many secrets?

6

———

LAWRENCE

I woke to the golden light of late afternoon breaking through the clouds. It gilded the exposed top of the mountain I could see outside my hospital room.

"That's rare," the Italian-accented voice from earlier said. "The clouds hang thick here."

I turned my head to see a tall, olive-skinned man with curly, dark hair and intense, black eyes. He wore blue scrubs and a stethoscope around his neck, and his badge said, "Barton Lucia, M.D., Pulmonology/Internal Medicine" in large letters with something along the bottom I couldn't read. The hospital symbol to the left of his name looked familiar, but I couldn't place it.

"Micro-climate?" I croaked out.

"In a sense. Here, have some water. I'll raise the bed slowly. Let me know if you find it as hard to breathe as I do."

My mind whirred with questions, which I shoved aside to pay attention to the basic function of breathing. I counted my length of inhale, then exhale, as the bed lifted my torso, and he paused when I reached a position where I could drink without choking.

"So far so good."

"I am glad." He handed me a cup with room temperature water and a straw. "I know you're parched, but take it slowly."

I did so, and the liquid flowed through my mouth with the ease of a fine wine.

He gently took the cup from me after I'd only gotten two long sips. "Let's see how that settles."

I wanted to argue, but I opted to save my strength. Besides, I understood. How often had I told pet owners to limit the food and water their dogs and cats had access to after medical procedures? Plenty before I'd joined the CPDC.

His next words surprised me. "The Fae is going to be here soon. I need you to ask her something."

I looked at his badge again, and the symbol clicked into place. "This is the Hospital of the Clouds, where tough paranormal cases come. I've seen reports at the..." No reason to reveal everything about myself.

But he was a step ahead of me. "Center for Paranormal Disease Control. Yes, I am aware of who you are, Doctor Gordon. And yes, this is Hospital of the Clouds, but around here, people call it the Aerie Hospital."

"So, you're..."

"Later Benandanti, healing wizard branch. Good thing for you, too, considering you needed an experimental treatment we've been working on for your lungs." He grinned. "Once you get back to work, you can look up the early trial results for yourself."

Getting back to work... After being in Faerie, then the Institute for Lycanthropic Reversal, this world felt comfortingly familiar, yet strange. Even if I could step back into my old life, could I? Should I? Did I want to?

"But I didn't consent to an experimental treatment." All right, that was pissy. I clenched and unclenched my fists, trying for some feeling of control, even if of my own body.

"You would have died. And your mother, as next of kin, gave consent for you."

Right, the mother I hadn't seen in a couple of centuries and who had come to The Aerie and started anew. I hadn't known The Aerie and the famous hospital for paranormals were so close together, but their proximity made sense. Gargoyles had the traditional role of guardians, so why not of a healing center? "What side effects can I expect?"

He shrugged. "Dry mouth, fatigue, mild headaches, maybe nausea... The usual. Considering the condition you came to us in, those may have happened, anyway. You're in tough shape. If you'd been human, you'd be dead."

I mentally digested that fact for a moment. "Thanks for the perspective. What do you want me to ask Reine?"

"Yes, the Fae in exile."

"Wait, you've heard of her?"

He swallowed before answering, and I made note that he'd let something slip he hadn't intended. "Surely you don't think she could have been in the earth realm so long without anyone noticing."

I hadn't noticed her until she walked into my life in the Atlanta airport, bringing one suitcase and a whole luggage rack of complications. But then, I had gotten very involved in my work, apparently to the point I had missed the fact that my family lived a short distance away. Or did they?

"Are we... In the earth realm?" Now that I had been awake for a certain amount of time, I could tell that there was something off, something weird in the air.

Barton ran a hand through his dark hair, and the angle of the light caught his face such that I saw the shadows under his eyes. "So, you can sense it, too? Something dangerous has taken up residence in The Aerie, and I fear for your Fae friend."

"If it's here, wouldn't it be more dangerous to the gargoyles? Why else would it set up here?"

"Because it's been here for several years, but something about her being here has changed it."

I recall the gravelly voice saying, "I want her," but I couldn't place where and when I had heard it.

My inner gargoyle stirred, and my protective instincts awakened. Barton put a hand on my chest. "No changing yet, my friend. The best thing you can do to protect her is to warn her to leave."

"But we're bonded. I didn't think we could be far away from each other for too long."

"I think I can take care of that. Again, experimental treatments can come in handy." Before I could protest, he added, "Be assured, this time I will ask your consent."

I felt Reine getting closer, and I struggled to sit further upright. Barton helped me by raising the bed again.

"This is as far as I feel comfortable raising you. If you feel short of breath at all, lower the bed, and call the nurse."

I nodded, half hearing him. Every part of my being reached out to her.

Barton touched my arm. "I mean it, seriously consider what I offered. It would be best for you both."

He left, nodding to Reine on his way out. I was pleased to see that she barely gave the handsome physician any acknowledgment before turning her wide smile on me. She carried a couple of bags from what I presumed were the boutiques in town.

"There you are." She took my hands and squeezed them gently. "You look like you're feeling much better. How are you doing?"

Fae couldn't lie, but I couldn't help the half-truth that came from my mouth. "Better." And confused. "What is The Aerie like?"

She paused before answering, and I wondered what had

happened to have her already concerned. Had she noticed something amiss as well?

"It's like a small southern mountain town, a little like Helen, but it's weird and magical."

"How so?"

She went and closed the door. Then she swept her right hand in a motion that caused the lights to dim briefly. "Wanted to make sure nobody was listening." She took my hand again, and I pressed her fingers between mine. I suspected we had the same look in our eyes, that of wanting more contact, which had started, not from our bonding, but from the point when we realized we didn't hate each other.

Or maybe even before that.

She took her bottom lip under her front teeth, not a usual gesture for her. Something must've really disturbed her. And after what we'd seen and experienced, especially in Faerie, that made me worried.

However, the next words out of her mouth were more disturbing than I could have imagined. "I've met your mother."

"And...?" I couldn't even begin to guess how that went. Talk about a clash of two alpha females.

"She told me something about the town, and now that I've been there, I can see that there's something wrong. Apparently, the Wonder Twins were some of the last babies to be born here."

So she'd met my siblings as well, and it sounded like she didn't really like them. I could see how perhaps they had conveyed my mother's prejudice against the Fae in dealing with her. Again, my inner gargoyle stirred, wanting to protect her. He and I would have to have a talk about how sometimes battles could be too big, and support rather than protection was the better course.

Meanwhile, apparently The Aerie had its dirty secrets. "So gargoyles have an infertility problem? That's weird."

"I agreed to help your mother get to the bottom of it, and I did find something strange. There is a certain energy field over the town." She motioned to the clouds, which had returned, outside the window. "When I crossed it, the sky went from cloudy to pristine blue. Sir Raleigh was also disturbed by it."

"This hospital is known for serving those of us of a more magical nature. I wonder if it's something to keep the humans out, so that the paranormals can heal and live in peace in the town."

"That's what I thought, too, but I don't know how it could be causing an infertility problem."

A knock on the door startled both of us. I recalled Dr. Lucia's warning.

"You need to get out of here, Reine."

"Why?"

"You just said that there is something off, something wrong. This is gargoyle country, and I'm guessing you've already found that they don't like Fae here. I don't want you to get hurt. I'll come find you after I'm better."

I thought for a minute she would become mad. Instead, she shook her head with a smile. "Tell your inner gargoyle thank you for trying to protect me, but I can handle myself."

Another knock preceded Barton opening the door without waiting for us to invite him in. "Visiting time is over. I don't want you wearing him out with too much talking."

Reine started, but didn't let go of my hand. "He's doing just fine. I would be able to tell if he wasn't."

"That said, visiting hours are still over. You can come back tomorrow."

Reine leaned over and kissed my forehead. "Rest well. I'll see you tomorrow."

She walked into the hall, followed by Barton. I felt annoyingly awake, not ready to rest. However, she had given me an interesting problem to chew over. What was going on in The Aerie, and did it have anything to do with why my mother hadn't summoned me here?

7

REINE

I kept it together until I walked into the hallway and out of Lawrence's sight. Then I almost collapsed with relief at how normal he looked and sounded. I didn't let Barton see it, though. A Fae queen didn't demonstrate emotion to others... Well, not yet, anyway. I wanted to change the perception of Fae, but not outside of Faerie. Not for a while.

I followed Barton to an office notable for how neatly everything was organized, not a bit of clutter anywhere. So Doctor Lucia liked everything in its place. Including Fae?

Apparently, and my place turned out to be humble. He gestured for me to sit in a plastic chair in front of the desk, and he took the plush leather office chair behind it. I gently lowered myself and found that he towered over me.

"What do you think?"

"That you should have a better chair for a fellow physician." *And Queen of Faerie.* No, I wouldn't pull that one out yet, but I regarded him with a haughty stare, or at least my best attempt as my insides still quivered with the emotion of seeing Lawrence and knowing we'd almost lost him.

Barton's lips curled in a half-smile, and he leaned back and steepled his fingers. "You're being stereotypically Fae right now. I do apologize, though. I'm aware that you're not a fan of plastic, but I assumed a Fae who carries a cell phone and credit cards would tolerate some modern conveniences."

I crossed my arms. "And I assumed a Benandanti would have more respect for an Old One." I hated using that term, but sometimes one had to do what one must to put inferior beings —albeit very handsome ones—in their place.

"Oh, I do. And I'm aware you could probably kill me where I sat, and no one would be the wiser. 'Oh, poor Doctor Lucia, died of a heart attack at his desk.'" He mimicked clutching his chest and keeling over.

I snorted to hide my laugh. At least he knew the threat I posed. I reached down and touched the edge of the ugly orange plastic with my finger. Then I stood as it disappeared. There. Now I towered over him.

"Where did it go?"

"Back to wherever awful chairs come from."

He shook his head. "Look, Doctor River, I don't have time to play these games with you, as funny as they may be. I do need to know what you think about Doctor Gordon. And if you're okay with dissolving the bond between you."

His words jerked me away from my fantasy about what silly picture to replace the one on his badge with. "Wait, what? Is that what he wants?"

"We're still discussing it."

All right, not a yes or a no. I should want our bond dissolved. It made things damned inconvenient for me as Queen of Faerie, but... Oh, gods, I had feelings for him. Strong feelings. Damnit.

"Obviously I need to discuss it with him."

"Understandable." The twitch at his lips told me he had caught on to my consternation at the idea. He must be terribly amused by the situation—a Fae in, ah, strong like with a gargoyle. I'd given away too much by not immediately jumping on the idea or acting interested. Plus, there was another problem...

"Do you have a way to do that? There haven't been any Fae/gargoyle bonds in almost a millennium, and I never heard anyone talk of dissolving one."

"An experimental treatment. I can explain more if you decide to do it."

I almost revealed my royal title to force him to say more—that procedure would be an amazing asset to have—but I opted not to. I could find out more later. "I'll let you know. As for Law, er, Doctor Gordon, he looks much better, and I can feel him growing stronger by the minute. I'll keep in mind that the *cryo fidelis* is a treatment possibility for gargoyles who have Faerie-related lung damage."

"And he went in because of his friend, not you?"

"That's the story."

"A long one, you said."

I shrugged. "Yes. Not one I'm interested in telling right now. Don't you have patients or something?"

He stood and looked around. I didn't tell him that his chair was now in the office closet, which I'd guessed would be neat like the rest of the space.

"I do. I wanted to warn you, however. The Aerie won't cause the same kind of damage that Faerie did to Doctor Gordon, but it's not a safe place for Fae. Please be careful and let me know the moment you agree to allow me to help dissolve the bond."

He and I both exited the office, and I couldn't help but ponder over his words...and how confident he seemed that I would want to be un-bonded from Lawrence. Doctor Barton Lucia definitely knew more than he let on.

~

I FOUND myself exhausted after visiting Lawrence, which was odd since Fae didn't need to sleep much. Perhaps it was because it had been a very long day, starting early in the morning in Scotland, and then being whisked away to a different continent and a strange situation. Both Lawrence's and Barton's warnings played in my head. Was I really in danger? From what or whom?

All signs pointed to one thing: I needed to get Lawrence better and out of there so that we could go back to Atlanta or Scotland and figure out where things stood between us. Our situation obviously was not going to change, not easily, although I was afraid I would need to break his heart...and mine.

I stopped by one of the restaurants in town and grabbed a salad that they claimed came from a local farm with organic practices. When I asked if they'd been certified, the hostess said they were working on it, so I opted for takeaway. If I couldn't eat their food, I didn't want to call attention to myself. Not that causing a scene had ever been an issue for me, but apparently something was watching me, so I desired to keep a low profile. Well, as low-profile as a Fae with long, curly, white hair and pointed ears could be.

I stood by the door and watched the diners laughing and talking. My mind wandered back to the first meal I'd eaten in Atlanta at the start of this whole adventure and how I'd resented Lawrence for thinking he knew all about the Fae and what we needed. Now I wished he was there to take care of me, not because I needed it, but because it would be nice.

A chill against the back of my legs preceded the gentle pressure of Sir Raleigh rubbing against them. Sweet grimalkin—he must have sensed my loneliness. Had I been lonely before, in my little cottage in the woods in Scotland? I couldn't remember the feeling, but that had been before I'd been forced to work with others. I'd always kept to myself, even during my medical training, especially after the shark incident with Max.

The hostess handed me my food, which she pointed out was in a biodegradable container in a paper bag, not plastic. I guessed I'd offended her, so I thanked her and complimented their commitment to the environment. Then I followed a path out of town, sensing the direction from the instructions that Astrid had given me.

Typically, when I entered a new forest, the trees rustled and greeted me. Here, however, they remained silent, with no extra motion beyond the slight waving of their leaves in the cool breeze. It's not that they were dead, more like they ignored me. Was it possible that Agnes's prejudice against the Fae had poisoned the whole area against me? That would make sense in the context of the warnings I had received.

Sir Raleigh padded along beside me, and since he remained in house cat form, I surmised he sensed no threat.

As I drew closer to the cabin, I did sense some sort of energy beneath the ground. Not quite Ley line, although I could feel one close by. This energy had a signature more like ancient rock or crystal. I knew there were caves in the mountains, so perhaps there was one here as well. I pulled out the town map I'd gotten at the visitor's center, but I couldn't find any indicated in the area. There was a network of caves near the hospital, so if there were some nearby, they hadn't been found yet. The thoroughness of the map made me suspect that there weren't any. The gargoyles had explored the area, and if anyone could find large chunks of rock, it was a gargoyle.

Another mystery.

As promised, the cabin, although charming and decorated in rustic log, hadn't been cleaned for a while. I set my dinner down on the wooden table and looked around, my hands on my hips. The main living area contained a large screen television, fawn-colored microfiber couch, and coffee and end tables of light wood. I could see a checkered bedspread on a queen-size bed in the bedroom, and the kitchen, although basic, had good quality appliances and marble counter tops. I snapped my fingers, and the dust lifted from the surfaces and whirled into a mini tornado, which I then sent out the front of the cabin and had dissipate. I had never been able to do that so thoroughly or quickly before, and I suspected my queen powers continue to grow. Ironic since a Fae queen should never have to clean her own space.

I handled the bathroom and kitchen similarly, then put my new clothes in the washer to get the manufacturing residue out of them.

With my chores done and environment clean of dust and dirt, I could no longer deny the fact that I would be eating alone. Well, aside from my grimalkin companion, whom I shared the grilled fish on the salad with. We ate our dinner on the screened-in back porch and listened to nightfall. I closed my eyes and leaned back, allowing the sounds of the summer bugs in the southeast to wash over me. After disposing of my leftover containers, taking a shower, and transferring my new clothes to the dryer, I turned in early. Sir Raleigh's purring beside me on the pillow lulled me into sleep.

I had just started stirring in anticipation of dawn when something woke me. Definitely not a gunshot. I couldn't tell whether it was a noise, or something more subtle, like a shift in the energy that shouldn't be there.

I lay awake for a few minutes, waiting for the fog of sleep to return, but it never did. I recognized that I was awake and rolled over to sit up and put my feet on the cold floor. I found myself oddly sore, probably due to the activities of the previous day, specifically being magically yanked a few thousand miles. Fae didn't travel well like that. At least it was still better than flying in an airplane.

Sir Raleigh prowled around the cabin, grumbling in a way

that only cats and grimalkin can. Something had disturbed him, too.

"Do you think we should go see what it was?"

He didn't speak to me, but he paused, his tail lashing. I was getting good at reading his expressions. This one told me he thought it was probably not a good idea to go outside, but we also needed to know if something threatened us.

I waited a few minutes for dawn to give way to sunrise, and I breathed in the energy of the new day. Fully charged, and fingertips tingling for action, I walked outside.

THE MORNING AIR greeted me with the freshness only found at the start of a new day. A few late crickets and cicadas sang a sleepy hello, and the wind whispered through the leaves. The trees themselves remained quiet, rude things. The previous evening, their disdain for me had both amused and saddened me. This morning it pissed me off. When I reached the edge of the cabin's clearing, I put my hands on my hips and scowled up at the silent giants.

"So you don't recognize a Fae, an elemental of your kind?"

No answer, although it seemed like the wind picked up a bit. It stirred my hair around my face, the individual strands like fingers that attempted to caress and calm me. I brushed them away.

Tired of being ignored, I demanded, "What is the meaning of this rudeness?"

The trees didn't answer, but the ground underneath did. *"You bring trouble, Your Majesty. Trouble that needed to come, but trouble nonetheless."*

I should note that some areas of the Earth itself didn't have a great vocabulary, and trouble could mean many things. However, since it repeated the word three times—a significant number—something big must have been about to happen.

"What kind of trouble, friend? And is there a place of power beneath you?"

"Trouble, trouble, trouble... Old secrets hidden. Prices too large to be paid."

Then a tremor shivered through the clearing, rocking me through the soles of my boots, and the Earth's voice went silent.

Sir Raleigh and I looked at each other. "Well, then. Old secrets, hidden as they tend to be. Another emphasis. But I think it wants us to investigate. What do you think?"

The grimalkin nodded, and I followed him into the gloom. At least I could release my anger at the trees. If something tainted the air and threatened them, they would be cautious and not inclined to talk to strange Fae. I put my hand on the rough bark of an oak and promised, "I'll figure out what it is and help you."

It dropped a twig on my head.

So the trees here had skepticism toward magical beings like me. Interesting. What had happened to them? What was happening? It must have something to do with the mysteries I already sought the answers for.

We walked through the trees for about a mile. The trunks stood silent and dark, and a mist wove through them, the fog thicker at the top of the undulating landscape. As the air around us lightened, rustling and chirping replaced the bug-song. I counted at least three kinds of sparrow, a thrush, and others, who went about their day like nothing had happened. Could I have imagined something? No, my gut told me that an event of import had occurred, and Sir Raleigh and I both had something driving us, whether mere curiosity or some larger purpose, I couldn't tell.

The trees thinned to another clearing. The center of this one held a small chapel, of whitewashed wood that had faded and greened so it looked like part of the forest itself. The windows had stained glass framing, but the centers had been left clear, presumably to allow the beauty of nature to illuminate the space. Had Agnes married for the second time here? How was Lawrence doing with all the family news? I almost envied him, but I had lived long enough to discover that every family had its problems, some more severe and overt than others. Agnes might not try to kill him, but she could still hurt him emotionally.

We walked around it, but I didn't go inside. I sensed that I might eventually, but it wasn't time yet.

Sir Raleigh found the path on the other side of the chapel clearing, and we resumed our journey. Softness crept in over the crispness of the morning, especially in the places where the forest canopy allowed dappled sunlight to fall across the trail, and I shed my faux leather jacket. I wished I could unfurl my wings and fly over the forest to see where we were heading, but I refrained from trying. While winged creatures might be common here, a Fae with rainbow wings would be remarked upon. I again shook my head at how the gargoyles had created a place safe for paranormals, as strange as it was, but not secure for all of us.

That Sir Raleigh wasn't a true cat was evident by how he stalked ahead and didn't pay attention to the squirrels and other wildlife that would have distracted a typical feline. It reminded me that I shouldn't underestimate him, and not only because he could turn into a bat-winged panther or teleport, both potentially deadly talents. No, he had his own mind and agenda, only part of which I knew.

We came to another clearing, this one empty. A hill rose on the other side of it, and dark splotches resolved into cave entrances when I narrowed my eyes to focus on them. I shouldn't have had to squint, but yet another odd thing occurred. While we were well beyond the energy barrier, some sort of obfuscation spell hung out there. I could peer through it, but I guessed that humans, and perhaps weaker paranormals, couldn't. They'd see a hill with grass and boulders, not caves.

"What do you think is in them?" I asked Sir Raleigh. He sat and licked one paw, apparently not concerned. "All right, then. What do you think we should do? We still haven't figured out what woke us."

The look he gave me reminded me that he'd already been awake, thank you very much, lazy Fae. Or maybe that's how I interpreted it. A sense of guilt flitted through my chest. Here I was out on a lovely morning having a walk through the woods with my beloved feline-ish companion, and I should be at home in Faerie being the queen and helping to prepare the realm to deal with a major event, possibly even a battle.

But I couldn't have loose ends. My mother had put that condition on me, and although she had proved to not be on my side, I still had to honor it. And right now, one of the major ones would hopefully be getting something appetizing— always a crap shoot in a hospital—for breakfast.

"Oh." I turned around and oriented myself. "The hospital is up the mountain from here. The caves are underneath. That's intriguing."

We crossed the clearing and started up the hill. The obfuscation spell caused more of a mental fog than a physical one, but I still tripped over something and almost landed on all fours. I righted myself with effort.

"What was that?"

Sir Raleigh sniffed at something that lay across the path— a boot. It wasn't attached to anything that I could see, but he darted back down the hill, his nose to the ground. He skidded to a halt at a spot about twenty feet off the trail, directly below one of the cave entrances, which loomed another twenty feet above us. The intersection of path and woods completed the even Y twenty feet in the other direction, and all the hair on my body stood alert as I approached whatever he'd found.

The first thing I saw was a hand, facing up, its fingers slightly curled. I swallowed, recognizing the stillness of death. The wrist disappeared into a navy-blue sleeve, and my gaze followed it to a chest and finally a head, facing away from me. The dark hair lacked any kind of gray, but then, gargoyles didn't age quickly, so there was no telling how old the man had been.

Then a familiar male voice startled me. "Step away from the body, Doctor River."

Oh, Hades.

8

REINE

I turned to see Barton Lucia walking across the clearing from the other side, where the path disappeared into the woods again. He carried two small animal traps in one hand and a rifle in the other.

Sir Raleigh growled, and I shot him a mental command not to go into full-on grimalkin form, at least not yet.

I gave Barton my coolest, haughtiest expression, which I hoped didn't translate into, "Oh, no, what body? No body here," and said, "Doctor Lucia, those are some big words coming from a guy with a gun."

"And was the unfortunate person you're standing over shot?" He kept the rifle pointed downward, but I could tell from how smoothly he moved that he'd had some training and could probably drop the traps, raise the gun, and shoot in a half-second.

"I don't know. I just got here."

"And you can't lie, so I believe you, even if I should mistrust such a direct answer from a Fae."

I put my hands on my hips. "This is no time for insults. Shouldn't we call someone? Like the police?" Oh, gods,

Minerva had told me the Aerie hadn't had a murder in twenty years. I couldn't imagine that she'd take this well. But I didn't know if the gargoyle had been murdered, or even if he was a gargoyle, although that seemed most likely.

Barton placed the traps and rifle on a boulder beside the path and came to join me. "It looks like they're already here. Or he is, at any rate."

I walked around the body so I stood beside him on the level ground, and I saw what he meant. The deceased guy wore a uniform and badge, on his jacket, which had been folded under on that side so the badge wouldn't show. From this angle, the dead man seemed to stare straight ahead with the typical slate-gray gargoyle eyes and mouth open. Shock or something else? A dusting of dark hair covered the lower half of his face. Stepping off the hill had taken me out of the breeze, and I wrinkled my nose against the smell, not of death—although that increased by the minute—but of electricity and burned flesh. What had happened to this man?

"What are your thoughts, Doctor River?"

"You're asking me that a lot these days, Doctor Lucia."

He gave me a small smile. "I may not trust you, but I respect your obvious intelligence, and I suspect this isn't your first corpse. Trust me, if we want useful information, we need to get it fast."

"All right, I'll let you clue me in as to why later. The whole scene disturbs me, but two elements stand out. First, the uniform and badge—he was a cop of some sort. Second, the bullet hole rimmed with blood in his right pectoral area. There should be more blood. So, if he's been shot, how or why had he also been electrocuted?"

Barton raised his eyebrows at my last sentence. "How can you tell he was electrocuted?"

"I feel and smell the energy around him. Fae senses."

He didn't argue. "Why, indeed?" He knelt and used a stick to probe the wound. "You're right, there isn't as much blood as one would expect, even if the exit wound, if there is one, is in the back."

"Do you know him?" I squatted beside him.

"In passing. His name is—was—Deputy Daniel Sturgeon. He's one of the younger gargoyles here. Rumor had it he was Minerva Gordon's protégé, which didn't set well with the sheriff. There's some competition between our two law-enforcement organizations."

"Great," I said with a sigh. "She already hates me as it is." Even if she had helped me.

"How do you know?"

"She seems annoyed by having to deal with me."

He chuckled. "That's Minerva's default. If she says more than two words to you, it's a distinct possibility that she likes you. She just doesn't show it. She's afraid to be accused of playing favorites, even if those of us who know her know better."

I scanned the body for other clues but didn't see any. I didn't want to touch him and contaminate anything, although I had no idea how advanced gargoyle forensics might be. Plus, there was definitely something magical going on here.

Barton and I both stood, and he held out the stick. "Do you mind?"

"Not at all." I swirled the tip of my finger around the end, and the part with the deputy's blood incinerated in a little flame that emitted both smoky and metallic odors. The wisps of smoke coalesced into a face, a laughing crone, but then dissipated before I could get a closer look. "Barton, did you see that?"

"Oh, so you're calling me Barton, now?" This time his chuckle had a warmth to it that part of me wanted to respond to, but the face in the smoke had disturbed me.

"Yes, but did you see it?"

"See what?"

"In the smoke." I didn't want to tell him what I saw in case it influenced him to imagine he'd also seen it. If he had noticed something, I wanted him to remember it without being cued.

"Just wisps of it."

"Quick, find another twig." We looked around, but suddenly they all seem to have disappeared. I walked to the forest and met with a wall of hostility. "All right, not going to get one there."

"Why?"

"We need to repeat that, but with a longer branch so I can see more clearly what was looking back at me."

The roar of a pair of all-terrain vehicles shattered the quiet of the morning.

"It's too late, Reine. Come back here and let me do the talking." He walked to the boulder where he'd set his stuff.

"Why? And what's with the traps?"

"I'll explain after."

"After what."

He looked toward the path that led to the hospital. "After we talk to the sheriff."

Two tan-colored ATVs rumbled into the clearing, both ridden by white men. The first guy had shifter energy, but something or someone had stifled it to the point I couldn't tell what kind of shifter. The stubborn set of his jowls under his aviator sunglasses made me want to guess bulldog, so I settled on some sort of canine. The other one was definitely a gargoyle, a familiar one—Micah Gordon, Lawrence's younger half-brother. Both vehicles slowed to a stop, and the men dismounted.

"And what do we have here?" The first one swept his

sunglasses off. He wore a dark-blue uniform like the deputy, but instead of a badge, a silver star winked on his breast. How very Wild West of him, I wanted to say, but as Barton requested, I let him do the talking.

"We were out for a walk and found the body, Sheriff Jones."

"We?" I asked under my breath.

"'We?'" Micah asked out loud. "Do the two of you have some sort of thing going on? Does my brother know?"

"We don't, Agent Gordon." I assured him. I pressed my lips shut to resist the urge to take control of the situation. I had to let Barton lead since he knew better whom we were dealing with.

"No, we were discussing her brother's case away from the hospital and the prying ears there." Barton shot Micah a challenging look.

Huh. Yet another thing I'd have to ask clarification on.

Meanwhile, the sheriff had gone over to the body, and his face, in profile, hardened for a second, then fell. Regardless of whatever conflict had occurred between him and the deputy, he was truly saddened by the man's death. That made me soften toward him, but only slightly. I couldn't trust someone who denied part of himself, and the longer I observed him, the more it became apparent that he didn't acknowledge his shifter side.

"Gordon, get over here."

Instead of arguing at being ordered around, as I expected a sort of federal agent to do, Micah joined Sheriff Jones. They both stood and looked down at the body for several minutes. I couldn't feel any kind of magic or spell-work.

"What are they doing?" I finally asked Barton.

"Memorizing as much detail as possible before the medical examiner takes over."

"Where's the medical examiner?" I listened for another ATV.

"He'll be here in a minute."

A dark shadow passed over us, and I looked up to see an unusually large raven carrying a knapsack in its intimidating beak. Sir Raleigh squeaked and darted into the trees. I guessed he was trying to act like a normal cat since we weren't alone, although I couldn't blame him. If I were that size, I'd hide in the presence of a giant bird, too.

The raven landed, and the energy of its impending shift tingled through me. I looked away, and Barton focused his gaze on me, which meant I got a deep look into his dark-brown eyes rimmed with green. My cheeks heated, and I dropped my gaze to the hollow of his throat, and then the tanned skin of his chest, which showed above his open shirt.

"Uh, so what are the traps for?" I asked to give myself something—anything—else to think about. This was not a convenient time for my flirty Fae tendencies to appear.

His voice rumbled through the air between us, dark and caressing. "Some sort of rodent that's been wreaking havoc in the hospital stores."

"And you're trapping them down here?"

"I think they're coming from the caves. I need to catch one here to make sure it's the same kind."

I returned to looking him in the eyes and leaned back from the proximity that had grown too intimate. "You can see the caves?"

"Yes, I can. But the gargoyles can't. Neither can the sheriff."

"Y'all can look now," a voice said from behind us, then added mockingly, "If y'all want to."

I turned toward the newcomer. The young man's broad grin stood out against his ebony skin. Rather than a uniform, he wore a navy-blue tracksuit with the Aerie "A" embroidered on the breast pocket in silver. As he approached, the sun gilded the script underneath it, "D. Eath, MD, Medical Examiner."

In spite of the seriousness of the situation, a laugh escaped me. "Your name is really Death?"

"Desmond Eath, at your service. Would you prefer for me to be called Edgar?"

"Never, er more, that would be too cliché." I stood, and we shook hands. "I'm Doctor Renee River. And this is—"

Barton cut me off. "We've met. Many times."

They nodded at each other but didn't move to shake hands or otherwise make physical contact. I sensed respect of the very grudging variety between them, which meant there must have been a story. Another one.

What sort of place had I come to? Desmond joined the sheriff and Micah, and I could only catch snatches of their conversation, which meant one of them was creating a quiet bubble. Or perhaps the magic of the place helped obscure the words. As it was, I got the gist—Desmond would have to have his men bring the body back to the hospital, where he could do a full autopsy. Ah, that made sense, and the hospital politics around it possibly explained the tension between Desmond and Barton.

The conversation wrapped up, and Sheriff Jones swaggered over to us. "Now don't neither of y'all leave town. We're gonna have some questions for you."

I refrained from telling him he couldn't stop me, but I couldn't resist an, "About what?"

"We'll want to get your official statements." And, I guessed, question us apart.

I didn't have time to play human detective games. "I can tell you everything you need to know here, Sheriff Jones. I was taking a morning hike along with my cat, and we found the deputy's body."

"And this gentleman?"

Barton held up his traps. "I was trapping small game."

"So y'all weren't walking together?"

"No," we both said, me with exasperation and Barton sheepishly.

"I should have said we were out for walks," Barton added. "Sorry for the confusion."

The sheriff narrowed his eyes at the two of us. "Something about all of this doesn't add up, which makes the two of you persons of a lot of interest in my eyes, if you catch my meaning. I'll be in touch. You're staying at River Cottage, young lady?"

"Yes."

"And you know where to find me," Barton snapped. "At the hospital. Taking care of people, as my Hippocratic Oath ensures."

A frenetic anxiety, like a sense of being trapped, emanated from him, and I stepped away. He obviously didn't want to have to deal with the sheriff. I couldn't blame him, but if he was innocent, he shouldn't have had anything to worry about. If. On the other hand, he, like I, was an outsider. Had he had problems before?

And worse, would he throw me under the bus so he could escape?

My whirring mind almost made me miss when the sheriff said he didn't want me and Barton talking to each other until I met with him or a deputy to give my statement. I agreed, and Barton had assured him it was his day off, and I'd likely be at the hospital most of the day, anyway. It felt like he was trying to hint something at me, but I didn't get it, and I didn't trust him, anyway, even if he had saved Lawrence's life. Whatever games Barton Lucia played, I wanted no part of them. After I promised the sheriff I'd come to the station later that day, he dismissed me from the crime scene.

I trusted my sense of direction, even though it felt muted like everything else in the clearing by the caves. Sir Raleigh and I walked along the path that Barton had come from. As I expected, it led me to the hospital and came out on the other side of the parking lot from the path that Sir Raleigh and I had taken to town the day before.

"A strange full circle, huh?" I bent down and scratched him behind the ears, more to comfort myself than to reassure him. When I'd left, my biggest worries had been about Lawrence and how I'd manage the feelings almost losing him brought up, especially since I belonged in Faerie, and being there had almost killed him. Now I was *a person of very strong interest* in a murder investigation of someone I didn't know.

We crossed the parking lot and entered the hospital through the main lobby, which was empty except for three people in an intriguing interaction. Two deputies talked to a young woman with a dark bob and wan, thin face. She toyed with the hem of her work smock—the hospital uniform for non-medical staff—and nodded, her lips pressed together. I didn't want to walk straight through their conversation, so I ducked behind a large potted plant and listened.

"We'll let you know what we find out when we can," the female deputy, whose long brown hair was pulled back in a ponytail, said. "In the meantime, Sheriff Jones would like for you to come by the station when you get off from work."

"I don't get off 'til seven."

"That's fine, Mrs. Sturgeon. Someone will be there to take your statement."

"But I don't have anything to say."

"You never know, you may remember something helpful."

The name made me flash back to the murder scene—the deputy had been Daniel Sturgeon. Was this his widow?

The two deputies murmured the sort of platitudes and condolences that don't really mean anything and left. The young woman sank to a chair and buried her face in her hands.

I emerged and approached her cautiously. She lifted her

face, and her lack of tears surprised me. Maybe she was still in shock.

"Are you all right?" I asked. "I'm sorry for your loss."

She squinted at me. "Are you...Fae?"

So, another resident who could see through my glamour. "I am. Are you a gargoyle, or a witch?"

"Little of both, supposedly." She gestured for me to sit beside her, but her expression never softened to friendliness. "So you heard all that."

"Yes." There was no reason to lie. Perhaps I shouldn't have eavesdropped, but we Fae had never been known for resisting our curiosity, especially about human or other non-Fae drama.

"Look, I don't have any money or even anything to threaten you with, but please don't tell anyone here that I know. I suspect word of Daniel's murder will be all over town by lunchtime, but I can't have people coming here and bothering me at work."

I held up my hands. "I won't tell anyone what I saw, I promise. But why the need for secrecy? You're the widow. People are going to assume you know, that you were the first person they told."

"Because we were about to not be married anymore." The tears I'd expected leaked from her eyes. "He ran around on me, and he wouldn't let me leave, so..." She swallowed, and when she turned her head, the bruise under her makeup on her jawline became visible in the harsh hospital lights.

"Ah, I understand." And I suspected Barton and I wouldn't be the only people of *very strong interest* in this case for long. But there was something else... If he'd beaten her, and she wanted to leave him, why wasn't she more relieved? Well, aside from the murder suspect thing. I recalled the rhythm of a typical hospital. If she got off at seven, that likely meant her shift had started at seven that morning, and although I was no coroner, I could use my Fae sense to pin the time of death at around seven-thirty—plenty of time for her to have gotten to work and had plenty of witnesses to attest to that. The murder site wasn't that far away, though, and there wasn't anyone in the lobby beside the two of us, even now. The one thing that made me sure she couldn't have done it was her lack of energy talent. Her aura told me she was more gargoyle than witch and would have weak magic, if any, beyond ability to change.

"Thanks. Well, bye. I gotta get back to work." She stood and walked away, then whirled around. "Do you...grant wishes?"

I swallowed the mocking laugh that reflexively rose through me. "No, sorry. Not that kind of fairy."

"Damn." She turned back and grabbed a laundry cart that had been sitting by the empty reception desk, which indicated what kind of hospital staff she was. She wheeled it out, and I waited a beat and followed her into the hallway, intending to go to the elevator. But the laundry cart stood in a small alcove, and she was nowhere to be found. I looked down at Sir Raleigh, whose tail twitched.

"I know. Something isn't adding up." The only place to go beyond the elevators was through double doors, on each of which a taped sign read, "Closed wing. Do not enter."

With classic cattitude, Sir Raleigh walked up to one of them, put his paw on it, and disappeared. After a couple of seconds, it swung open outward, and he leaped down from the security guard podium just inside the doors.

"Nicely done, Kitty." I walked into the gloom of the abandoned ward.

9

REINE

My eyes adjusted to the dim lighting, provided by emergency bulbs, and I shivered. The bulbous eyes of cartoon characters stared at me from the walls, and an echo of lost laughter hung in the air. The place had once been a pediatric ward, now closed since the Aerie didn't have any children. Would it open during tourist season for kids who got hurt or sick while visiting? Or would they be sent along to their home hospitals after leaving the emergency room or ICU? I'd have asked Barton if I'd been currently allowed to speak to him. Even once I was, I didn't know if I wanted to. Well, not beyond what Lawrence would need me to.

The murmur of voices drew me along beyond the empty nurse's station, and the hair on my neck stood, each follicle prickling and alert. This would be a good place for ghosts, and kid ghosts creeped me out the most.

I turned a corner, and a dark shape jumped out, yelling, "Boo!"

I gasped, and Sir Raleigh jumped straight up in the air. He transformed mid-leap into his bat-winged panther form, and I caught his tail before he could lunge at the small figure, whose laughter had turned to terrified screams.

"Raleigh, no!"

"Monster! Mommy, monster!" He ran back into the light, which I now saw came from the ward's play room, and into the arms of the Sturgeon widow. She clasped him to her waist.

The air around Sir Raleigh rushed in to fill the void left from his larger grimalkin form as he poofed back to his cat form and left me holding empty air with one hand. The other hand lay clutched against my chest over my pounding heart.

"What were you thinking?" the widow demanded. "You could have killed him! Well, your monster cat thing could have. What is that?"

I managed to choke out, "I'm thinking it may be a good thing we're in a hospital." It took a few deep breaths, but I finally regained my composure. "And what was *he* thinking?"

"He's been told to try to scare off anyone who comes down here." She smiled fondly down at the little boy and smoothed his dark hair—the same color as hers—back. "I don't know how effective he'd be. Especially if someone is traveling with a devil creature."

"He's not evil, he's just gray Fae." Then the odd detail of the situation hit me. "And that's a child. Yours?"

"Yes, mine and Daniel's. I was just coming down here to tell him..."

The boy turned from his mother and said with seriousness odd for someone so young, "Daddy is dead, isn't he?"

"Yes, Eddie. He is."

"Did the cave monster get him?"

"What cave monster?" I asked.

Little Eddie frowned at me as his mother replied, "It's a story that Daniel used to tell him. I think it was to make sure he didn't wander away from here. It was about a beautiful witch who turns into a horrible creature and sucks the marrow out of children's bones."

"And I need to keep my marrow," Eddie added. "Isn't that right, Mommy?"

"Yes, baby. That's right."

There was something about the boy... I knelt to get a better look at him, and his mother clutched him tighter. "I won't hurt him, I promise. Is this the wish you were asking about?"

"Yes." Now real tears came to her eyes, and she dashed them away and inhaled deeply before saying, "I want him to be healthy, and I want us to be able to get away from here."

"And how did you know about your daddy, Eddie?"

He leveled his dark gray gaze—so similar to that of the other gargoyles—at me. "Because he came to say goodbye."

Another child medium. Gabriel McCord had found one at the school in Scotland. It was a rare talent, especially manifested by one so young. What could it mean?

The widow shook her head. "That's not possible. You must have suspected something since he hasn't been to visit you in a while."

"No, I saw him. He had a hole here." He touched his chest where the bullet hole had been. "But that's not what made him dead."

I asked as gently as I could. "Did he tell you what had done it?"

"No, he said he had to get away, and he loved me, and he wanted me to be a good boy for my mama. He said she was right, and he was no good, and he's sorry."

The widow covered her mouth, her eyes wide and still streaming with tears, and she and I both knew it was too late for her to hide her sobbing from her son.

What could I do? Both the boy and I hugged her until her crying subsided into hiccups, and then long, deep breaths.

"How long has he been able to do that?" I asked, figuring that getting her to talk about Eddie would calm her.

"Since he was old enough to talk in real sentences. And thank you..."

"Doctor Renee River, but you can call me Renee. And you are...? I won't use your name against you, I swear."

"Eliza Crabb-Sturgeon."

The names in this town... "You were a crab and you married a sturgeon?"

She shrugged. "It seemed funny at the time. Until nothing about the relationship made me smile. Except Eddie." Her lips stretched into a true grin at the little boy. "I got him out of it, so it wasn't all bad. But now..." She looked at her watch and gasped. "Oh, hell, I've got to get going. Be a good lad, Eddie."

Eddie nodded solemnly, and he reminded me of someone, a child from another era. "I will. Nurse Grayson is going to come soon for my treatment."

"You're right, she is. You're such a big boy to remember."

Did the treatments hurt? Was that why he tracked them so well? Or was it part of his otherworldly personality? There was definitely something odd about the kid.

Eddie walked back into the empty playroom and sat at a table stacked with brightly colored, interlocking blocks.

Eliza sighed. "He can play with those for hours."

We walked down the garishly painted hallway, and I blurted out, "I have questions. How did you manage to conceive? I thought—"

Her sharp nod cut me off. "So did we all, and I don't know, only that I've had to keep him a secret from most everyone except for Doctor Lucia, Nurse Grayson, and the techs who give him his treatments."

"And his father. He knew, right?"

She didn't say anything, so I pressed, "What would happen if knowledge of him got out?"

Eliza stopped, and I paused as well. She turned to me and said, slowly and clearly, "You think you're so clever, but you don't know about the lies in this town and the promises we have to keep. If anyone finds out about Eddie, the whole house of cards will come tumbling straight down, and don't be surprised if you and your precious boyfriend end up crushed at the bottom. There are some who aren't happy there's another prince in town." She stalked off, leaving me to move her back to the top of my suspect list, as much as I didn't want to. Sure, she had an alibi, but no creature was above murder for hire.

Not even my mother.

I brushed the painful memories away and waited a minute after she left, then sent Sir Raleigh to scout out the hallway and make sure no one would see me. With his help, I sneaked out of the closed ward and back to the elevator, which I should have taken instead of indulging my curiosity. How many more secrets would I be burdened with?

WHEN I ARRIVED at Lawrence's room, I found the bathroom door closed and heard running water. Good, he must have been feeling better if he was washing up. I walked to the window, where I admired the view. That morning, the sun had come out and illuminated everything from the smallest curve of the leaves to the rounded, bald tops of the mountains. I could see why the gargoyles had settled in this place. They'd like the exposed heights to sun themselves and to look over the majesty beyond.

The events of the morning and Eliza's threat/warning kept me from admiring the view too much. I had to remember that the tall hills hid deep shadows and foul deeds, and as someone had cautioned me, a web would always try to trap me in its strands and destroy me.

I shivered and turned away from the view as Lawrence emerged from the bathroom. His furrowed brow told me he had expended more energy than he'd expected. I wanted to rush to him, but I didn't want to bruise his pride.

"Are you all right?" I asked instead.

He smiled at me, and it still lacked some of the brightness of how he used to grin at me, before I'd kept a big secret from him. It was the same secret I now kept from all the gargoyles, although he knew—that my brother Rhys had killed his father in a case of mistaken identity. I doubted Agnes would have given me any leeway for the actions of my brother, and I could feel Lawrence's heart-pain through our bond. Had being back among family made him miss his father all the more? Or was he thinking of staying, which would mean the end of us?

And possibly of him because he wouldn't tolerate secrets, lies, or the shadows where distress festered.

He braced himself against the bathroom door. "I have a confession."

"What?"

"I absolutely had to brush my teeth, and I couldn't wait for an orderly or nurse. Now I find that the distance between here and the bed has stretched to insurmountable."

I didn't make him ask me. I rushed to his side and supported him back to the bed. He'd definitely lost weight and muscle mass. Still, my heart thrilled at holding him, touching him through his hospital gown, and if my hand slipped to grasp his rear end, well, he still had some bulk to him that made balance awkward.

After he'd settled in the bed, he asked, "Was that on purpose, Doctor River?"

"Was what on purpose, Doctor Gordon?" I batted my eyelashes.

"The extra, ah, support you provided to my nether regions."

"Well, I didn't want you to fall. That's always a risk in a hospital with a fragile patient, you know."

"Right." He leaned back and laughed. "I've missed flirting with you, Reine."

I took his hand. "Same. When do you think you can bust out of this joint?" I bit my lip so I wouldn't add, *and go anywhere but here so we can figure out this thing between us?*

He sighed. "I don't know. Your friend Barton Lucia is being cagey about that. What do you think of him?"

"I don't trust him."

He raised his eyebrows. "That was a fast answer."

"That was a strange morning." I went on to tell him everything that had transpired. Well, not everything. I didn't tell him about Eliza and Eddie, not because I didn't trust him with the information, but because of something Barton had said about the hospital having ears. I also left out the strange electrical residue on the corpse for the same reason. He nodded as he listened, and occasionally quirked an eyebrow when I glossed over a detail. It was hard to believe we'd known each other for a scant month, and yet he understood me so well. Or was that our Fae/gargoyle bond at work? What else could he tell about me?

The thing was, I didn't mind. I couldn't remember a time when someone listened so attentively to me and didn't do so out of obligation or want something in return.

And if it got back to Barton that I didn't trust him, let him take that as its own warning that I wasn't going to just play along with him and let him throw the blame on me.

"So the sheriff thinks you and Doctor Lucia have something to do with the murdered deputy." Lawrence drummed the fingers of his right hand on the thin blanket. "Do you think you were set up?"

"I hadn't pondered that far, but it's a possibility. But by whom? I haven't been here long enough to make enemies." I didn't think his family would kill someone to get rid of me. I hoped.

"No..." He furrowed his brow, which meant he was trying to remember something. "It keeps escaping me, like a dream."

"Don't strain yourself. It will come back to you when it's time."

He set his jaw, obviously intent on teasing it out. Time to distract him so he didn't wear himself out too badly.

I took his hand and squeezed his fingers. "I can tell you about my dreams. They may be naughty."

That got his attention. He focused his gaze on me. "Oh?"

"Yes, and they may have started with..." I leaned in and brushed his lips with mine. He captured my mouth with his, and we'd just gotten to the best part of the kiss when the sound of a displeased mama gargoyle clearing her throat jerked us apart.

10

———

LAWRENCE

I'd never had the occasion for teenage embarrassment over being caught snogging a girl by my parents, so the chagrin that flooded through me surprised me. At least my adult self tamped it down quickly. While Reine and I didn't have a formal verbal arrangement, we did have a bond, and I suspected it went deeper than the mystical Fae/gargoyle thing that had happened to us in Faerie. Right, Fae/gargoyle thing. My mind still hadn't returned to its previous sharpness, and I swallowed my frustration at my inability to define exactly what had happened between us and what we meant to each other.

Maybe that had nothing to do with my persistent brain fuzziness. I'd never been good with emotions, at least not the positive ones.

As for frustration, I had lots of familiarity with it. I didn't bother to hide the scowl at my mother, who stood in the door and frowned at us. The planes and lines of her displeasure looked all too much like the ones I'd noticed in the mirror, and yet I couldn't feel much of a connection with the woman who had given birth to me and with whom I'd shared the biggest trauma of my life—losing my father.

Oh, gods, she couldn't find out that Reine's brother had killed him. Even though it had been a case of mistaken identity, she would still hold it against Reine and her family, and that would kill any future we had.

My mother, whom my mind told me to address as Agnes, at least internally, narrowed her gaze on me. Had she somehow sensed my thoughts, discovered that I held the answer to her biggest question and didn't want to tell her? That childlike guilt welled up again, and as before, my adult self had to suppress it. Did this programming never cease to affect us?

"Lawrence, don't waste your energy on frivolous activities. We need you well and whole." Agnes couched the words in a caring tone, but both Reine and I stiffened.

Reine squeezed my hand. "Nothing is more healing than love, Regent."

Wait...did she just say love? Her eyes widened, and she shot a quick look at me. Had she meant to use that word? I wasn't sure, but I heard a faint murmur of secret conversation.

"Play it off. We can talk about it later."

"Got it."

She dipped her chin in acknowledgment. Well, then. We could communicate telepathically, at least when we touched. That could be fun.

Agnes motioned between the two of us. "Doctor Lucia has told me he can dissolve this...whatever it is...between you. And the sooner you go, Fae, the better. Something about you being here has disturbed the balance our little area has enjoyed for the past twenty years."

Reine didn't show it, but the sting of my mother's dismissal whipped through her. Another thing I felt through our connection, and this time I squeezed her hand.

She gave me a quick smile accompanied by a shot of gratitude for the support. "You mean the murder this morning. I can assure you, I had nothing to do with it, and you know I cannot lie to you."

"Yet you discovered the body. It's possible for you to have influence without recognizing it. You're aware that no one has died by the violence of another's hand here for two decades."

I caught her qualification—another's hand. What about self-inflicted wounds? Had The Aerie experienced suicides? Or murders masked as suicides?

Reine nodded. "I am aware. Minerva told me yesterday. I thought it was interesting she brought up that fact, and yet, here we are, having to reset the 'blank years since a murder' clock."

"What are you saying? And I resent your flippant tone. Deputy Sturgeon was one of our rising stars. Minerva is devastated."

I did feel a pang of sorrow for the little sister I barely knew. Even if I hadn't been a gargoyle with my own natural protective instincts, I wouldn't want anyone to hurt a sibling.

"I apologize, Regent. And I will assist with the investigation if you allow."

I expected my mother to argue that Reine needed to leave, and I half-hoped she would. While I wanted to have Reine here with me, I also didn't want her to be hurt, and Doctor Lucia's warning played in the back of my mind.

"*What are you doing?*" I asked through our telepathic connection.

"*My path dictates no loose ends. If I were to leave—and I don't want to, for many reasons, including you—it would be seen as guilt, and I'd be wanted for the murder.*"

"*But it's dangerous here, and I can't protect you. Not like this, with my current limitations. I can barely manage to brush my teeth!*"

"*No loose ends...*"

Agnes considered Reine's offer. "You can't lie. And can you tell if others are?"

"Generally. I can read some emotions, and they often indicate to me whether someone is hiding something. The problem is that everyone is hiding something, including you."

Agnes laughed. "Well-played. We all have our secrets, don't we?" She focused her gaze on me again, and I tried to appear as innocent as possible. I needed to get better and get out of The Aerie soon, regardless of what they expected.

I cleared my throat, which was still dry from the breathing tube that had been in there. "There's no need to tell everyone everything about ourselves."

"Very true, son."

Of course my mother saw the flicker of shame across my face. She spoke with a cajoling tone that did little to hide the hardness in her words. "There's something you're not telling me, and all evidence points to poor choices on both your parts. You think I was never young? That I didn't make impulsive decisions?" She took a deep breath. "You think I don't regret every single day that I didn't do more to protect us, didn't insist that we get the hell out of that cottage after your father had drawn the attention of the Fae who killed him?"

Reine spoke gently. "There was no way you could know, and Fae are very determined creatures."

I held my breath, willing my mother not to ask if Reine knew anything about our family tragedy. If Reine was pushed, she'd have to tell the truth, and then...

Luckily Agnes went for the condescending tone. "Encounters with the Fae have never ended well for our family. There's no way you could know that, but it's true. There's a reason gargoyles and Fae took different paths long ago—they're not meant to be together."

"Then I appreciate the opportunities you've given me to help right the wrongs."

This time I frowned at Reine. "Wait...opportunities? As in multiple?"

"Yes, son, and this is why we need you here. No gargoyle has been born in our town in two decades. A curse of infertility has descended upon us, and even without violent deaths, our town is dying."

Awkwardness flooded the room, and I heard what she didn't say—she hoped that I would be willing to stay awhile and try to father some gargoyle babies. "You're telling me that since I was away, I haven't been affected by whatever is going on here, and that you want me to help you, what? Breed? Like a stud horse?"

Reine's hand vibrated in mine, and I glanced up at her to see she'd pinched her lips together, and she blinked, apparently trying hard not to laugh.

"What's so funny?" Agnes and I both asked.

"You're talking about me tricking him into bonding with me, and you have plans for him to be a stud gargoyle, but you haven't bothered to ask him. You're making a lot of assumptions this morning, Regent."

Agnes drew herself up, and I could tell she wasn't accustomed to being confronted or challenged.

"I'll concede that to you, Fae. I want my son to make the decisions about his future with a clear head and heart. If you do truly love him, you'll allow Doctor Lucia to dissolve the bond between you so if he does choose you, it will be because he truly wants it. Meanwhile, I look forward to what you can find out about our curse...and our murder."

She swept out of the room, leaving me and Reine in awkward silence. Whereas my initial question had been whether she meant to use the L-word, now I had a bigger concern.

"Am I just a loose end to you, Reine?"

She let go of my hand and sank into the chair beside the

bed. "No, of course you're not a loose end. You're my bond-mate, however that plays out."

"You don't sound very happy about that." I blinked my suddenly heavy eyelids. Reine's kiss had invigorated me, but then my mother's visit had drained me.

She stood and kissed me on the forehead. "I should go and let you rest. Barton will be grumpy if I exhaust his patient."

"Barton? You're on a first-name basis with him?"

She shrugged. "Physician courtesy. Rest well. I'll be back this afternoon."

A knock on the door heralded the arrival of my little brother Micah. "Reine? Mum said you may need someone to help with your investigation. I'd like to talk to you about a few things from the scene if that's okay."

"Of course." She ruffled my hair and left me to my thoughts, which swirled around one important question—how would I respond if she told me she loved me? Could I tell the truth and not get my heart broken?

11

———

REINE

I followed Micah out of the room, which was the last thing I wanted to do. My head swirled with questions and the many secrets I found myself having to keep from Agnes. Ugh, why wouldn't she accept me? She didn't need to like me. I could argue that I'd never cared what people thought of me, but I now questioned the reason for that.

Micah's deep voice gently plucked me from my mental tornado. "Penny for your thoughts, Doctor River?"

I smiled up at him. "Oh, you know, there's been a lot to take in this morning." Now that I knew of the genetic relation, I couldn't help but notice the resemblance and differences between him and Lawrence. They both had the same wavy, dark hair and stone-gray eyes, but Lawrence's face was more chiseled, his bone structure more pronounced, especially now with the illness-induced weight loss. Micah's skin, while tan, didn't quite reach Lawrence's olive. I'd not pondered the gargoyle genetic ancestry, at least how it related to their human bloodlines. That might be an interesting project for my Fae scholars once I returned. Plus, it would give me an excuse to come back to the Earth realm. Fae, being a curious bunch, could justify almost anything in the name of research.

I turned my face forward, my smile lost. No, I'd be sending representatives. My duties as queen of the light Fae would keep me busy...and trapped in Faerie.

"It's definitely been a lot," Micah agreed. "I haven't even had breakfast yet. Have you eaten?"

My stomach growled in answer, and he laughed.

"Noted. Would you prefer to eat here or in town? The bakery is closed this morning, unfortunately, so we'd be stuck with hospital food."

"Then that decides it. Let's go into town." Plus, it was better for me to resist the temptation to check on and disturb Lawrence again. I hoped he slept, although I suspected he'd be pondering my letting the L-word slip. Hell, I didn't know what to make of it. I'd never used the word with anyone else in my long life, at least not outside of my family, and even then, it was rare. Fae didn't do love well. We preferred relationships of a more transactional nature.

That reminded me—I needed to be careful around Micah, as easygoing and charming as he seemed. However, he'd invoked the age-old principle of breaking bread together, which put us in a situation of sharing and some level of emotional intimacy. I'd use the informal ritual to get whatever info I could and not feel guilty for it. When dealing with gargoyles—aside from Lawrence—I could be as Fae as I needed to be.

He led me out of the hospital and to a nondescript dark gray sedan. Once inside, he opened the windows. "It's too pretty a morning." Then his face flushed. "Well, aside from, you know..."

"Yes, and thanks. I prefer the fresh air."

I observed the scenery as we drove away from the hospital down the narrow road that led across a bridge and into the town. An arch over the road just beyond the bridge proclaimed,

"Welcome to Aerie! All are welcome and accepted here." Except humans and Fae? I decided to save that question until later.

We drove down the main street I'd walked along the day before, and he parked in the public lot by the visitor's center. He cut the ignition before we rolled the windows up, which I pointed out with a gentle, "Should we leave these open?"

"Yes, the people of the town know it's my car. They'll leave it alone."

"Are you sure?" I tried to think of a delicate way to remind him that their town wasn't as secure as they made it out to be.

"Yes, don't worry. I'm sure this morning was an anomaly. And no one is going to mess with Agnes' kid or his car." Was that an intriguing hint of bitterness in his tone?

"All right."

We got out and walked through the park. He motioned to the shops lining the main street.

"Where to? And have you gotten a tour yet?"

He had looked over to the Fudge Shoppe a few times, but I didn't want to face the mercurial Astrid again quite so soon, so I suggested the coffee shop.

"Sounds great to me!" But his smile appeared forced. Hmmm, could the lovely Astrid have this young gargoyle under her spell?

I ordered a large tea and cranberry-orange scone, and he got a blueberry muffin and coffee, and we went outside to sit on the patio. The air smelled fresh and of spring, although I still felt the odd magic that hung in the air. We were the only ones sitting outside, so I asked, "Do you want to discuss the scene while we're alone out here?"

He blinked. Where had his mind gone? Could he be sulking that we hadn't grabbed breakfast from the Fudge Shoppe instead? I had to remind myself that while he appeared only a few years younger than Lawrence, Micah was in fact a couple of centuries behind his older brother in both maturity and physical age. What had Lawrence been like at only a few decades old? Probably mature before his years after his father's murder. But Micah had also lost his father, although as a baby. Gargoyle psychology would make another interesting study.

"Yes, thanks." He removed the wrapper from his muffin with long, tapered fingers similar to Lawrence's. "Sorry, now you've caught me with a lot on my mind."

"That's okay. I sense that there's more than just the murder."

He shuddered. "That was awful. I'd never seen a dead body before. At least not a dead gargoyle."

So he definitely didn't remember his father's death. "Yes, I understand there's not much violence here."

He shook his head. "There isn't any, not even random muggings or bar brawls."

"Your mother and sister must work very effectively with the sheriff to keep things under control." I hoped he'd argue with me and reveal something about the magical force field over the town.

He cocked his head at me, then shifted in his chair. "That's one way of saying it. You could also say that there's not a lot of excitement here. In fact, The Aerie could advertise itself as the most boring place on the planet."

"What, no scandals or gossip? That's typically how things go in small towns."

"Oh, there's always that. We have a small newspaper, but people only take it for the coupons. Everyone knows everything before they can print it."

Yet Eliza had managed to keep Eddie a secret, but at what price? "So news of what happened this morning has gotten out." It wasn't a question.

"Oh, I'm sure it's all over by now. And it will quickly be followed up by you and I having breakfast, and speculation there as to whether you're trying to get in good with the family by assisting or something else ridiculous."

I sipped my tea so I wouldn't give away that yes, I was trying to suck up to his mom by helping. He didn't need to know I acted as a ruler trying to court a potential ally. I decided to direct us back to our original topic of conversation. "What did you want me to tell you about the scene?"

"It's not just that, it's that, well, the way you and Doctor Lucia were looking at each other. And that he said you'd gone there together when you found the body. Do you know what that place is called?"

"No, it's not given a name on your town map."

He snorted. "That's the one for the tourists, so it doesn't have any of the interesting labels. The locals call it Lover's Caves even though there aren't any."

"What, lovers or caves?"

"Either. There are holes on the surface of the hill, but they don't go very far in."

I wanted to argue with him, but he'd been fooled by the magic of the place. Was it connected with the electrical residue around the body or the energy dome under which we sat? I'd have to find out.

"There is nothing going on between me and Barton Lucia. I'm in—I'm bonded to your brother."

He nodded. "Good. That's what I was hoping." Then he dropped the volume of his voice. "Watch out for Doctor Lucia. He's a man with his own agenda."

I took another sip and a nibble of my scone. "Do you know what it is, his agenda?"

"No, and neither do my mother or sister. He showed up one day looking for a job at the hospital. No one knows where he came from or why, only that he's Benandanti-descended and is a very good doctor, especially for those like us, so that's why Mother let him stay."

"Because he's a competent medical professional?"

"And is a wizard-shifter hybrid, so he's good with all kinds of problems, not just physical ones. But he won't talk much about his past or how he found out about The Aerie."

I felt that Micah had warmed enough to me that I could ask him about the strange aspects of The Aerie, but he checked his watch. "Hell, I'm supposed to be at the station in five minutes. You're coming by later, right?"

"Yes, I promised the sheriff."

"Good. I'll see you then." He stood, shoved the remaining half of his muffin in the paper bag they'd given it to him in, and brushed his hand on his pants. Then he picked up his coffee and held it up in mock salute before rushing off with the remnants of his breakfast.

I took my time finishing my tea and scone so I could mentally sort through what he'd revealed, both through what he'd told me and what he hadn't said. I came to one interesting conclusion—Micah Lawrence felt trapped by being in The Aerie and under his mother's influence, and for some reason, he couldn't leave. That led me to the question of whether he was desperate enough to kill to ruin the image of the paranormal Stepford-type town and escape.

WHEN SEEKING information in a small town, I'd often found it most useful to go to the town's hub of information. In this case, it wouldn't be the newspaper, but the heart of the gossip network itself, which I had quickly surmised on my previous stop at the visitor's center to be Karen Lovejoy.

"Are you ready to be your charming self?" I asked Sir Raleigh, who dozed in the sun beside my chair. He opened one eye, then the other, and yawned, which in the language of cats could mean many things. I chose to interpret it as, "If you insist."

I brought my trash inside and separated what I could into the recycling bins.

"Thank you for keeping The Aerie beautiful!" the barista called and gave me a big grin and a thumbs up.

"You're welcome." I smiled at the young man, whose hair was lighter than most gargoyles, but who had the same stone-gray eyes. "It's a lovely town."

"Yes, and we're happy for a Fae visitor. We haven't had one in, well, ever."

I would imagine not. "Do you have many other types of paranormals come through?"

"Yes, definitely. They like it here since they can be more *out*."

"And the humans don't freak?"

"Oh, no." He shook his head so emphatically he almost dropped the mug he was drying. "The humans usually can't find this place, and if they do, they're so magic-blind they don't see us. They may see you, though. You're very, um, distinct."

"There's a glamour for that."

He gestured for me to approach the counter, so I did. He leaned over and whispered, "Check your magic. Something about The Aerie makes it wonky for a lot of us, but we accept the trade-off to be safe and seen."

"I will. Thank you."

It occurred to me once I stood outside and fished in my purse for my sunglasses that I hadn't seen any gargoyles in their shifter form. Was that what he'd meant about the "wonky" magic of The Aerie? I thought about asking him, but that felt like too personal of a question. Again, not something I'd typically concerned myself with, but I didn't want my behavior to reflect badly on Lawrence in case he decided to stay.

That thought made my heart plop into my stomach. Would he choose to stay? Would he want to after being among his own kind?

I wandered along the sidewalk for a minute or so trying to really *see* The Aerie. The dome overhead shimmered like the inside of a soap bubble against the clear blue sky, and I tested my magic by making a flame dance over my fingers like I had when attempting to train Kestrel. It took a few seconds to get going, and the flames only appeared as half their typical size. So, I had magic, but muted. I didn't dare try something else in case the magic of the place refused to tolerate spectacle.

"What do you think, Raleigh?"

He looked up at me, and his tongue flicked over his nose.

"Yes, I agree, the air smells weird here." Then I remembered I needed to ask Astrid about grocery staples for the cabin, so I steeled myself, crossed the street, and went into the Fudge Shoppe. Sir Raleigh settled into a cat loaf outside.

An electric bell sounded when I crossed the threshold, but I didn't see anyone. The lights were on, and the same delicious assortment of goodies sat in the case. I took a deep breath, noticing cinnamon scented the air that morning. Astrid came out of the back, wiping her hands on a towel.

"Oh, good, it's you!" Phew, she'd returned to being friendly Astrid. "How did your night at the cabin go?"

"It was great, thanks. I slept really well."

She gestured to Sir Raleigh, whom we could see through the front door. "And your friend?"

"He slept like normal, as far as I know." In truth, I didn't know if he always ran around like a nut just before sunrise. It was something I'd known cats to do before.

"Good, I'm so glad. I'm happy you're here because I just pulled some cinnamon rolls out of the oven for you to bring to the cabin with you. I typically do it for my guests, but since I didn't know you would be here..." She shrugged. "I hope you don't mind them with raisins."

"Not at all. In fact, I prefer them that way."

"Great! Did you need something? Another snack, perhaps?

I can add it to your bill, so you don't have to worry about paying now."

Again, that strange energy from her, like she tried to get me out of her shop before I noticed...what?

"I was going to stop by the grocery store to get some staples for the cabin, like tea bags, sugar, and powdered creamer. Do you have any brands you prefer I grab since I likely won't finish all of it?"

She blinked, and for a second, I thought she would start crying. "Oh, that is so sweet of you. I don't have any strong opinions of them, so get whatever you prefer. And if you bring me the receipt, I'll take the amount off your bill."

"Okay, I'll do that. Thanks. And can I have a brownie to go?"

"Coming right up! Please do stop by later to get your cinnamon rolls. They'll go great with coffee for breakfast tomorrow." She reached under the marble-topped table to her left and pulled out a flattened white cardboard sheet, which she folded into a box with deft movements. "How is your friend at the hospital doing?"

"He's improving quickly." I opted not to give her any more information. In fact, it surprised me that she hadn't asked me for any intel on what had happened that morning. Surely everyone must have heard by now. And now I had a quandary —should I bring it up? But how? *Hey, I stumbled upon a dead body, well, not literally, I saw him before I found him, but..."*

But if I didn't, she might find out later, including that I had been there, and she might feel like I'd held back or hidden something from her. I wished I knew how she would respond either way. Her going hot and cold the day before hadn't made me any easier in her presence, even though she seemed to be in friendly mode today. Either way, I didn't want to make an enemy who could endanger my chances to convince Agnes to help me.

Since she seemed to want me to move on, I opted not to say

anything. I took the boxed-up brownie she handed me and thanked her. Then she asked, "Did I see you crossing the park with Micah Lawrence earlier?"

"Yes."

"Isn't he the sweetest? If you happen to see him later, please ask him to come by. I have something for him." Her expression didn't indicate whether it was something from her pastry case or something...sweeter. His lingering looks toward the Fudge Shoppe earlier made me think it must be the latter.

"I'll pass the message along if I see him," I promised. "And I'll be by later for the cinnamon rolls. My sweet tooth is my weakness."

She grinned and said, "Thanks, and I'm counting on it. Have a great morning!"

Then she walked back into the kitchen, leaving me to wonder what was going on between her and Micah, what Agnes must think...and why Astrid's words struck me as sinister.

12

REINE

S ir Raleigh and I crossed Main Street again and sat on the same bench as before. Although I hadn't eaten breakfast too long before, I found myself craving the sweet treat in the bag from the Fudge Shoppe. I ate it piece by piece and pondered over everything I'd learned that morning. No matter how hard I tried to focus on it, I found my mind wandering. Before I knew it, I'd finished the brownie and wished I had another so I could see what the first one tasted like. And what had I been thinking about? I never missed the opportunity to savor chocolate.

I licked my lips to seek any stray crumbs and found myself disappointed I couldn't find any. The flavors of bittersweet chocolate chips and sweet fudgy brownie still lingered, but they faded quickly. Strangely quickly, in fact. What kind of brownie had that been?

"We should go to the visitor's center," I told Sir Raleigh, but my voice sounded far away, and my ears felt muffled. What was happening?

Sir Raleigh put a paw on my thigh and looked deep into my eyes with his green ones the same color as mine and Ellerin's.

The disorientation vanished, leaving me as quickly as it had come. I scraped my tongue against my teeth to dispel the too-sweet brownie aftertaste. Barton's warning echoed through my mind, and I made a note to strengthen the wards in and around the cabin that night. I'd decide whether to take Astrid up on the cinnamon rolls later. The strange thing was, I didn't sense any overt ill will from her. So had what I experienced been a result of the brownie, or the strange energy of this little town under its magic dome?

I took a few deep breaths and anchored myself to the earth, which I could still sense beneath me. At least I could count on it as a constant. The river nearby also helped, especially as it had a branch that flowed into the main waterway, so I could draw strength from both sides.

Raleigh jumped down and walked a few steps, then looked behind him to make sure I followed. He seemed eager to get away from that spot, so did the park harbor something sinister? I wished that the grimalkin would just talk to me, but he had returned to his inscrutable self. Perhaps he could only communicate so much outside of Faerie. Or maybe our current level of mental intimacy satisfied him. He did have the form of a cat, after all.

As we crossed the public parking lot, I looked for Micah's gray sedan. It had disappeared, and annoyance stabbed through me. I didn't know where the sheriff's office was, or how to get there, and even if I did, I didn't have any transportation, and I wouldn't dare to try to teleport myself.

We strolled to the visitor's center, Raleigh because he didn't seem in a hurry and me due to wanting to draw as much energy as I could before facing Karen Lovejoy again.

She looked up and greeted us when we came in. "Oh, hello there! You're back. How did things work out with the cabin?"

"It's great, perfectly cozy. Thanks again for recommending it."

"Oh, of course. And hello, kitty."

Sir Raleigh had jumped up on Karen's desk and presented himself for a scratch behind the ears. I suspected he didn't mind as much as he wanted me to believe he did.

"Do you smell my boys?" Karen asked him. She grinned at me sheepishly. "I have, uh, five."

"The more, the merrier." I didn't have to force the cheerfulness in my tone. I found the thought of a gargoyle cat lady amusing. What must they think when she transformed? Or did she?

She smiled so sweetly at Raleigh, she almost took me off guard with her questions, "How is your friend in the hospital? Is it true that he's the Regent's long-lost son? And did you really discover the body of poor Deputy Sturgeon?" She blinked at me with wide eyes and looked so innocent I had to laugh.

"You don't waste any time, do you?"

Her face lost a little of its sweet expression as she met my gaze with a serious one of her own. "I'm the town secretary as well as the visitor center manager, so it's my job to find things out. And of course, it didn't take me long to figure out who you are, Madame Fae, also known as Doctor Renee River. But you're a real doctor, too, aren't you?" She motioned for me to take a seat in the reading area, and she went to turn the sign on the door to Closed.

Well, this was easier than I'd expected. Therefore, I knew there would be some sort of catch or trap to watch out for. Sir Raleigh seemed to agree. He twined around my ankles but wouldn't settle by my feet or on my lap.

I spoke while she moved around. "Yes, I'm a physician. Internal medicine, specifically, so I could have a broad focus for human and Fae issues."

"Do you know much about us? About gargoyles?"

I shook my head ruefully. "Not a lot, but I'm learning. I hadn't encountered many before Lawrence."

"Oh, that's too bad. I've been told we're similar to other shifters, but with better mental control." She grinned, and I could practically sense the species pride flowing from her. Then she sighed like a teen girl over a celebrity crush. "And Prince Lawrence. Such a wonderful name. Do you want any tea or coffee?"

It took me a second to follow the bouncing trail of her sentences, but I had to grin at the thought of what Lawrence would think about being a heartthrob. I imagined he would not be thrilled.

After the brownie incident, I hesitated to accept anything from anyone, but Sir Raleigh nodded at me, so I said, "Yes. Tea, please. English Breakfast if you have it."

"Well, I've got black, green, and sweet and unsweet iced."

"Black would be great."

"Great, just a sec! Your timing is perfect. I was just making some for me, and I always fix extra." An electric kettle whistled, and a minute later she brought out two ceramic cups with tags dangling over the side. I ignored the stain on the inside of mine and trusted it had been cleaned before she made my tea in it.

"Thanks."

"No problem. I was wondering how to find you so I could talk to you." She dunked her tea bag up and down so vigorously a few drops splashed over the side.

"What do you want to know?" I raised the hand that didn't have my mug. "And I do want to let you know that I'm seeking information, too, about your town and the Regent if you feel comfortable." I blew across the top of my tea and took a tentative sip. Phew, generic, but not terrible.

She shrugged. "No problem. We don't have any secrets here."

I almost did a spit-take. "No?" I asked around coughs.

"No, none at all. It's a perfectly quiet, peaceful little place.

No crime—well, not usually—no drama, just..." She gestured with a palm up. "What you see is what you get."

I almost asked what spell she was under and took a little pleasure in popping her cheery bubble. "That doesn't seem to be the case after this morning."

Her entire posture deflated. "No, it's horrible. We haven't had a murder or even a violent death in twenty years." Then she leaned forward. "What was it like? Could you sense anything with your...?" Her free hand fluttered at me, which I took to mean my Fae senses.

"Maybe, but I don't know what it means, or even if it had something to do with what happened or the place where it happened. What do you know about the Lover's Caves?"

"Oh, not much. Just a silly local legend, that each of the holes in the hill holds the broken heart of a gargoyle who'd been betrayed by their true love." She placed a hand over her heart and sighed. "But it's better to have loved and lost..."

I didn't finish the quote, mostly because I didn't know if I believed it. Trying to get information from her was like tracking a butterfly—lots of flitting about, but unpredictable where it would land. I decided to apply some subtle flattery to see if she'd stay on course with the murder.

"You seem very connected with the gargoyles here. Was Deputy Sturgeon liked? I heard he was a favorite of Minerva Gordon's."

"Oh!" Her cheeks reddened. "Well, ah, I can't say anything about Agent Minerva's pref—er—business, but I can say he was one of those people we all knew, but no one knew well."

"What about his wife?"

Another blink. "What about her?"

I sensed the flow of information drying up, but I pressed on. "I'm sure she'll be very upset." I didn't specify about what.

Karen shrugged. "They had a good relationship as far as I know. Couples in The Aerie tend to stay together. So, what's going on with you and Prince Lawrence? He is the Regent's oldest son, right?"

"Yes, he is, and I can't say." Mostly true because my slip that morning had pushed our relationship into unfamiliar territory, so I didn't know.

"Are you going to stay? It would be exciting for you to be here, although..." She trailed off and looked away.

"Although...?"

"Well, that murder twenty years ago? That's what's so strange. It was the last time a Fae was here, a guy with a scar, and it happened at the Beltane festival, which is just a couple of days away."

Her words hit me with a punch to the solar plexus. "A Fae with a scar? Was he accused of the murder?"

"No... Not really. But there was a suspicion that him being here had somehow caused it. By unbalancing things, you know, with the energy of the town."

All right, time to go for it. "Is there a spell or something over the town that would require a delicate energetic balance?"

She stood, all traces of friendliness gone. "I'm sorry, but I have to get back to work." She plucked my now-empty mug from the small table where I'd set it. "It was lovely chatting, and I hope you enjoy the rest of your visit." Then she disappeared into the back room.

Sir Raleigh and I exchanged bewildered glances, then walked out. I had apparently stumbled upon something sensitive, and I mentally kicked myself for not being more subtle in my interrogation, but I had been shocked by the news that Rhys —what other scarred Fae could it have been?—had visited The Aerie. What had he been doing here? I had a guess—looking for the gargoyle who had helped to maim him, or relatives. But why hadn't he told me?

∾

THE SECOND I stepped outside of the visitor's center, I remembered that I hadn't gotten around to asking Karen about where to find the sheriff's office. The map had something on it labeled, "Administrative Complex," but it was a good walk to the other side of the river, and I didn't want to be late in case that wasn't it.

Sir Raleigh and I headed back into town, and I stopped by the coffee shop since I guessed the cinnamon rolls might not be cool and iced yet. I didn't know how long it would take, but I also didn't want to face Astrid again, and I hadn't made up my mind whether I wanted them. The same barista was there, and more patrons sat at tables and stood in line. A glance at my watch told me it was lunchtime, although for the first time in memory, I wasn't hungry. Something about the atmosphere of the place—not just magical, but interpersonal—made my stomach twist. It reminded me of facing the obsidian spike at the gate into the dark Fae city of Cruaidh—hostile and potentially lethal. That was odd because earlier the vibe of the place had been fine, neutral if not friendly.

When I reached the front of the line, the young man looked at me without any trace of his previous smile. "What do you want? To order?"

I almost stepped back from the anger that emanated from him. "It's me, from earlier."

He rolled his eyes. "Yes, I know who you are. What do you want? As you can see, we're busy."

"Uh, black tea, please."

"We're out. Next in line!"

How dare he? Fury bubbled up through my gut, and I half-considered smiting him. Luckily for him my rational side took over. Striking him down or turning him into a worm definitely wouldn't make me any friends. Plus, I didn't know what would happen with my magic being stifled. Earlier the fact had disturbed me. Now, the unfamiliar feeling of vulnerability pushed to the surface.

My hands trembled, so I shoved them in the pockets of my new jeans. Then I pivoted and walked out through the whispers and hostile looks of the townspeople, head held high. I wouldn't let these peasants get the best of me, but the idea of going back to an isolated cabin felt more like a trap than an escape. Would they be coming after me later with torches? What in Hades had happened?

Sir Raleigh joined me on the sidewalk with a look of concern, and I picked him up and held him close. His rumbling purr soothed me, and he allowed me to place him so he draped across my shoulders, which he hadn't done since he'd been a kitten. As sensitive as he was to others' emotions, he must have been shaken, too.

As a Fae princess, I'd endured worse, but I'd been prepared for it. Would Astrid know what was happening? What if she had turned on me, too? I'd be without a place to stay. I decided I couldn't discount her as my only source of information, and she seemed eager for my money for the cabin, so even if it would hurt, she'd let me know what had changed the town's attitude toward me. But when I crossed the street and tried to go to the Fudge Shoppe, I found it closed and dark. Could Astrid's absence be connected to the strange events of the past half hour? Or had Karen Lovejoy been at work, texting and causing trouble? If so, she'd worked fast.

Without any options and afraid to ask someone for directions, I made my best guess that the sheriff's office would be in the Administrative Complex. I wended my way through town and by the large grocery store, which I made a mental note of. I'd be fixing my own meals and drinks the rest of my stay, if only to make sure no one spit in my food. A path through the woods brought me to a bridge, and then over it to the Town Administrative Complex, a three-story red brick building. At least a sign out front confirmed that The Office of the Sheriff and The Aerie Agency of the Regent, which I guessed was what Minerva headed up, were inside.

When I entered, the middle-aged clerk looked up, and his friendly expression melted into a scowl.

"Well, well, well, look what the cat dragged in."

I'd had enough attitude for that morning, so I gave him my haughtiest glare. "I'll thank you to speak to me with respect. I'm here to see the sheriff."

"I know. He's looking forward to it. We had bets as to whether you'd actually show."

"And why is that?"

"Because you're now the prime suspect in Deputy Sturgeon's murder."

13

REINE

Every village had an idiot, and I pegged Sheriff Buck Jones as the one for The Aerie as soon as I saw him again in the interrogation room. Barton had warned me that somehow, he managed to remain oblivious to the gargoyles. I admitted to only minimal training in psychiatry, but my now several-centuries observation of humans had given me some insight.

Jones stood tall and skinny, his Adam's apple prominent on his stubbly neck, and ran a hand through his thinning buzz-cut hair. He matched the gargoyles in coloring—dark hair and tan skin—but his black eyes had a hardness to them that, ironically, the gargoyles lacked. He had a restless energy that quivered around him, obscuring his aura and anything else I could have been able to tell about him magically. Not that it would have been much. He'd managed to stifle the non-human part of himself so thoroughly, it didn't show through.

He tossed a manila folder on the metal table. I declined to touch it.

"Aren't you going to look at it, Miss River?" he sneered.

Don't smite him, don't smite him... I smiled. "Why should I, Sheriff? And that's Doctor River."

"All the doctors I know are in the business of saving lives, not taking them." He clenched his teeth together and swallowed, then ground out. "I thought you'd want to get a nice, close look at your victim."

I didn't let my smile waver. "What victim is that?"

He shoved the folder toward me, then when I didn't move to take it, opened it. A picture of Deputy Sturgeon while he was alive grinned up at me. There was also a picture of him, Eliza, and a much-younger Eddie. They all smiled, but Eliza already had sadness in her eyes.

"They were a lovely family, but I fail to see why you're showing these to me. I didn't know Deputy Sturgeon or his partner or child." I tried hard not to give away that I'd met Eliza, which unfortunately meant Sheriff Idiot might have picked up on the fact I was hiding something.

"You're telling me that the body you just-so-happened to discover in an out of the way place that just-so-happens to be where lovers go to have trysts is someone you didn't know previously."

"That's correct. As I recall—and I'm sure you'll tell me if I'm wrong—you need to have a motive and means to pin a murder on me. I'd never seen the man before this morning, and you know I can't lie."

"Everyone lies, *Doctor* River."

Oh, Hades, he didn't know I was Fae, and even if he did, I couldn't tell him. How did he manage to do his job with all these paranormal creatures right under his nose? And why did Agnes keep him around?

"I don't." I shrugged and decided to try a little feminine charm on him. "I have a terrible poker face. That's why I don't ever play strip poker. I end up cold."

His Adams apple bobbed with his emphatic swallow. Aha!

I'd scored a hit and distracted him, at least for a moment. I gave him my most innocent, helpless look, which, truth be told, didn't do a great job of making me appear innocent or helpless. My fingertips tingled with the desire to put some sort of spell on him, but something subtle, like a terrible jock strap itch.

"Well, Doctor River, if you're so innocent, then I'd like to search the cabin you're staying at. Assuming you have nothing to hide, of course."

"You assume correctly."

He hooked his thumb through one of his belt loops and leaned his other hand on the table. "And remind me what brought you to The Aerie?"

"My partner is in the hospital here. I accompanied him."

"And why aren't you with him now?"

I blinked. "Because you wanted to talk to me."

"And yet you don't seem upset or eager to get back there. How did you get to The Aerie?"

I couldn't tell him we'd made a magical transfer, so I gave him the truth in a way I hoped he could digest. "Agents Micah and Minerva brought me and my partner to the hospital. They were quite insistent that this was the best place for him to get care." This time when I blinked, I let two tears escape and flow down my cheeks. "He almost died."

He stared at me for a full minute, and I refused to break eye contact. Damn, I wanted to do something to retaliate. Instead, I decided to turn the tables a little and confront him with, "I thought you were going to ask me for any details I may have noticed at the crime scene."

"You're right, Doctor River. I was, and I still am. You're a cool cucumber, and I don't know if you're making crocodile tears."

A little electrical energy escaped from my folded hands to the metal table, and he jerked his hand back from the shock. "Dry air," he muttered, his denial a reflex. Interesting. Then he continued, "Most women would be upset or at least weepy at seeing a man who'd been brutally murdered. Yet you were sitting there making gaga eyes at Barton Lucia over one of my best men. Did you manage to notice anything else of interest?"

Well, I couldn't point out the odd electrical energy now that I'd given him a taste of my own. "The bullet hole was very clean. I didn't touch the body to check for an exit wound."

He nodded. "You're right. He was shot after he'd been killed. You don't own a gun, do you?"

I stifled a sigh. "Check the accent, Sheriff. I come from Britain. We don't do guns over there, but again, you're welcome to search the cabin."

The door to the interrogation room flew open and hit the wall with a bang, and I jumped to my feet as the sheriff leaped behind the table.

Minerva strode in. "What is the meaning of this?" At least this time her anger was directed at Sheriff Jones, who turned a shade of red I'd only seen on roses.

"If you don't mind, Agent Gordon, I'm interrogating a murder suspect."

"And did you read her rights to her?"

"No."

"Or ask if she wanted an attorney?"

He went from rose to beet. "No, ma'am."

"Then I'll take it from here."

MINERVA GOT me out of there so fast I didn't register my surroundings until we reached her office on the top floor. It had a lovely view of the river and the town with the mountains rising behind all of it like a background put into a picture. She pointed to a chair and handed me a mug of fresh black tea.

She picked up the phone and dialed. "Bring up the scones."

Then she set down the receiver, folded her arms, and scowled at me.

"Um, thanks?" I didn't know what else to say in the face of her brutal hospitality.

"What were you thinking, talking to him?" She gestured toward the floor, which I determined must have meant the sheriff. "Don't you have crime shows where you come from? Always, always ask for a lawyer. It will buy you time, if nothing else."

"I have nothing to hide, and I thought I was being interviewed as a witness. Plus, what if I was trying to get information from him?"

"That's my job, not yours." She sighed with a huff and raked her fingers through her dark bob. Her hair fell neatly back into place, of course. I couldn't imagine anything about Agent Minerva Gordon daring to be askew. Did the woman ever let loose, have any fun?

I might have wondered the same thing about Lawrence when I first met him. And then I'd found that, oh, yes, he did have the capacity to have fun, even if it took some effort to draw out of him. Recalling our dances and other moments of intimacy reminded me not to underestimate his younger sister. In fact, I wanted to help her break out of her hard shell and become...something.

Wait, what was I thinking? Was I developing fairy godmother tendencies? I definitely didn't want that job.

Micah knocked on the door, then entered carrying a bag, from which emanated the scent of fresh blueberry scones.

He handed the scones to Minerva and frowned at me. "What did you do? The whole town is pissed at you. Can't leave you alone for half an hour, can I?" His frown broke into a grin, and I reflected that whereas Minerva had Lawrence's seriousness and earnestness, Micah seemed to get the charm.

"Hades if I know. I went to talk to Karen at the visitor's

center, and by the time I got back to the coffee shop after, the attitude of the whole place had changed."

They exchanged glances—more telepathic twin-talk? Sir Raleigh looked up at me, then jumped on to my lap, and I stroked him. Again, I didn't know if it bothered me more that I'd suddenly become the town pariah or that I cared so much.

I had to pose the question. "Did Karen do something to make everyone mad at me? I seemed to have offended her when I asked about..." Did I want to reveal the contents of the conversation? It did have something to do with what Agnes wanted me to find out, but I didn't want them turning on me, too. As independent as I prided myself on being, I also had to admit that Karen's sudden coldness and the town's new demeanor had shaken me.

In truth, my control of the situation slipped more each minute, and the warnings I'd received played on a loop in the back of my brain. If it wasn't for Lawrence, I'd be out of there in a heartbeat. All right, Lawrence and the loose ends I needed to tie up. Plus, if we could get to the bottom of why the gargoyles had been banished from Faerie and why it had become poisonous to them, they'd be powerful allies in the Great Battle on the horizon.

Minerva put a scone on a plate and handed it to me. I found myself surprisingly not hungry in spite of it smelling so delightful, of butter, the raw sugar sprinkled over it, and blueberries.

"About what?" Micah sat across from me and crossed his right ankle over his left knee, making him open, but also partially closed. I kept myself from mirroring his posture, but I did wrap my fingers, which had gone cold, around the mug.

I took a deep breath. "About the spell that's over the town." I met both their gazes directly. Neither appeared surprised. "I asked if there was a spell over the town that would require a delicate energetic balance." I braced for them to turn on me as well, but neither did. They only looked at each other, and this time I sensed they engaged in what we Fae called secret conversation. To me it sounded like overheard whispers, and I could tell they spoke, but not what they said. Then they turned back to me.

"I'm going to be honest with you, Fae," Minerva said. Micah winced.

"I'd appreciate that." I tried to smile, but I suspect my expression landed more in the territory of rueful. "It's been a tough couple of days."

She nodded. "I bet. Please understand it's been odd for us, too. We never expected to meet our brother under these circumstances."

That rang true. Apparently, they'd known about him, but Lawrence hadn't been aware of his siblings. Nor had Agnes been in touch with him in several decades.

"As you can probably tell, our mother has her own secrets and agenda," Minerva continued, and a chill ran through me —had she somehow read my mind to know I'd been thinking about her mother? "But she means well, and the safety of The Aerie means everything to her. Unfortunately, she's an old-fashioned gargoyle in a modern world, and much of what she's done has been driven by her fear of the Fae and her dislike of both them and humans, who could turn on us at any moment."

"I know the feeling," I muttered, then said at normal volume, "So she somehow put a spell over the town to keep humans out? But it obviously doesn't repel Fae. I'm here." And my brother had been here, but I didn't mention that.

Micah responded, "No, but it could have odd effects on them. Have you had any dizzy spells?"

"Yes, actually. I had one in the park this morning." Good, it hadn't been Astrid's brownie.

Minerva nodded. "We can't duplicate what Faerie does to us, but we can at least do something to make it unlikely that

Fae would come. But there's always a price." She hardened her jaw, and her lips pressed into a line.

"Minerva doesn't like secrets," Micah explained. "Especially not as our mother's main enforcer."

"Don't call me an enforcer, Micah."

He winked at me, and I hid a grin. They sounded so much like siblings, and he knew how to push her buttons.

Minerva glared at him for a second, then returned her attention to me. "So yes, there's a spell. No, before you ask, I don't know where it comes from or who's feeding it, but I aim to find out. It may have protected us at some point, but now it's causing more harm than good."

"It's the infertility, isn't it? You two must have been some of the last gargoyles to be born." Except little Eddie. The longer I stayed here, the more it became apparent that he could be the key to solving this and finding out the driver of the spell.

Minerva nodded. "That and other things. You've met our sheriff. He was one of the last outsiders to move here, and you've seen his inability to perceive—or believe in—the paranormal."

I shuddered at the memory of our encounter. "That makes no sense. Yes, I got he's a stifled shifter, and he's majorly in denial, but why wouldn't he be able to see what's right in front of him?" Then I recalled the weird energy around him. "Or he's been bespelled. I couldn't tell much about him due to whatever's interfering with his aura."

Micah clapped his hands. "I knew it! Sis, you owe me five bucks."

Minerva rolled her eyes, then told me, "We had a bet, whether it was something congenital or something external that messed with him."

"It could be both. The spell around him is likely amplifying what's already going on inside. Why does your mother keep him around?"

Micah slumped back. "Damn, there goes my lunch money. And she keeps him as sheriff because his myopia makes him easy to manipulate. She pretty much aims him at whatever she perceives as troubling her, and he takes care of it until Minerva or one of our agents steps in."

I frowned. "Is that what happened to me?"

"No." Minerva let out an exasperated sigh. "That was something else, too. As was the murder of the deputy. Just like before, the arrival of a Fae in our little town is leading to trouble, and I don't like it."

Could this be my chance to confirm that Rhys had been the previous one? I enjoyed our detente and took a nibble of scone while I thought.

"You need to explain that, sis."

"Right." She raked her fingers through her hair again. "Twenty years ago, a Fae with a nasty scar on his face came to the Aerie just before Beltane. That was our last murder."

"Who was the victim?" I asked. Karen hadn't told me that part.

Micah and Minerva looked at each other again, then Micah answered, "Our father."

14

LAWRENCE

I woke to Doctor Lucia adjusting the IV that... Wait, I hadn't had an IV to this point, at least not here. I still had the port from the hospital at the ILR, though, and he'd already hooked me up to something clear that dripped from a bag hanging on a typical rack.

"Please tell me that's saline." The words came out gummy, and after one more flick of his fingers against the port leading out from the bag, he handed me the cup of water that had been just out of reach on the small table beside the bed. I sipped, swished the cool liquid around in my mouth, and swallowed. Then I repeated the process. No matter how much I tried to hydrate the dried tissues, they refused.

Doctor Lucia watched me and then took the empty cup, refilled it, and handed it back. "Go ahead and drink all you want. You're going to want to flush your system after what I'm about to do."

I arched an eyebrow. "That doesn't sound sinister at all." Then I took another gulp, not bothering with the swishing procedure. If my stomach rebelled, so be it. "Seriously, Doc, what are you giving me? It feels like it's turning me into a desert from the inside out."

"It's a cousin molecule to luridatone, which they're using at the Institute for Lycanthropic Reversal, but has a different effect." He flicked the tube again. "And it is sometimes more cooperative at coming out than others."

I tried to pull the needle from my skin. "You didn't ask me about this first. I didn't consent to this. I read the journals, Barton, I know there's no approved use for that."

"You read the regular medical journals. Yes, this is experimental. But necessary. Your Fae friend is walking deeper into a trap, and I need you well to help her." He shook his head. "I don't know why she won't leave."

A languor spread through my limbs, and he took the cup from me before I spilled water all over the bed. I flopped back, every muscle in my body except the ones necessary for basic life functions relaxed, and the room blurred. The words, "What are you doing to me?" floated from my lips in a raspy whisper.

"You need to connect with your inner gargoyle. I don't know what's wrong with you that you're disagreeing, but you need him, he needs you, and Reine needs you both."

"How do you know her..." The room went dark, or, more accurately, the red-orange of the inside of my eyelids. I tried to stay aware, to remain in the room and present as long as I could, but first my toes went numb, then my fingertips. I heard them scraping against the sheets as I moved my hands, but the shuffling noise sounded like it belonged to something else, someone else.

Doctor Lucia chanted something in Latin, but nothing I knew. Old Latin, the ancient part of my mind told me. The language of the earliest of the Benandanti, before they'd been cursed and changed. There are two sides to every legend, I remembered someone telling me. Or had they? Were those my thoughts?

The orange darkened to red, then brown, then black. When I scraped my tongue against my teeth to get saliva to wet my mouth, the sensation echoed as sound rather than feeling, a large door opening over stone floors. The odors of candle smoke and incense filled my nostrils, and I finally opened my eyes, but not to my hospital room.

I sat on a stone throne in a room so cavernous the ceiling and far corners lay shrouded in shadow. Robed figures moved about me, disappearing and reappearing through the smoke that hung heavy like mist throughout the space. One approached me. It stood larger and broader than the rest, and when it came to the foot of the dais upon which my throne sat, it tilted its head back and removed its hood to reveal a face I'd seen a thousand or more times in the mirror—my gargoyle self. His wings burst through the robe, leaving it in tatters on the floor, and he flexed his giant hands and claws. Watching him filled me with a mix of pride and a sense of my own puniness, especially now, in my weakened state. When I'd been in my human form before going to Faerie, I'd been a young-looking man in his prime. Now I felt like a worm, and Gargoyle Lawrence regarded me with a mix of contempt and predatory calculation.

I sat as straight as I could, although the hard surface upon which I sat dug into all the places where muscle had atrophied to leave protruding bone. I told him with as much force as I could, "I will not be afraid of you."

He threw his head back and laughed, and his mirth echoed through the cavern. The other robed figures—my thoughts? My dreams? My fears?—disappeared, and the mist thickened so that when the echoes stopped, the silence, no longer broken by the shuffling of footsteps on flagstone, pressed in on my ears.

"You have always been afraid of me." His voice, which should have been familiar, sounded strange as it landed on my ears instead of coming from inside me.

"That's not true. I have controlled you, as I was taught by my father in my childhood."

He studied his claws in an almost coy gesture. "Not always. Not with her." He pointed, and Reine appeared. Except I knew it wasn't her. While I had no doubt she had the ability to land in my head in some form, I knew this was a representation of her. She looked from one to the other, then folded her arms in her classic, "What now?" gesture.

Shame flooded through me. "No, not with her. I allowed you to take me over."

"You were weak. I took control when you wouldn't."

"And there was an enchanted dessert," I argued. I could still evoke the intoxicating taste of berries, chocolate, and whipped cream. It would always be entangled with the memory of that night, of her wearing that sheer lace thing while she gazed up at the moon on her balcony, and then her skin flushed with pleasure.

I unclenched my hands. She'd known she couldn't get pregnant during our encounter, but I hadn't, and I'd been too weak to fight my gargoyle self as he took possession of her—of us. Or perhaps I hadn't tried hard enough because I hadn't wanted to, hadn't cared. I'd hungered for her from the moment we'd met, and our dances and our fooling around in her hotel room had only served to whet my appetite.

"You knew what you wanted. We knew what we wanted. And she offered. She knew the effect that dessert would have, so there was no question of consent. She. Gave. It."

Effigy Reine dipped her head, and one corner of her mouth curled into a sly smile.

I buried my face in my hands. "It still wasn't the honorable thing to do. I should have at least asked."

Gargoyle Lawrence's growl rumbled through the floor. "Stop being useless, human!"

I snapped back to straight posture, my hands on the arms of

the throne. "There's no need to yell. And how can I possibly be useful when I can barely make it to and from the bathroom?" That had been embarrassing. And yet she'd helped me with compassion and humor. If I had to pick one favorite thing about her, it was—

"Her humor," Gargoyle Lawrence finished for me. "She's a snarky lass, but you—*we*—need someone to help us laugh, to see the fun in life." He stretched his wings. "And to fly."

"You're not wrong. What do you want? Why are we here?"

His gaze met mine, and a wave of disorientation washed over me at the realization that the movement of his facial muscles didn't match my own. "Because you need to accept me. You heard what the lass said—she loves us. And I need to protect her from whatever is out there putting her in danger."

"I can't... I'm too weak to change."

"I know that, dummy." Even though he insulted me, he spoke gently. "You need to accept me, to join with me fully instead of keeping me in a cage inside your mind. Only bringing me out when you need me or can't stand my scratching and clawing at your brain."

"But Uncle Augie... He didn't change back."

"He had the same problem, and eventually he couldn't fight anymore." He walked up the steps and towered over me, his hands on his hips. I could see the appeal to Reine. He stood strong, powerful, magnificent... And I cowered in front of him as a weakling worm.

"You wouldn't be weak if you let. Me. In." He tapped my chest with each of the last three words. I looked down to see my hospital gown. "That's why the Benandanti wanted me to talk to you, for us to speak with each other and come to an agreement. If you stop fighting me, you'll be able to draw on my strength and more quickly recover your own." He spread his arms. "Look at me. I haven't sustained any damage to my physical self, and he healed my lungs as well as yours."

"But you're irresponsible, animal..." I slumped back, and the back of the throne made me feel every one of my vertebrae. "And not under my control."

He knelt so I had to look him in the eye. "Why don't you trust me? You know you're in truth not trusting yourself. I didn't kill that Fae even though we had the chance."

"You mean Rhys, when we flew with him on our back."

He nodded. "If you need just one reason to accept me, I have a good one."

"What's that?"

He jerked his head toward Reine's image. "Because even though you haven't admitted it to yourself, you love her, too."

15

REINE

After they dropped the information bombshell on me, Micah and Minerva brought me back to the hospital so I could see Lawrence. Thankfully we didn't have to drive back through town. I didn't think I could face the townspeople's ire and not react. The longer I stayed in The Aerie, the harder I fought to not embrace my Fae queen side and do what all the Fae queens before me had—treat other races as inferior and punish them for their insolence, even if it would drain me of my strength.

When I reached Lawrence's room, I found the door closed, so I knocked. Barton Lucia opened the door.

"Oh good, it's you."

I put my hands on my hips. "Isn't this supposed to be your day off? And I thought we weren't supposed to be talking to each other."

"I don't follow the directions of that idiot sheriff." He pulled me inside and shut the door behind me. "And I snuck in, so no one will disturb me with patient questions. I'm trying something on him, and it will be helpful for you to observe and monitor him mentally. His vital signs are stable, but he keeps frowning."

"He does that," I said, but I only half heard him over the pounding in my heart. "Did he say you could do this?"

"Well, yes and no."

That did it. I turned to him, grabbed him by the throat, and lifted him. I still had my full physical strength, and outside the boundary of the spell, most of my magic. "What do you mean?" I spoke softly, coldly. "I am not fucking around, Barton. Tell me what you're doing to him and why, or this will be the end of you."

He motioned to his throat, so I dropped him.

He gasped, "Right, don't piss off the Fae." After drawing in a long breath, he staggered to his feet and said, "You and I both need him at full capacity. Things are coming to a head here, and I don't know what's going to go down at the Beltane ceremony tomorrow, but it's likely to not be good."

"I don't disagree with you, but I need to know what's happening to him right this minute. And don't try to talk around it, Benandanti."

He nodded and rubbed his neck. "I gave him a dose of luridatone, and he's currently having a discussion with himself. His gargoyle self."

My cheeks heated at the memory of the last discussion I'd had with his gargoyle self, which had involved very little clothing and a lot of pleasure. And then Rhys had busted in on us. For good reason, but still... Sometimes, I hated my brother.

I walked over to Lawrence and put my hand on his forehead. I could sense something happening, but he wasn't hurting. "What are they discussing?"

"Hadn't you noticed a certain distance between Lawrence and his gargoyle self?"

"He doesn't appreciate that wild, unpredictable side of his personality." I couldn't help a grin. "But I do."

Barton cleared his throat, and my mischievous side thrilled at having made him uncomfortable. Barton went on, "It's quite likely that his childhood trauma caused him to bury the part of himself he felt he couldn't control. If something bad happened again, he didn't want it to be his fault."

"Thanks for the armchair analysis, Doctor. You're not wrong." Lawrence's forehead muscles moved under my hand, and I stroked his hair. "How long is this going to take?"

"You'll see."

I narrowed my eyes at him. "You really aren't that attached to your trachea, are you?"

He dropped his hand from where he'd been massaging his throat. "I could have you arrested for assault."

"You'll have to wait in line, I fear. The town has decided it doesn't like me." Now that I'd gotten confirmation about the spell over the town, I tried to think about it rather than the individuals, who couldn't help but be influenced by it. I was glad I hadn't given into my impulse to smite the barista.

To my surprise, Barton nodded. "I was wondering how long it would take you to find the town's magical bubble."

"I noticed it immediately. I'm guessing it spotted me, too. The question is, how did it get there, and who set it up?"

"That's two questions."

I ignored him and turned my attention back to Lawrence just before the heart rate monitor increased its beeping. Barton grabbed me and dragged me away as Lawrence arched off the bed, supported only by his head and his feet. His gargoyle wings emerged, spread laterally, and knocked over an empty cup on the table by the bed. Luckily, they missed the equipment, and the bed rails had been lowered, so they didn't get entangled in them. His muscles moved under his skin, growing large and strong to replace the ones that had atrophied, and his face filled out as well. Gargoyle Lawrence flopped back on to the bed, then disappeared, leaving human Lawrence, but a healthier version.

Barton released me, and I ran to Lawrence. I smoothed his hair back and murmured, "Come on. Open your eyes. Wake up. Come back to me."

His eyelids snapped open, and his irises faded from his shifter black to their usual gray before his eyes focused on me, and he smiled. Then he grasped my head and brought my lips to his. Just before our lips touched, he whispered, "I love you, too."

Alas, our kiss didn't last nearly long enough before Barton cleared his throat. "Ahem, I'm glad that worked, but I need to get the IV out. And we have work to do."

Lawrence dressed in one of the sets of clothing that Micah had brought for him. Holding hands, we followed Barton down to the morgue. I kept sneaking glances at Lawrence. The change in my gargoyle lover from weak and barely recovered from his ordeal to strong and vigorous would have blown my mind if I hadn't seen him in his gargoyle self before. We'd definitely have to have a chat about what had happened...and other things like the fact we'd now both used the l-word. I didn't know where that would lead us, but it further complicated an already complex situation.

As if my feelings hadn't been swirled enough, Eliza got on the elevator with us at the third floor and rode it down to the second one. She barely acknowledged any of us although she and I had met, and I knew Barton treated little Eddie. Her emotions had the same quality as that morning—tight and protective. She had a secret she would likely take to the grave with her, and I suspected it held the answer to what I needed to know. How had she managed to conceive a kid in spite of the spell? Did she have some contact with the paranormal spell-maker, and if so, were they still around?

We rode the elevator all the way down to the morgue, which was on a floor below the cafeteria, laundry, and other non-medical parts of the hospital except, I assumed, administration. Hospital CEOs and their minions felt they deserved windows even though they were the least directly useful hospital employees. No, I hadn't lasted long working in a traditional healthcare setting. I'd only done so long enough to satisfy training requirements.

Desmond Eath, Doctor to the Deceased, as the plaque on the suite door proclaimed him, looked up when we walked in. He motioned for us to approach the body on the metal table in front of him. He nodded to each of us in turn.

"I assume you're here for the results of the Sturgeon autopsy, Doctors?" Then he looked Lawrence over. "Glad to see you're feeling better, Prince Lawrence. I was hoping I wouldn't be seeing you down here for a while, but I'll take you in this state of life."

I almost asked how he knew who Lawrence was, but hospitals were sometimes like small villages, and no matter what the confidentiality protocols, the arrival of a person of note would be discussed. Or perhaps there had been a warning—"Don't mess up with the Regent's son."

Lawrence shrugged, and when he smiled, the resemblance with Micah showed through. They definitely had the same charm, although Lawrence didn't display it as easily. "Better this way than the way this poor fellow arrived. Is this the victim from this morning?"

I pointed to the bullet hole in the deputy's shoulder. "Yes. See? There's the hole from where he was shot. After he died, is that correct?"

Desmond nodded and cleaned his scalpel with a damp cloth. "It is, Doctor River. And you knew that because...?" He flashed me a feral smile, and I sensed he taunted me. Did everyone know the sheriff had his eye on me? Again, small town, big gossip... *Mental note—don't smite Karen Lovejoy.*

Barton cleared his throat. "I told her." He shifted his weight from side to side, and I again felt the friction between him and Desmond Eath, Master of the Morgue, as the sign on his office door said. The guy liked his funny signs. Perhaps he liked to balance out his grim job with some reminders that humor, even if of the gallows variety, existed in the world.

"And I could tell by looking at him," I added. "If he'd still been alive, there would have been more blood. So what did kill him, Doctor Eath?"

He put the scalpel on the instrument tray, sanitized his hands, and then handed me a manila folder. "I was hoping you could tell me. I understand you've done some investigative work and have the ability to hear the singing of blood. Is that correct?"

I looked up from the lab results in the file, then at Barton and Lawrence. "I, ah, have been known to do that."

Barton nudged me, and I handed the file to him. Lawrence shot me a quizzical glance.

I couldn't resist the opportunity to show off for both of them. "It was a murder in Scotland, at the ILR. I helped put Gabriel McCord on the right track with some magical sleuthing." I'd also saved Max Fortuna's ass, but they didn't need to know that detail, as it was tied to proprietary information about the cure for lycanthropy. I shot Desmond a thought via secret conversation, although I didn't know if he'd pick it up —*"Don't say anything else about it."*

He dipped his chin slightly, but I couldn't tell if it was in agreement to my request or in acknowledgment of what I'd asked. He said, "I have a hunch, and I would like your confirmation."

"All right, I'm game." I frowned down at the corpse, seeking the song of his blood, which should have still been present at that point, although it would fade as the individual cells died. If there was one, it came through as the barest echo of a chime. "But there's not much blood in him, is there? Was it already gone at the murder site?"

Again, a grin, but this time he appeared delighted. "Very good, Doctor. Much of it was. What does that tell you?"

I couldn't attribute the chill that shivered down my spine to the temperature of the morgue. "That whoever did it may have known of my ability."

"Yes, Doctor River, that is correct, and also what occurred to me."

A rumble came from Lawrence, and he pulled me to him. "You're the second person to mention she's in danger. What do you know of it?"

Desmond held up his hands. "Now, now, guardian. You and I are on the same side. I, too, would not like to see this not-so-young lady down here before her time."

"I'll ignore that not-so-young comment," I grumbled. "Mostly because you're right. I'd forgotten how perceptive raven shifters are."

"Even after Edgar Allan Poe described it in his poem?" he teased.

I wasn't in the mood to discuss literature. "That raven was downright mean. All right, Mister, er, Doctor Perceptive, what do you make of all this? And what about the strange electrical energy that surrounded him at the murder site?" I looked down. "It's more of a tingle now, but still there."

"It took me a while, but after I examined the entrails, I came to the conclusion that it's the remnant of an ancient spell."

"What kind?" Barton had stayed interestingly quiet until that point, and I had the disturbing sense that he studied me in interaction with Desmond as much as he did the body of the murder victim.

"Something only a truly powerful creature could concoct—a love spell."

Eliza had mentioned that her husband was cheating on her. Did she know who the other woman was?

"Right." Lawrence said. "Ancient, powerful, and without ethics. Reine, do you know of any such creature?"

I couldn't help the snort that escaped me. "There are many, including some of my kind. This does help, though."

All three men looked at me and asked, "How?"

"Because now I know the rules for drawing them—probably her—out and fighting her."

Lawrence rubbed my back, and I relaxed into his soothing touch. "Can you defeat her?"

I looked down at the now peaceful visage of Deputy Sturgeon. "I hope so."

Desmond pulled the sheet over the deputy's face with a snap, and I jumped back. "If you'll excuse me, doctors, I have work to do."

"Of course," I murmured, and I didn't wait for Barton to lead the way this time. I walked toward the door, followed by Lawrence. If I hadn't had such excellent Fae hearing, I would have missed it when Desmond said to Barton, "You need to tell her who you really are."

"Not yet."

I paused and opened the door slowly.

"She needs to know."

"You know my reasons." He turned to follow us out, and I again found myself questioning whose side he was on.

16

LAWRENCE

We walked out of the morgue, and while I couldn't speak for Reine and Barton Lucia, I could only watch the parade of thoughts in my mind with a feeling of impotence. I stifled my urge to growl and pull Reine close against me again and then find my mother and siblings to guard them. I can confirm I did not like the idea of a threatening ancient being in the town. Accepting my inner gargoyle and allowing him to truly be a part of me should have made me feel more powerful, but instead I found myself frustrated at my helplessness. Brawn wouldn't cut it here, so I turned to a more appropriate, and my preferred coping method—seeking information.

Reine hadn't said anything, and the line between her brows that indicated something bothered her had appeared. It had taken me a while to figure out that little tell. She typically kept her Fae poker face on, but the crease became evident when something deeply disturbed her. I couldn't blame her.

Barton turned to us when we reached the elevator and said, "Perhaps we should convene in my office and figure out our—your—next steps."

Reine put her hands on her hips. "And what about you? Who are you, really, Barton Lucia?"

A flush came to his cheeks like he'd been caught at something. "I can't give you the whole story yet, but please trust me that we're working toward a similar goal."

The elevator doors opened, and we stepped inside. No one said anything until we reached his office. He frowned, then went to the closet and pulled a plastic chair out of it. "Very funny, Doctor River."

Reine smirked. "I thought so. And pray tell, what is the goal we're working toward? My primary aim for coming here was to make sure Doctor Gordon was all right, and that he'd be well on his way to recovery before I left."

Before she...? "Wait, you were going to leave me here?"

She squeezed my hand. "You know our situation is complicated."

"That is the truth." I sighed and ran a hand through my hair. "Yes, Doctor Lucia, what is your aim here? I suppose you're more than a doctor. Does it have something to do with the Benandanti?"

He gestured for us to sit, but neither of us did. I didn't trust my gargoyle weight to the flimsy plastic chair.

"Fine." His shoulders lifted and dropped with his exasperated sigh. "I'm here primarily as a doctor with expertise in the supernormal, but also because I'm investigating the spell over the town and the loss of fertility among the gargoyles here."

"On whose authority?" Reine challenged. "The Benandanti haven't been active in centuries."

"Do I need any authority but my own?" He arched an eyebrow at her, and her lips curled into a smile.

"Touché, Doctor Lucia. But I have my reasons."

"As do I, Fae. And together we have a much greater chance of success."

I expected her to argue further, but she crossed her arms,

and the line appeared again. That was different, a new, more patient side to her. She'd always been calculating, but this... This was strategic.

Like a queen.

I resisted the urge to let forth a frustrated sigh and decided to point out the obvious. "How do you know you can defeat the creature if you don't even know what it is?"

Barton nodded to me. "That's where we can work together. I've been narrowing down the possibilities based on what I've observed, and as you pointed out downstairs, the manner of Deputy Sturgeon's death and the spell he had around him gives us an important clue."

Reine tapped a finger on her lips. "I'm thinking ancient witch or demigoddess, and it would help to know what culture she comes from."

"I suspect the rodents I've been seeing may tell us, but I still haven't been able to catch one." Another frustrated sigh.

Reine looked down at Sir Raleigh, who sat and appeared to follow the conversation. No, not appeared, *did*. "Well, it's a good thing I have the world's best cat on my side."

Sir Raleigh regarded her with one of those classic cat expressions that said, *"Don't forget who I am, woman."*

I stifled a laugh. "Okay, so where do we find these rodents?"

Barton pulled out a map that looked like something tourists would get. "The town has a network of caves. These are the ones that are marked..." He pointed to some directly south of the hospital.

I studied the map with interest. As much as I'd heard about The Aerie, or earlier versions of it, I still hadn't been to it.

"And where the deputy's body was found," Reine added. "That seems too obvious."

"I agree, although I suspect our target was trying to either send you a message or get your attention."

"Or both." Reine spoke in a resigned tone. Was this one

more loose end she'd have to tie up before she went back to Faerie? As much as I wanted—needed—to protect her as my bonded Fae, I acknowledged my own selfish desires not to be hurt more than I needed to be.

"What about the springs on the other side of the park?" I asked. "Do they connect with the spa at the inn?"

Barton traced a line on the map between the two. "They do. But I don't know if they connect with the ones nearby. I suspect that there are more that aren't on the map, but I haven't been able to get close enough to the locals for them to tell me. Or perhaps any knowledge of them passed away with the older generation, with the help of our witch or demigoddess."

The thought of tangling with a demigoddess didn't thrill me, but what could I do? I'd take Reine's lead on this, but after a long conversation.

I also had a question about what she'd said earlier. "You mentioned something about playing by ancient rules the creature would understand. What did you mean?"

She smiled at me, and the return of her confident air eased some of the tension in my chest. "I'm glad you brought that up because you're definitely a needed part of it. As the oldest child of the regent, you're the crown prince, at least according to traditional protocols."

I'm sure my expression betrayed my horror at the idea. Barton turned away and tried to hide his guffaw with a cough.

Reine suppressed her chuckle. "Don't worry, I doubt your sister would be thrilled with that idea, and she seems very much in charge."

"You say that, but my mother seems to assume that I'm going to stay and take my rightful place here. I mean, I'm sure it's charming, but..." My bachelor house in Atlanta suddenly seemed more appealing than it ever had, especially if I had a certain Fae to help me redecorate it, and did grimalkin scratch furniture?

Oh, right, normal life wouldn't be for us. The daydream that had just intruded into my thoughts wouldn't happen, and a pang of sorrow stabbed through my heart.

Reine put a hand on my arm and looked up at me with her big, green eyes. "Breathe, Lawrence. You'll figure it out. She can't force you to stay."

I followed her suggestion and gulped in a deep breath, then let it out. "You don't know my mother. That gargoyle has a force of will stronger than the mountain we're standing on."

Barton said, "Unfortunately I can't argue with him there. Regent Agnes is a tough cookie. It's only by her grace that I'm here."

Reine's mouth rounded into an *O*. "You're the witch she brought in."

"Well, I'm the one who appeared. I think she'd go for this plan if she thought it was possible Doctor Gordon would stay."

"Wait, what plan?" I needed to get my head out of the future that couldn't happen and into the present that moved too fast. Or was I still mentally recovering from my ordeal?

Reine gestured to the map. "You, the crown prince of the town, need to make an official appearance and show you're allied with me. That would turn the energy of the town back in my favor."

"You mean it's not?" I clenched my fists as a wave of fury rose through me at the thought that the townspeople had mistreated her.

She nodded, her mouth set in a grim line. "Yes, someone's been causing mischief. At first I thought it was your sister, or the Fudge Shoppe proprietor, or the town secretary, but I think I know who's behind it."

"The Fudge Shoppe? Town secretary? Are we in an episode of some English cottage mystery?"

"If that's how you want to think of it." Barton pointed to an area on the map labeled, *Beltane Field*. "And there's where the battle for the minds and hearts of the people will be won or lost, tomorrow at the celebration."

"Yes." Reine glanced outside, where the sunlight had warmed to the golden of late afternoon. "We have work to do. Lawrence, do you agree to the plan?"

I took a deep breath and nodded. "I'll do what it takes to make The Aerie safe. We can't forget, though, that our foe isn't above taking innocent lives."

Barton and Reine both snorted, and Barton said, "Deputy Sturgeon wasn't exactly the nicest or most innocent man, but I take your point."

Reine argued, "But if he was under a love spell, there's no telling how much of it was under his control." She looked like she wanted to say more, but she looked at me, then shook her head.

Immediately the old suspicions popped into my head, about how no one could trust a Fae. I pushed them back down. She'd tell me when it was time.

She wrapped her arm around me and looked up at me again. "So... Shall we invite ourselves to dinner with your mum?"

A QUICK CALL to my mother's office confirmed that we were on for dinner at her house, which lay outside of town south of the Admin Complex. Minerva would come get us at seven o'clock, giving us enough time to go by the cabin and get cleaned up. Micah picked us up at the hospital, handed me a bag of clothes, and sized me up. All right, it was mutual. I could definitely see the resemblance, but he looked like he had more fun. The wink he gave me when he dropped us off at the cabin where Reine was staying irritated me. Did he think she and I were going to just throw each other's clothes off and fuck like wild animals?

I rubbed my eyes. The thought had come through in my thought-voice, not that of my inner gargoyle, but I knew he was in there, and that the integration wasn't going as smoothly as I'd hoped.

"You all right?" Reine unlocked the door of the cute little cabin. Sir Raleigh darted in, his nose working. "What is it, Raleigh?"

The grimalkin circled the interior of the cabin, which had been decorated in Mountain Chic style. I barely took note as I beelined for the shower.

"Do you need help?" Reine asked, her voice husky and suggestive.

"I…" I ran my hand through my hair and grimaced at the sensation. "Not this one. It's best if I get the hospital—hospitals—off and out of my hair on my own."

"I understand. I'll fix us a snack."

I wasn't sure what a Fae could understand about the experience of *being* in a hospital, but I didn't question her. I also acknowledged my grumpiness. She'd probably seen enough in her training.

Sir Raleigh gave me a quizzical look just before I shut the door of the small bathroom. Reine had spread her toiletry stuff on half the counter, leaving the other half empty. Had she been expecting me, hoping I'd join her there?

Guilt at my snappishness spread through my chest. I had to remember she'd been through a rough time, too. Hell, her mother had tried to kill her on more than one occasion, and yet here she was, in a hostile place, trying to help my mother save her community.

Or was she trying to butter my mother up so she could have the gargoyles as potential allies in the upcoming battle with the Fae revenants? I wouldn't put it past her to do that and try to figure out a way to make Faerie inhabitable for gargoyles again. Indeed, some sense deep in my gut told me the two problems were related somehow, but I couldn't figure out how or what to do about it.

I stripped out of my borrowed clothes and stepped under the warm water, which poured forth in a glorious, strong stream. I shampooed my hair twice with the stuff in the shower —travel-sized bottles that looked like they'd been placed there by whoever owned it. The bathroom door opened and closed, but Reine didn't join me.

When I finally felt like I'd removed all traces of my hospital stays—first at the ILR and then at the Aerie hospital—from my body, I turned off the water and opened the door to find a glass of white wine on the counter. I dressed in the other clothes Micah had given me, a white button-down shirt, khaki pants, and socks and shoes that fit surprisingly well. If I'd been here, would I have helped to raise the twins, even to the point of sharing clothes with Micah? That seemed an odd thing to do, but I didn't have any idea as to the customs of gargoyles in the twenty-first century.

Reine looked up from her phone when I walked out of the bathroom. I took a look at her sitting on the sofa, the open bottle of wine in the kitchen, and the light slanting through the windows. It felt for a second like we were a regular couple on a vacation in the mountains, and my heart thudded with the desire for that to be true. I'd loved John and Beverly Graves, my longtime friends and colleagues, but I'd also envied their domestic moments and comfort with each other. Was I doomed to only have pretend moments like this?

I saluted Reine with the glass, from which I'd only taken a sip. "Thanks for the wine, but I'm not going to be able to drink much without getting tipsy. Lunch at the hospital was a while ago."

"I figured as much. I have cheese, charcuterie, and sliced baguette here. Astrid must have come by and stocked the place while I was out. Sir Raleigh keeps running around like he can tell someone was here."

Indeed, the grimalkin prowled along the exterior walls and sniffed at corners.

I walked around the couch and joined Reine, who wore a blue and white striped dress with more ruffles than I'd ever seen on her. She must have bought it in town. She also had her hair up with curls dangling to frame her face. All parts of me took note of how feminine she looked.

My attraction to her must have shown on my face because she gave me a soft smile as she motioned to the cheese and meat tray in front of us. "Please, go ahead. I've been nibbling already."

"Has he ever done anything like that before?" I popped a slice of salami, a square of Havarti, and a piece of baguette in my mouth and closed my eyes. I almost growled with satisfaction at the combination of salty, creamy, toasty tastes that had more flavor than all the hospital food I'd eaten combined.

When I opened my eyes, I found she grinned at me, obviously pleased with my reaction. "No, but then, this is the first time we've traveled someplace like this."

"Who's Astrid?"

Reine filled me in on the people she'd met and their reactions to her. She tried to hide it, but I could tell how much the anger of the townspeople and their resulting rudeness had bothered her.

"And then that twerp of a sheriff dared to accuse me of killing the deputy! And I couldn't tell him I wasn't lying to him —couldn't lie to him—because he's so stifled in his own magic that he can't see it in others. Minerva thinks it's part of the spell that's over the town."

"I can't imagine that anyone could look at you and see what an amazing magical cr—er, being, you are."

She glanced up at me sideways. "I know you weren't about to call me a creature."

I leaned forward, teased her with our lips only a couple of inches apart. Now that I was clean, I found myself aching to experience her again, this time in my human form. "And what if I was?"

Her breath caressed my face with her reply. "I may have to spank you. I don't care if you've got a big, bad gargoyle hiding inside you."

"Oh, that's not all I have for you, missy." I leaned in to close the distance with my lips, but a yowl from Sir Raleigh broke us apart.

Something small and white streaked out of the corner he'd been sniffing. It moved so fast I couldn't get a good look at it, but it appeared to be longer and narrower than a rat. Some sort of ferret or mink, perhaps?

Raleigh ran after it. He remained in house cat form, likely because he was more agile and could duck under the furniture that way. He chased it through the cabin, under the coffee table, and around table legs. Reine pointed her finger and mumbled something, but frustration crossed her face as her spell missed. I ran to the front door and opened it. The white thing ran outside with Raleigh after it.

Reine glared at me. "What did you do that for? He almost had it."

I couldn't keep my vet voice from coming out. "When dealing with a wild animal, the best place for it to be is outside."

"But what if that was one of the rodents Barton was trying to catch? We could have had another clue as to who our foe is. It could have been spying on us!"

Sir Raleigh returned to the porch and spat out a hunk of flesh with hair still attached to it. Then he sat and looked at me like he expected praise.

"Oh, good kitty!" Reine scooped up the sample and brought it inside. She put it in a plastic container and then into the fridge. "I'll do a spell to see what it was later," she told me as she washed her hands.

"Right, good."

If I didn't know better, I'd say the grimalkin gloated at me.

A knock at the door preceded Minerva opening it. Instead of her uniform, she wore a dark blue dress with a halter top. "Ready to go?"

"Yes, thanks." Reine grabbed her purse and faux leather jacket. I followed her out, then waited as she locked the door.

"Just a warning," Minerva said and started the car. "Mom's in a mood tonight."

MOTHER'S HOUSE turned out to be a Tudor-style mansion in a gated estate in a neighborhood that looked like it had perhaps been built to support a logging town. In other words, she had the biggest, newest, and most ostentatious property there.

"Do you have a big family?" Reine asked as Minerva drove us up the long, winding driveway.

"No, just the three of us."

The house loomed larger as we approached, and my anxiety grew with it. I hoped it didn't show too much in my voice when I asked, "And you all live here? How many bedrooms is this?"

"Five. One for her, one for each of us, a guest room...and one for you." Minerva caught my gaze in the rear-view mirror. "Fair warning, y'all—she was not happy when she found out you went back to the cottage rather than home."

"Great." I slumped back against the seat. "I'm already disappointing expectations I didn't know were there."

Minerva shrugged. "Welcome to The Aerie."

I didn't have time to ask her what she meant because the car rolled to a stop on the drive between the steps leading up to the house and a fountain filled with cavorting stone fish that spit water at each other. Minerva and I got out, and a butler or some other servant in a tuxedo opened Reine's door. She stepped from the vehicle, her Fae mask in place as she surveyed the scenery and the surroundings. She looked unimpressed, and I swallowed my anxiety as we ascended the stairs. What would happen in an all-out war between Reine and my mother? I knew one thing with certainty—the house might not be left standing.

17

REINE

Lawrence put his hand on the small of my back when my foot hit the first stair. I didn't show it, but some pretty angry butterflies had taken up residence in my stomach. I recognized the arrival procedure for what it was—a power move designed to impress and intimidate me. If it had just been Lawrence, I had no doubt he would have been brought in through a side door or garage, like family.

The foyer echoed the grandness of the house's façade. My heels clicked on the marble floors, and brass accents gleamed over mahogany and other dark wood. The butler led us beside the staircase and into a parlor, where Agnes stood talking to a tall older gargoyle, who turned, then bowed when he saw me.

"Your Highness," he said.

"Doctor Renee River," I corrected him. "Although you can be forgiven for the mistake. My mother and I look very much alike."

I didn't know whether news of my ascent to the throne, bypassing my mother, had gotten out, but I didn't want to make that announcement until I had to, and I certainly didn't want it to be to a bunch of gargoyles I didn't know. One of them could be spying for our enemy.

"I meant Prince Lawrence."

"Oh, of course." I anticipated the heat in my cheeks must match the hue of the red roses in the vase on a nearby end table.

Agnes walked over to us, her hands held out. I almost raised my hands to meet hers, but she grasped Lawrence's. "Lawrence, Reine, I'm so glad you could make it. I took the liberty of inviting a few of my close friends so you could meet them. Lawrence, this is Harvey Hollis, the architect who designed the house…"

She took her son around the room and introduced him to the various gargoyles present, six or eight in all. I lost track of them. Everyone oohed and ahhed over Lawrence's miraculous recovery out loud. I caught the subtext—he must have been doing better because he was back where he belonged. I grabbed a glass of sparkling wine from the tray one of the servants passed.

Minerva joined me with her own glass in hand. "Why did you even come?"

"Here tonight?" I sighed. "Because I need her blessing and help with something. We think we know what kind of paranormal enemy we're dealing with, and according to the old laws, we need the blessing of the ruler, in this case the Regent, to draw the creature out." I glanced at Minerva, expecting to see a scowl or skeptical expression, but instead, found she looked… interested, perhaps even intrigued.

"Why can't you just go after it directly?"

"Because when you're dealing with a creature that old, there's a certain dance, a protocol. It has some investment in this town, so it's going to take some effort to extract it."

Minerva nodded. "I'll try to get you a few minutes alone with her."

"Thanks. By the way, I understand you were close to the Deputy. I'm sorry for your loss."

Her brows rose, and she blinked, then said, "Thank you. He had great potential."

What had she seen in him? Had he been a good deputy even while under the influence of the love spell? Did she know about Eliza? I needed to find out where the woman lived since trying to talk to her at the hospital would be too difficult...and might lead the wrong people to Eddie.

Minerva wandered off, leaving me standing with my wine in hand. Lawrence would glance over to me, a pleading expression on his face, but I wasn't going to rescue him. No way would I get in the middle of the relationship between a stubborn woman and her son. He needed to negotiate that for himself.

I wandered to the window, which looked down over the sloping lawn.

"Any luck yet?" a familiar voice asked. I turned to see Barton Lucia, handsome as ever, this time wearing a shirt, tie, jacket, and slacks.

"Not yet. Letting them have their mother-son time and negating the hard work you did to get him better."

He didn't seem annoyed. Instead, he clinked his glass to mine. "Here's to misfits. We always seem to find each other."

"Don't try to charm me, Benandanti."

He had the audacity to laugh. "It's a dirty job, but someone has to do it."

"And what other dirty jobs do you take care of for Regent Agnes?"

Now his eyebrows moved up his forehead. For a second, I imagined myself as Reine, eyebrow herder of the evening.

"I assure you, I'm my own man."

He looked hurt, so I said, "I'm sorry. I didn't mean to offend you."

"A Fae apologizing? Now I have seen everything."

I scanned the room again. "I like to keep humans and paranormals guessing."

Minerva waved me over, so I left Barton standing by himself. He had a point—Fae didn't apologize, at least not usually—but I wasn't a typical Fae.

Minerva leaned over to me, and I couldn't help but notice how pretty she was, even with her simple haircut and the hardness at the sides of her mouth. "She's going to check on dinner before inviting everyone to the dining room. It'll be a good time for you to follow her and ask your favor."

Lawrence joined us, and he ran his finger around the side of his collar even though it was open. "Do you have a cheat sheet for all these people, sis?"

Now it was his turn to get a surprised glance from Minerva, and then her face softened with her rare but lovely smile. "I'll go over them with you later. You'll need to know who they are if you stay."

Lawrence's expression said that was a big *if*, but he choked out, "Thanks."

Agnes slipped out as the butler and maid brought out another round of champagne, and Lawrence and I followed her. I didn't ask him to come along. Maybe he could tell I needed the moral support...or his ability to charm her. We caught up to her before she entered the kitchen.

"Mother, may we have a word?" He grabbed my hand.

"Yes?" She turned and scowled at me, then smoothed her expression for him. "What do the two of you want? I hope it's not to announce an engagement."

My cheeks heated, both at her disapproving tone and at the thought of betrothing myself to Lawrence. My heart filled with sorrow, not joy, considering it would never work out, at least not with our respective responsibilities. Okay, at least not with my responsibilities.

"No, Mother, we're not there in our relationship...yet."

Lawrence smiled down at me, and I returned the expression with effort around my anxiety. "Reine?"

I took a deep breath. "Regent, you asked me to help you find the source of the town's infertility problem. I believe it's tied to the spell over the town, which I've heard originally served a protective purpose. But something has twisted it and is using it for their own nefarious ends."

"That's not helpful information, Doctor River. I need you to help me fix the problem, not tell me fairy tales about it."

I winced at the term *fairy tales* but pressed on. "Creatures like that play by a certain set of rules. I believe I can defeat it, but I need your blessing. Well, Lawrence does. We need to appear together with him as crown prince to turn the energy of the town back in my favor."

"Crown Prince?" Agnes' face lit up with joy. "So you're staying? What about her?"

"I'm not committing to staying, at least not right away. But I do want to help."

"So you don't want to be crown prince." She looked back and forth between the two of us. "What are the two of you playing at?"

Why couldn't she understand? "We're trying to help you, Regent. Lawrence needs your blessing, just for a few days."

She turned to Lawrence. "Of course, I'll give you anything, son, but I have to warn you. I've found out something interesting about your Fae friend here. Did you know she's royalty? Specifically, that she should be on her throne and not here in our humble little town?"

Oh, Hades, someone had outed me. But who? "Everyone's path to their destiny is different. I am still on mine."

"Well, don't try to use that to your advantage. I cannot respect someone who is running away from their responsibilities, even if my son has a thing for her."

"Mother!" Lawrence didn't shout, but his voice carried, and

I thought I heard a reduction in the noise from the kitchen. "You don't know the whole story, and I resent that you're questioning my judgment."

Agnes put her hands on her hips. Was she mocking me, mimicking one of my favorite gestures? "And yet, here you are. You show up on death's door accompanied by a runaway Fae queen, and you've somehow been tricked into bonding with her."

Lawrence spoke with patient firmness he must have invoked many a time when dealing with the administration in the government agency he worked for. "There was no trickery. Both of us entered into willingly with consent."

"And did you make sure you couldn't get her pregnant?" She dropped her voice to a stage whisper. "They can control that, you know."

Lawrence's face reddened, and my heart clenched. He'd been in gargoyle form, which meant he'd been in fuck-and-claim mode. He gave a Fae-worthy answer. "She was making sure she wouldn't."

Agnes looked back and forth between the two of us. "Fine, I'll give you my blessing—my *temporary* blessing—on one condition. That you seriously, with full gargoyle honor, consider staying, Lawrence. As for you..." She turned her fierce, gray gaze on me. "Know that your authority means nothing here. This is my kingdom, and you are here because of my grace. Fae always bring trouble to The Aerie, especially at Beltane."

She stalked into the kitchen.

A bewildered Lawrence turned to me. "What does she mean?"

I sighed. "I think my brother was here around the time of the last murder."

"Reine..." He shook his head. "I'd ask why you didn't tell me, but I know you have your reasons. I just..." He sighed. "I just wish you trusted me more." Then he left me alone in the dark hallway.

I RETURNED to the parlor and accepted another glass of wine from Barton, who raised his eyebrows. I declined to clue him in beyond a slight nod to indicate that Agnes had agreed to our plan. Lawrence came in a second after me, and he avoided me. Dinner passed in an awkward blur, and Barton drove us back to the cabin.

"So Agnes was agreeable?" he asked once we were off the property.

"Yes, she was, if reluctantly." I relaxed slightly into the front passenger seat, although Lawrence faced forward and stared at the back of Barton's head, likely refusing to look at me.

Lawrence spoke through clenched teeth. "Yeah, I'm ready to get this over with. Defeat the witch. Get back to Atlanta, and..." He rubbed his eyes, and my irritation melted. What awaited him back in the place where he lived? His two closest friends had died, his boss was still probably going to go to prison, and his goddaughter...

I sat upright. "Lawrence! You need to call Kestrel, let her know you're okay."

He looked at me, and the pain in his expression made me wince. "You're right. I can't believe I forgot." He looked at his phone. "Damn. It's late over there."

"She's probably back in Atlanta by now. Max was going to arrange it."

"It's late here, too, especially if she's been traveling all day. She'll be tired." Lawrence scowled at me, and I drew back. "Is there anything else you're not telling me?"

This time I turned away and faced the woods illuminated

by the car's headlights. "Not that I can think of. I'll let you know if anything comes to me."

Barton shot me an amused glance, and I reminded myself that if I were to smite him, he'd likely wreck the car. Hades, that smiting urge came up more and more, and I couldn't tell if it was the result of developing a Fae queen's sensitivity to insult or my own frustration at the situation.

Plus, I didn't know what Barton played at. I was sure he'd noticed the chill that had arisen between me and Lawrence before dinner. All right, I couldn't smite him. Barton had sat beside me and kept me involved in the conversation, which was an act of kindness I owed him for.

He dropped us off at the cabin and said, looking only at me, "Let me know if you need anything."

I hoped that my tired smile, all I could muster, conveyed my gratitude. "I'm sure we'll be fine."

Then Lawrence and I ascended the steps and entered the cottage in silence.

"I'm going to take another shower," he announced. "I'm still feeling..." He shrugged. "I don't know. I need a few minutes to myself."

"You don't have to hide in the bathroom. I can take a walk or something."

He growled, and Sir Raleigh darted into the bedroom and under the bed. "You're not going anywhere. It's dangerous for you here. In fact, I don't know why you don't just leave. You've solved the mystery—leave the cleanup to your friend Barton and his Benandanti buddies, assuming he still has some."

Stung, I crossed my arms and met his fierce expression with one of my own. "I don't leave loose ends. I can't. You know this."

"Yet you somehow forgot to tell me that Rhys had been here."

"To be fair, I don't know that it was Rhys. But he had a scar."

"Oh?" He crossed his arms. "How many scarred Fae do you know of?"

"Just the one, but there are a lot of us, as you saw. It's possible that the man dressed as a Templar and the gargoyle wandered around and hunted down others to maim them, keep them exiled." I shivered at the thought. I'd always assumed Rhys' injury had come as a result of the battle we were spying on, but anything was possible. Could there be another maimed Fae, or a whole community of them?

If there were, I could welcome them back, perhaps even heal them as their queen. Assuming they were light Fae.

"And how many more loose ends are you going to have before you disappear back to Faerie forever?" He rubbed his eyes. "That's what you want, isn't it? It's what you've always wanted."

"I..." I didn't know how to argue with him. Yes, I had wanted to go home to Faerie, but it hadn't been what I expected, and when I'd left, it was with more of a burden of responsibility than a joy of returning to my realm of origin.

He walked over to me and placed his large hands on my upper arms, then squeezed with gentle pressure. I knew he had the physical capability to hurt me, and yet I also knew he wouldn't. The pain in his eyes told me that if anyone was hurting, it was him.

"What do you want, Reine?" he asked, the resonance in his voice telling me that it wasn't just his human part talking—it was all of him asking.

I struggled to find an answer, but the overwhelming weight of my responsibilities choked me. "I don't know. I'm sorry, but it's the truth, and it's not like it matters. Can't you see? I have to go back to Faerie to rule. Things are coming to a head there, or they will soon, and they need their leaders."

"You're not the only queen there." He grimaced. Did he recognize what a stupid thing he'd just said?

"No, but you remember what Troubadour and Rhys told us —the dark Fae princess Desdemona has allied with the revenants, or at least is keeping them as pets or something. I don't know that her mother is going to be much help if she's allowing her daughter to act like that." I sighed and tried to turn away, but he held me firm.

"And Fae queens can always control their daughters."

I winced. "That's not fair."

He bowed his head. "I'm sorry. That was out of line. I know you want what's best for Faerie. But do you know what's best for you?"

I shrugged. "Does it matter?"

"It does to me."

Then he let me go and walked into the bathroom.

18

LAWRENCE

I stood and let the water run over my face, my eyes closed. Dammit, why did seeing her standing there in the cabin get to me every time? It was all too easy to imagine the two of us in a place like that, in a cottage of our own. Well, us and Sir Raleigh. I knew the cat/grimalkin wouldn't be going anywhere. He was too attached to her to leave her.

Unfortunately, I felt the same, but she'd probably be leaving me. And what if it hadn't been Rhys who came to The Aerie two decades previously? The thought of him, my father's murderer, so near my mother and younger siblings made me want to hit something in frustration that I hadn't been here to protect them. Even if I knew he hadn't posed a real threat.

I reminded myself to take deep breaths and focus on the sensations around me. I recognized my anger as irrational, arising from the part of myself that was going to be protective no matter what. I had to have faith that I could do this, could control my reactions. I had to believe it was possible since my self-doubt had led to the psychic and supernatural wound that had caused my inner gargoyle to separate from me.

The bathroom door opened and closed, and then the

shower door did as well. I found myself with a naked Fae's arms around my torso, her breasts pressed against my back. My cock immediately stood to attention. Okay, I couldn't control that particular reaction, but I didn't want to. Memories of our previous times together flashed through my mind. The last time, we'd decided to each get the other out of our systems through a night of passion. Obviously, that had not worked like we thought. Instead, we'd ended up with an old-school Fae/gargoyle bond.

"I'm sorry," she whispered so softly I barely caught it above the water noise. "I wish I had easy answers for you, but I don't. I wish I could promise you forever, but I can't."

I turned and took her in my arms. I relished the softness of her against my hardness, her tits against my chest and her belly against my erection.

"Is that to be how it is between us? Only a night here and there?"

She looked up at me, the green of her eyes like the ocean on a perfect day. "I wish it could be different."

"That's new, a Fae wishing rather than granting wishes."

Her lips curled into a rueful grin. "Unfortunately, I can't have a fairy godmother. That would be too meta." She looked down, then back up at me, and her smile stretched into a naughty expression. "Nice wand. I'm sure you could grant a few of *my* wishes."

This time when I growled, it was of possessiveness, but a worry wiggled its way into my mind. "I hope you won't be disappointed. It's not as impressive as the one I have in my gargoyle form." A stab of satisfaction at the memory of my size and performance the last time we'd been together only made me grow harder, if that was possible.

"I won't be disappointed, believe me. And I have a few tricks of my own." She placed her hands on my shoulders, and the glow from her skin illuminated the inside of the shower. She levitated such that she hovered just over my cock, then wrapped her legs around me and, Fates bless her, took possession of me. I held on to her, but didn't have to support her weight, which worked out since I didn't know how well I could. I had more strength than before I'd accepted my inner gargoyle, but I could tell I still wasn't at a hundred percent.

I braced her against the wall, and we moved together as the water flowed over us. When she came, she leaned her head back, giving me access to nibble her neck, and the clenching of her muscles drove me over as well. We held each other in the running water for a few minutes, and it felt like some sort of benediction.

She raised herself off me, and we cleaned up. Then, wrapped in fluffy towels, we made our way to the bedroom. Sir Raleigh lay curled in a cat-circle on the bed and opened one eye when we came in. We slid under the sheets and tried not to disturb him, but he huffed and leaped down, anyway.

She wriggled against me, and we spooned, her back to my front.

"At least this time we don't have to worry about your brother interrupting us," I said. Then I groaned. "I didn't call Kestrel."

Reine spoke with the huskiness of sleepy sexual satisfaction. "I sent her a text and let her know you're okay, and that you'll call her tomorrow. She said she's glad you're better, and she's looking forward to talking to you."

I relaxed, relief washing over me, and I kissed the pointed tip of her ear. "Thank you. I appreciate you taking care of that. Of her. And me."

Now sleepiness took over as the dominant force in her voice. "Maybe she will someday, too."

Did she mean Kestrel would appreciate her, or would take care of me? She breathed evenly against me, and I didn't want to pull her out of her well-deserved rest to ask for clarification.

The problem with having basically slept for a month was that I found it difficult to drift off, even when I tried to inhale and exhale along with her to mimic her rhythm. How long had it been since I'd had a woman in my arms? All right, never like that. I'd not yet found someone I wanted to share such moments with.

Sir Raleigh jumped on the bed and curled up on Reine's pillow, on the other side of her. I reached out and scratched his ears, and he purred. His rumbling finally put me to sleep.

The next thing I knew, sunlight stabbed my eyes. I pried my eyelids open to find Reine standing beside the bed wearing a green terrycloth robe and holding a cup of coffee.

"Good morning, Prince Lawrence. Are you ready to meet your people?"

I rolled over and covered my eyes with my right forearm. "Can't this wait?" Then I peered out from beneath my arm. "Want to take another shower?"

She laughed, and the sound made me grin. "Nice try. Come on, I've got breakfast ready for you."

She left the coffee on the nightstand and left, closing the door behind her, but not before I caught a whiff of bacon.

Sir Raleigh stood from his spot on her pillow and stretched, and then he looked at me.

"She may not have meant to say it, but I think she does love me."

He looked at me with the classic cat expression of, *Ya think, dumbass?*

I scooted to a seat and placed my head in my hands as the impossibilities of our situation washed over me. "The problem is, I love her, too."

Well, this was going to suck.

～

Minerva picked us up after breakfast and a post-breakfast bedroom interlude. When I made love to Reine that morning, it was just the two of us in my head, and I could almost fool myself into believing we were somewhere in the mountains on a honeymoon. Unfortunately, reality intruded all too quickly, and we scrambled to get dressed when Minerva's car horn jerked us out of our post-coital stupor.

If my sister noticed anything amiss in Reine's slightly swollen lips or the silly grin I couldn't seem to keep off my face, she didn't say so, which I thought odd considering she'd proved to be a direct communicator. Instead, she sighed and turned, but not before I caught the sadness flitting across her face. Was she worried about me? Grieving the fact she didn't have someone to sneak in a quickie after breakfast with? What would our mother do if Minerva dared to live her own life? From what I'd observed, Agnes treated Minerva as a personal assistant and head of her security detail, not much like a daughter. It didn't take extra special gargoyle alertness for emotional distress in those I was trusted to protect to figure out that there was some history there, an old wound that hadn't healed.

Minerva's first question indicated that she played the role of security that day, which I supposed was appropriate considering both Reine and I sat in the back seat. "Did you notice anything threatening or amiss last night, Lawrence?"

Reine bit her lip, and I could tell she struggled not to make some sort of smartass Fae remark, like the only thing that had threatened me was her desire to seduce me.

I poked Reine's thigh, which was covered in a lacy white sun dress under her leather jacket. "No, all was quiet." *Well, except...* I shook my head. I couldn't do that to Minerva. Even though we'd only just met, I didn't want to distress her by giving her mental images of her big brother's activities. No matter how they'd been separated, there were things that siblings just didn't need to know about each other, or have made obvious if they guessed. Reine took my hand and winked.

"Good. I'm taking you to the visitor's center. You two will start there and walk through town. Doctor River, have you thought about your route?"

"Yes. We'll visit Augie, then come back around by the visitor's center. We'll get coffee at the Dancing Dragon, then walk up and down Main Street, ending at the inn."

"Augie?" I asked.

"Yes, there's an impressively detailed stone statue of a gargoyle by a bridge that one of the paths from the hospital leads to. It's like he's guarding the town from that direction."

I'd of course heard the legend, but I hadn't thought about it actually being here until now. Past and present came crashing together in my awareness, and a wave of dizziness overtook me.

"You all right?" Reine squeezed my fingers.

"Yes... The legend is that Augie, who was an uncle of ours, was unable to fight the urge to remain a gargoyle." I had new sympathy for him, considering how strong my inner gargoyle-self had shown himself to be. "He ended up turning to stone one morning at dawn, and now he guards the entrance to the town."

Minerva nodded. "That's what I was told, too. When did you hear it?"

"Back in the late eighteenth century."

"You're that old?" Minerva's surprised look and question lifted my mood.

"Yes. And Reine is even older. Didn't you know that we live for a while?"

Her shoulders moved with a sigh. "Yeah, but I'd not seen proof, and Mum never answers any questions about her age. It's not like the good citizens of The Aerie walk around with their numerical ages on display. Great, just great."

We pulled into the parking lot by the visitor's center, and

Minerva parked the car. "I'm going to check on something. Y'all coming in?"

"It's worth seeing," Reine told me. "Although the timeline doesn't track with your legend of Augie, unless they moved him when they came."

Minerva walked ahead of us, then held the door open. "I suspect it's a cautionary tale told to young gargoyles."

A plump young woman jumped up from behind the desk, her eyes wide at the sight of Minerva and the two of us. Was this the clerk Reine had disturbed so much with her questions the day before?

Reine attempted a gentle tone. "Good morning, Karen."

"Good morning, Doctor River. Agent Gordon. And…oh! Are you Prince Lawrence?"

I winced, and Reine elbowed me. "I suppose I am. You can call me Lawrence. Or Doctor Gordon, if you want to be formal, but you don't have to."

"Oh! Welcome, welcome! Can I get you anything?"

"No, thank you. I'll just look around, get my bearings."

She darted out from behind the desk and almost stepped on Sir Raleigh, who squawked and darted out of the way. "Oh, I'm so sorry, kitty. Come here." She knelt and held out a hand. Sir Raleigh went to her and allowed her to pet him like they were old friends. "Such a good boy. Please forgive me."

Sir Raleigh rolled on his back and allowed her to rub his tummy. Reine and I turned to each other, and I'm sure my expression mirrored her shocked one. She said, "He's never allowed anyone to do that."

Karen put her hands on her knees and raised herself to standing. "Oh, I have a special way with animals, especially the grumpy ones." She slid a glance at Minerva, who cleared her throat.

Minerva ignored her and addressed me. "Do you have any questions for Miss Lovejoy? She's our town secretary."

"Uh, sure." I looked around. "Can you give me a quick and dirty history of the town? I feel like I'm walking into this blind."

"Oh, of course!" She walked to a photographic display. "The Aerie was founded in the late eighteenth century when settlers came from the British Isles, but also elsewhere. Our gargoyle forefathers and mothers came with the others seeking freedom from persecution from, uh..." She looked at Reine. "From those who didn't like them." She went on to tell a typical settlement story, and then how the town had originally been the site of a sanitarium for gargoyles who were ill or stressed in the nineteenth century, finally settling into a tourist spot as well as a place for healing after the Civil War. "And now that's our main industry, tourism for the paranormal types."

"No humans come here?" I remembered Reine telling me about the dead end she'd reached in her questioning and went for a more indirect approach. "That's surprising. Normally you can't keep them away."

Karen looked back and forth between Reine and Minerva. "Uh, well, we don't advertise to them, you see, and whenever The Aerie makes it on to one of their review sites, we always give it negative ratings so no one will want to come. But we always get excellent reviews among the paranormals."

"So, it's publicity."

She nodded, perhaps too vigorously. "Yes, you can't underestimate the power of the written word, especially among humans."

"Interesting."

Reine gestured to the woods outside. "What about the statue by the river? It's quite well done and beautifully detailed."

"Oh, yes, that's Uncle Augie. He's our town guardian against anything evil that may come from the mountains to the north and east. Legend has it that he's a gargoyle who refused to change back, and so turned to stone, but that's just a legend."

Reine nodded. "So you know who the artist was?"

"Some very talented gargoyle back in the day. His or her name was lost to history, unfortunately. Perhaps they didn't want to be recognized to give the legend more power."

Minerva chuckled, and I turned to her with a surprised look. "What?" she asked. "I can tell you it scared the giblets out of me when I was a kid. I definitely monitor my emotions during changes more carefully as a result. Hell, I don't change unless I have to."

"I do the same," I agreed, and Karen nodded again.

The thoughtful line between Reine's brows had reappeared. "Yes, when it comes to legends, it's interesting to tease out truth versus purpose. And then in the end, does it matter if it accomplishes the original intent?"

Minerva regarded Reine with a scowl. "Sure it does, if it means you're emotionally manipulating and unnecessarily frightening children."

Yes, there was definitely some history there.

Reine inclined her head. "Point taken, Agent Gordon. It's always important to remember the harm such things have resulted in or could cause."

Was she thinking about some of the legends in Faerie she'd accepted without questioning? And the nightmare of one that was coming to life?

Minerva's shoulders and jaw relaxed. "Thank you, Doctor River. You're turning out to be more reasonable than I'd expected for one of your kind."

I braced myself for a sharp retort, but Reine inclined her head. "I'm happy to surprise you."

Karen walked back behind her desk and audibly sighed at her computer screen.

Minerva arched an eyebrow. "I'm sorry, are we disturbing you, Miss Lovejoy?"

"Oh, no, but I do have a lot of work to do, mostly making

sure everything is in place for tonight's festival. Please let me know if you need anything. Otherwise, I'll be back here."

I placed my hand on the small of Reine's back. Her faux leather jacket felt cool to my touch, and her muscles moved underneath my fingertips as we walked toward the door. "I think we're good. Thank you for your help."

Minerva followed us out, and Reine brought me to the statue of Augie by the river. Whoever had carved him had done a bang-up job, even to the raised blood vessels under his skin, the surface of which had softened with so many decades of erosion. His eyes stared blankly ahead, and I imagined they had been even more piercing when the statue had originally been made.

I clasped one muscular shoulder. "Whatever you are, thank you for guarding The Aerie." Then I released him and held my breath for a second. Did I expect him to respond, to move for the Crown Prince, or pretend Crown Prince?

Even though Augie was supposedly a statue, I felt something watching me when we turned and walked back toward the town in silence. Or perhaps that was my anxiety at what lay ahead. Would the townspeople change their attitude toward Reine? Karen Lovejoy certainly seemed less hostile toward her than I'd expected.

And if they weren't nice to her, would my inner gargoyle threaten to take over and make sure they did? That would cause the kind of trouble no one could fix.

19

REINE

"**A**re you all right?" I asked Lawrence.

He nodded, but his mouth twisted into a grimace. "I'd always taken the tale of Uncle Augie literally, you know? It's tough to find out that a legend you took to be true is a fairy tale. No offense."

I squeezed his hand. "None taken. I felt that way much of the time I was in Faerie, but about my memories. At least your mother hasn't tried to kill you yet."

"Not that we know of."

Minerva caught up to us as we approached the visitor's center. "What exactly are you looking for with this tour?" She motioned to the building and the town beyond. "You're not going to find anything, you know."

I'd forgotten that Minerva's youth meant she hadn't been schooled in the old protocols. "I'm not looking for anything specific. I'm hoping to draw out our foe so she'll reveal something that will allow me to figure out what we're dealing with. What you've been dealing with."

"That makes sense, although I don't like you using my brother as bait." Her scowl reminded me of Lawrence's again.

Both were fiercely protective of their loved ones. I sensed there was more to Minerva than she'd allowed me to see. She must have wanted something beyond being her mother's enforcer and chauffeur, but I couldn't tell what. Gargoyles did like their rules and structures. Did Minerva want to better define the ones for her life?

Lawrence met her frown with one of his own. "I'm not helpless, sis, even if I was just in the hospital. I could probably take you in an arm-wrestling match."

She granted him a fierce smile. "You're on. After this charade, meet me at the River Pub. Then we'll see who's stronger."

Sometimes my bond with Lawrence allowed me a glimpse of his emotions, like an ethereal whiff of buttery pastry on the breeze outside a bakery. He enjoyed the banter with his sister, and his reaction to it reminded me of how isolated he'd been growing up, first with his mother, and then on his own. I shared in his happiness, but it gave me a pang of grief. Could I take him away from his newfound family, even if it was possible for him to not die if he came to Faerie? How could I go against my own value of family loyalty and do that? It would be no better than my mother's betrayal. Well, without the attempted slaying of the preferred heir to the throne.

We walked along the path that wound through the topiary garden and its oversized green animals, and I had the first inkling of something watching us. The leaves in one of the trees shaped as a seal balancing a ball on its nose rustled, but nothing emerged. In fact, not even the birds sang in this part of the garden. The hair on my neck prickled as we walked by. Minerva and I exchanged a glance, and she dipped her chin in acknowledgment. As much as I might have resented her presence, I added gratitude for the validation and extra security to my feelings about her.

Lawrence pulled me closer to him, so I knew he felt it as

well. Then, once we rounded a bend, the feeling subsided, and the sounds of birdsong returned.

"Did you feel that?" Lawrence whispered. Minerva and I both nodded. "What could do that? Shut the birds up and create that creepy sensation?"

I rose to my toes and kissed him on the cheek "Ah, you are, as ever, the scientist. We need more data."

A wall of hedges separated the topiary garden from the coffee shop patio, and I braced myself when we walked through the gap and on to the smooth concrete. Had the townspeople changed in their attitude toward me? What should I do if they didn't? I got another sense from Lawrence, this time determination, and I knew he wouldn't allow any offense to be directed at me.

The two tables of patrons looked up as we walked past, and their whispers held curiosity, not malice. I relaxed slightly but tensed again as we walked into the building and saw the barista who had been so rude to me. His face lit with a smile, and he walked around the counter to shake Lawrence's hand.

"Prince Lawrence, it's truly an honor. Thank you for coming in. What can I get you, Agent Gordon, and your lovely companion?"

The sense of being not invisible exactly, but definitely outshone, disoriented me. Did he not recognize me? Or did he not care?

"Why are you looking so surprised?" Minerva murmured in my ear. "Isn't this what you wanted?"

"Yes, it is." And it wasn't. I'd have to sort out my conflicting feelings from Lawrence's. It didn't require a special connection with him to see the tightness in his jaw and stiffness of his shoulders. He'd never been a celebrity before, poor guy.

"Try not to look so uncomfortable," I whispered to him, then added in secret conversation, *"These are your people. You need to be gracious and accepting of their adoration while conveying the assurance that you're here for them."*

"I don't know any of this stuff. You're the ruler, not me."

"You are today. Act as if you were taking on the role. Believe me, your mother's eyes are on us, even if we can't see them."

He rolled his shoulders back and managed a slight smile. "Thank you. I'd like a skim latte please. Doctor River?"

"English Breakfast tea, if you've gotten it in."

The barista's hair flopped with the force of his nodding. "Of course, of course, and for you, Agent Gordon?"

"Water." Of course Minerva wouldn't ask for something as frivolous as a coffee drink, at least not on the job.

We got our drinks and walked outside. Lawrence still moved stiffly, but he seemed to get some of his fluidity back when he looked up and down Main Street. I tried to imagine what it looked like through his eyes—a pretty little town full of creatures just like him on a scenic river. Was he thinking that the water likely teemed with trout and other nostalgic and delightful things that might remind him of his long-ago child-hood, those golden years before my brother had murdered his father?

Did he feel the tug of home like I did in Faerie? And had it faded for him like Faerie's appeal?

I breathed in the fresh air of the surrounding forest and grounded myself in the delightful energy I could still tap into in spite of the counter-effects of the spell over the town. The fog over my thoughts cleared along with the doubts and despair that had tried to creep in. That, more than anything, concerned me—what sort of witch or other powerful being could command so insidious a magic? Love spells, which most likely were lust spells, were one thing. Loss of faith in love spells was completely different and on a higher plane of ethical violation. Why hadn't the Truth Seekers gotten involved? Although this was a case of paranormal-on-paranormal interference, it seemed just the sort of thing they'd stick their noses into in case the trouble spread to the surrounding human communities.

I set my jaw. This bitch was going down.

Lawrence's chuckle brought me back to our present, and he squeezed my hand again. "You've got that look like when someone is about to be in big trouble."

I grinned up at him and then tugged his arm so we walked toward the park. "You know me well. What do you feel?"

His brows came together in his classic thinking expression. "It's like home, but a distorted image of it. I grew up on a river, and we had a cute little town like this we'd go into for supplies and social things, but the nearby city always loomed over us. That's how this feels—like something is hovering, and while it may not want to exert its power over us all the time, it knows it can."

"It already is." I nodded to a shopkeeper from whom I'd bought the dresses I wore that day and the night before. She swept the sidewalk in front of her store, and when she smiled, only had eyes for Lawrence. That was the case as we walked by the other boutiques on that side of the street. I could almost feel the energy clearing and turning as we passed. Yes, this magic responded to traditional stimuli, namely an heir returning to claim his birthright, even though he really wasn't. Or did the magic know something I didn't? Could Lawrence be falling under the spell of the traditions and connections that had been so deeply ingrained in him as a child?

We finished our drinks when we reached the park. Minerva took our cups and sorted the trash and recycling into nearby bins. Lawrence and I sat on the bench where I'd had the strange episode the previous day. Nothing happened except a bird tweeting nearby and two squirrels chasing each other.

"Are you all right?" I couldn't stop asking him that. "I mean,

I know you've gotten a dose of renewed vigor, but you were pretty sick."

He put his arm behind me across the back of the bench. "I'm here under the care of a good doctor. How could I not feel fantastic?"

A bright spot across the street caught my attention. Astrid emerged from the Fudge Shoppe, her copper hair catching and gleaming in the sunlight. She wore a white chef's top and turquoise pants underneath.

Lawrence sat straighter. "Who's that?"

"That's Astrid, the one I'm renting the cabin from."

He blinked and squinted like he couldn't quite make her out clearly. "Where did you say she's from?"

"Not from around here," Minerva practically growled. She hadn't reached for a weapon—if she even carried one, I didn't know—but a subtle shift in her stance told me she had moved to protective mode. Right, Astrid had told me she avoided Minerva, although I couldn't remember why.

She didn't seem to have any issue today. Astrid crossed the street and walked toward us carrying a white pastry box. When she reached us, she knelt on one knee and proffered the box to Lawrence.

"Prince Lawrence, I am honored that you've decided to grace the town with your presence. Please accept this strawberry pastry from my shop as a token of my respect and appreciation."

Lawrence accepted the box with, "Thank you. Please don't do that. I'm just a gargoyle like everyone else."

She rose, and the grass stain that looked like it had started on her knee faded. I felt the magic and had to admire her attention to detail. But then, I'd noticed it in the cabin and in her baked goods.

When Lawrence opened the box, Sir Raleigh jumped on to the bench and sniffed at it. Perhaps he remembered my reaction of the day before. He nodded like it had passed inspection, and Lawrence lifted out a layered pastry of cream, strawberries, and dense white cake. Although we'd had a substantial breakfast, our stomachs growled in unison, and Astrid smiled.

"It appears my offering is well-timed. Please, enjoy." She turned and walked away.

Lawrence held out the pastry to me, and I couldn't help but sniff as well, with all my senses. I couldn't detect anything amiss about it, so I took a bite, and then he did, and soon we'd finished the shortcake-like confection.

The sugar from the dessert and the caffeine in my bloodstream mingled in a happy tune. The air felt fresher, and the sky bluer. Minerva still scowled, but less fiercely than previously.

"What now?" Lawrence asked. "Have you noticed anything?"

"Not since the topiary garden. At least nothing I can put my finger on." But something had shifted, subtly but meaningfully. I'd own my addiction to sugar and caffeine and acknowledge I'd just gotten a good hit, but could Lawrence's presence be responsible for the almost euphoric feeling in the atmosphere?

Minerva checked her watch. "It's time to get moving."

We stood and followed her back to Main Street. She led us past the shops on that side, and this time the owners appeared to see me and acknowledge me more. What in the world was happening? We ended up looking over the river, and I again reached out with my Fae senses to call whatever nymph or dryad may be present, and received nothing.

The pastry should have held us, but I found myself hungry again. Could I be burning more calories in my efforts to counteract the spell over the town, even if they occurred mostly below my awareness?

Minerva checked her watch. "Y'all have reservations at the

River Rock Restaurant in ten minutes. That's Mum's favorite place, and the owner is excited you're coming."

I noticed she said *you're*, not *we're*. "Won't you be accompanying us?"

"I need to get back to work. This was all the time Mum gave me. Look, I want to help, I really do, but I feel like a third wheel here. Plus, there hasn't been any sign of a threat since the topiary garden unless you count Astrid and her diabetes-inducing treats."

Lawrence straightened, and for a second I saw the shadow of his wings on the ground. "Go on, sis. I can take care of us."

She nodded. "I'll take you up on that arm-wrestling challenge later."

Minerva left us alone, and Lawrence turned to me. "Whatever shall we do now that we've been left alone?"

"I guess we should have lunch. Then we have a spa date."

He raised his eyebrows. "You didn't tell me that part. I may have been more eager for the day if I'd known."

We turned away from the river, but a splash caught my attention. I turned to see a pair of transparent white arms emerge from the water. Time slowed, or seemed to, and the water quieted as I watched the limbs move together such that the palms of their hands met in an old signal I'd almost forgotten the meaning of—*Help me.* Then they vanished, and the sound returned.

"What was that?" Lawrence asked.

The warmth of the sunshine couldn't dispel the chill that flowed from the crown of my head to my feet. "A warning." Suddenly, I wished that Minerva hadn't left us.

20

LAWRENCE

I didn't know what Reine had seen, but she'd gone more pale than usual. I drew her away from the river, which she seemed determined to stare into until she got some answers. Once we reached the sidewalk again, she shook her head, and her gaze cleared.

"I don't know what that was, but I wish I did. I've been trying to reach the river nymph because it feels like there must be one. I don't know if that was her, or her ghost. Or a non-aware shade from the past replaying its last moments."

"In the middle of the day in the sunlight? I've never heard of a ghost or shade behaving like that."

She nodded, but she looked perplexed as well. "If the desire to get the message across is strong enough, they can appear at any time."

We walked to the River Rock Restaurant, which had a patio off Main Street with a large, black, wrought iron fountain in the middle. Water cascaded over its round tiers, and smooth river stones sat at the bottom of the lowest one.

The host approached us. "Ah, Prince Lawrence and Doctor River, welcome. I see you've noticed our fountain."

Reine spoke without sarcasm, "It's rather hard to miss."

He laughed. "The rocks on the bottom are from each of the rivers near each of The Aerie settlements. There's no major magic to them, but they help us feel connected to each other."

I looked back at the stones, admiring the variety of shapes and colors, all worn smooth. "So each of the Aerie villages has a fountain like this?"

"A fountain or some other installation at their own River Rock Restaurant."

I touched the fountain and had a pang of disappointment when I couldn't feel anything. I don't know what I expected, but I guessed I hoped for some sort of answer to what the heck I was supposed to do. Seeing the stones and thinking of the connection to the other gargoyles around the world highlighted how isolated I'd been, how focused I'd been on my task of finding my father's murderer, and then of trying to do some greater good through my training as a veterinarian and then with my work at the Center for Paranormal Disease Control. I'd made science my comfort and my guide when revenge had appeared off the table.

And then when I could have had revenge, I hadn't. What would my gargoyle kin think about that, especially since the situation involved a Fae?

I turned from the fountain, a strange shame blooming in my gut even though I knew my reasons for acting as I had were valid. "I understand we have reservations."

The host nodded, his expression serious and cautious. I tried to relax my face into a smile. I hadn't meant to scare the poor kid.

"Yes, would you like to sit outside since you have your animal companion with you?"

Reine gave him a soothing smile. "Yes, please. And if you have a table and chairs made of wood, not wrought iron, that would be great."

She'd stayed two yards back from the fountain, and I mentally kicked myself. Of course a Fae wouldn't react well to the iron. My shame intensified—how could I have forgotten?

"Of course, I have just the one." He led us to a wooden table with a round marble top. Even better, it stood in a corner in the shade behind a wall of terra cotta pots stacked to allow the plants in them some light in the gaps and the table behind them some privacy. Once he left us with menus. Sir Raleigh, who mostly ignored me, rubbed against my legs before settling under the table. Could he feel my mixed emotions?

I glanced over my menu at Reine. "Please don't ask if I'm all right again."

She rubbed her breastbone. "I don't think I have to. Something about the river rocks got to you, didn't it?"

I nodded. Could she feel everything I did? That could get embarrassing.

"Don't worry, I can't read all your emotions, just the strong ones. Well, unless you allow them to show physically, which you're definitely doing more of since leaving the hospital."

"Yeah, thanks inner gargoyle." Now I added vulnerability to my list of *Currently experienced uncomfortable emotions, Post-integration, Version one.*

She reached across the table and covered my hand with hers. "No, no, I like it. It's much better than your stone face. You look friendlier, too."

"Thanks." I pulled my hand back and turned my attention to the menu to distract myself from my thoughts and the hurt that flickered across her face. "Do they have stuff here you can eat?"

She rewarded me with a smile. "Yes, thank you. I picked dinner up from here a couple of nights ago." She returned her gaze to her menu, but she captured her bottom lip in her upper front teeth.

"What happened?"

She shook her head and didn't look up. "We can talk about it later." Then her eyes met mine over our menus. "Don't worry about it. The situation has already improved drastically."

"We hope." I still didn't have much of an idea of what we were doing, what we were supposed to be looking for. Reine was in her element with these games of subtlety and the old rules she could slip into without thinking about them. I suspected that if my inner gargoyle and I had maintained our separation, we'd agree that we wanted to just smash something and be done with it. Or he'd be trying to convince me of that, and I would be arguing that we needed to collect data before we smashed.

I put the menu down, the realization that I'd somehow lost my scientific focus hitting me like a boulder to the head. My scalp even prickled, and I resisted the urge to look up to see if something hovered over me.

Reine arched an eyebrow at me, asking whether I was okay without actually asking it.

"Yes, I'm still trying to figure out how to balance myself internally. Being here is confusing. I wish I could elaborate, but I can't."

A young female server came over with two glasses of water, and I took a long swallow of the cool liquid.

"Would you like to know the day's specials?" The corners of her mouth turned up, but her hand trembled as she pulled out her notepad.

Reine spoke in the gentle voice she usually reserved for animals when she said, "That would be lovely." I barely paid attention to the server's words as expressions of determination and anxiety fought each other for dominance. She looked back and forth between us, and I couldn't tell—was she more frightened of Reine, or of me? Sorrow added itself to my list along with unfounded guilt. It hadn't occurred to me that by acting as my mother's representative, I allowed myself to be compared to her, and gargoyles here might expect me to embody her traits, including the worst ones. Could that be the explanation for why Micah and Minerva had such different personalities—they rebelled and responded to the environment that shaped them as our mother's children. What had their father been like?

As though summoned, Micah strode on to the patio and waved to us. He leaned down and pecked the server on the cheek. "Got another chair for this tiny table, Lizzy? I'll have the trout."

"Of course, Agent Micah." She beamed at him, and she seemed so relieved at his presence that I couldn't argue that he hadn't been invited. "And for the two of you?"

Reine glanced at me before ordering a kale and apple salad with goat cheese and walnuts.

"Any protein on that, hon?" The server had definitely achieved a new comfort level with Micah there.

Reine raised her eyebrows, and I stifled a laugh. I doubted she'd been called *hon* much, if ever. "No, thank you. I'm mostly a vegetarian."

"Got it. And you, Prince Lawrence?"

I winced at the title, and Micah didn't bother to hide his amusement.

"I'll, ah, have the trout." I'd been eying it, and it felt simpler. Perhaps the root of my confusion lay in the fact that every time I thought I understood the situation, another layer of complexity added itself.

Another server brought over a chair for Micah, and he sat, then leaned back so the chair balanced on its back legs. "How's it going, *Prince* Lawrence?"

I imagined giving him just the slightest push to send him toppling into the wall of greenery behind him, but I didn't want to cause the restaurant staff any extra trouble with cleaning, not to mention the damage it would cause the plants.

"As well as could be expected, I guess. What are you doing here?"

"I was passing through and saw you sitting back here."

"How?" Reine asked. "The plants make for a nice screen." I couldn't read her expression. She said I had a stone face, but when she retreated into inscrutable Fae, there was no telling what she felt.

"Oh, I have ways."

I might have taken some delight in bringing his cockiness down a peg with, "You read our schedule, or Minerva shared it with you." Aha. Somehow, I knew she wouldn't abandon us completely.

"All right, fine, that may have been the case." He frowned. "You could let a guy have a little fun."

"And you could let me have a nice lunch with my..." My what? Girlfriend? Partner? Calling her my bond-mate would lead to more explaining than I cared to do, although I suspected he would know if Mother kept him and Minerva up to date with the situation. I settled on, "girlfriend." I'd never been one for casual sex, so I felt justified in claiming the title for her. A rumble of satisfaction deep in my chest indicated my entire being approved.

"Oh, we all know this is for show, and you'll be heading back to Atlanta or Scotland or wherever you two are going to settle once this is over or you give up."

Reine cocked her head. "What do you mean?"

He gestured upward, presumably toward the dome of the spell that kept the clouds at bay except for when The Aerie really needed rain. "Look, this thing has been here for forever, and it's not going to be easy to get rid of it. Do you think it's going to leave without a fight?"

Two servers brought our food over and set it down along with a mug with a tea bag and a small ceramic pot of hot water for Reine and an iced tea for me. Micah got a soda.

The trout distracted me for a moment. It lay perfectly cooked on a bed of wild rice and spinach and had been baked with a topping of crumbs, mustard, and herbs until done and crispy, but not dry.

"They do know how to do trout here," I acknowledged. "It's delicious. Reine, do you want to try some?"

"No, thanks." She sent a nervous glance in the direction of the river. Did she not want to eat something that came from waters she perceived as contaminated...or haunted?

I didn't mind, and neither did Micah. We didn't talk much as we ate, and soon our empty plates were whisked away.

"Would y'all like any dessert?" Lizzy asked. "We have a great chocolate mousse cake, and our seasonal offering is strawberry shortcake."

"Where do they come from?" Reine asked.

"From the Fudge Shoppe. Astrid bakes all the desserts for the places in town."

I jumped in to spare Reine the potential embarrassment of refusing and appearing like she had some sort of issue with the redheaded baker. "Thanks, but we already had the shortcake earlier."

Micah patted his belly. "And I need to stay in shape. You know my addiction runs to the liquid." He saluted her with his now-empty glass of soda.

"One for the road, Agent?"

"Always."

She left, and I turned to Micah. "Are you going to be our shadow now?"

"Well, the prince and his consort need a guard, right? Mum wasn't happy that Minerva left y'all alone even though she put the time limit on her."

And for some reason, I wasn't happy he sat with us now. "As much as I like Minerva and her dedication to her task, I believe we were doing just fine without a babysitter."

Reine continued to study Micah, then nodded at some sort of internal conclusion she'd drawn. "It's all right, Lawrence. It's all part of the performance. Royalty does need its guard."

She had a point. I asked her, "Have you noticed anything unusual?"

"Not since the river."

Micah leaned forward. "Oh, that sounds interesting. What happened at the river?"

Reine shrugged with one shoulder. "I'll let you know when I figure it out myself."

"Fair enough, dear Fae."

Now Reine gave him a dangerous grin. "Oh, haven't you realized? There's no fair in Fae." Now she mimicked his gesture toward the sky. "And in case you hadn't figured it out yet, we don't give up." She pointed a finger at his chair, and he jumped up and rubbed his bottom.

"What was that for?"

"To remind you that while you're for show, only one of us carries the true firepower here."

He looked at the chair, which still emanated heat. "Understood. I'll take my orders from you."

It should have bothered me that he recognized Reine as the true authority, but in fact, it relieved me. The sooner I could be done with this whole fake prince thing, the better.

We paid the check and headed back toward the park and the inn behind it, where we were supposedly going to relax in the underground hot springs. What did it say about me that I hoped it would be more interesting than relaxing?

That Reine and I made a perfect pair. The question was, would we get to be one in the end?

She grabbed my arm before I could walk too far down the path of melancholy. "Lawrence, look!"

"What?" I directed my attention to the spot where she pointed, under the bench where we'd sat earlier. A white rodent like the one that had been in the cabin stood on its hind legs, looked straight at us, and then vanished.

She grinned up at me. "Do you know what that means?"

"That the park needs more cats?"

Sir Raleigh gave me an unamused look.

"No, that we're on the right track, and the rodents are definitely connected."

Micah trotted up behind us. He'd lagged behind while flirting with a shopkeeper. "What'd I miss?"

21

REINE

Micah followed me and Lawrence to the Cloud Inn. The lobby itself had been painted a robin's egg blue with white, wispy clouds painted over it. The golden accents of brass hinted at sunbeams, and the furniture also had a fluffy cloud feel with overstuffed cream chairs and light-colored, wooden tables. All of it faced a stacked river stone fireplace that took up the whole of one wall. It felt too bright to me—what did they have to hide that they needed all this distracting lightness?—but Lawrence and Micah both twitched their shoulders and grinned at each other. Did the decor serve as a stimulus to remind gargoyles of their times in flight?

The clerks greeted Lawrence and Micah with surprise and warmth and confirmed our appointments in fifteen minutes. I spotted the brass sign for "Spa, Grotto Floor." It pointed to a stairwell beside an elevator, and I headed straight for that opening before they finished their conversation. Let them think me a rude Fae, I had to get out of there. It felt too exposed, and if my wings wanted to emerge, it would be to escape. I did pause to think once I entered the relative gloom of the stairwell, which was lined with pictures of the inn and various presumably famous gargoyle guests I'd never heard of. One would assume that a Fae would appreciate the sky, as air was one of our elements.

Lawrence's deep voice wrapped around me as he caught up. "Now it's my turn to ask—are you all right?"

"Yes, although something about the lobby disturbed me. I don't know why. Normally I love the sky."

He rubbed my lower back, and I relaxed into his touch. It never failed to calm me. "Is it because you don't feel safe here in The Aerie?"

I searched his tone for sadness or wistfulness, but he spoke with the assurance of a scientist seeking data. I appreciated that, and his attitude helped me to answer truthfully. "Yes. And I hate feeling like I need to hide, both physically and who I am."

We continued our descent into the spa, which welcomed us with the mingled scents of lavender and other relaxing herbs. Down here in The Grotto, the walls had been painted a dusky green with the silhouettes of branches. Dark wood made up the desk, accent tables, and chairs, which were also upholstered in forest greens and browns.

Lawrence took in the décor with a bemused expression. "Are you more comfortable down here?"

I inhaled deeply, both for the smells and because I could feel the Earth enveloping us. I could also track the caves and tap into their power. It wasn't the same as the ones in Scotland, but more in the sense of a different flavor of power rather than anything less, like the difference between two flavors of ice cream—both would give the same sugar hit, but with alternate experiences.

Why had I reacted so negatively to the décor on the main floor? Could I have gotten too much sun, or otherwise been weakened by the exposure to the taint of the spell in the air above? The question made me frown with a new sense of vulnerability. If something was going to affect me, I didn't want it to do so without my knowledge.

"Yes, it's cozy down here." I took Lawrence's hand. "I'm looking forward to relaxing a bit. It's been a stressful few days." But also with alertness for what might be watching me. I had to remind myself not to relax too much.

A male clerk with curly dark hair, the stone-gray eyes of the gargoyles, and nicely built arms—massage therapist?—emerged from the area behind the desk and grinned at us. "Welcome to The Spa at the Cloud Inn."

"Thank you." Lawrence returned his smile.

He handed us each a clipboard with the medical information forms and waiver paperwork, and once we'd turned them in, he showed us the men's and women's changing rooms. At that point, I realized that Micah hadn't followed us downstairs.

"Where's your brother?" I asked Lawrence once we met up again in the Inner Sanctuary to wait for our massage therapists.

"He's waiting for us upstairs. And, I suspect, flirting with the cute hotel clerk."

"Does he have a woman in every business?"

Lawrence chuckled. "Possibly. He does seem to have gotten around. I'm surprised they put up with it. Gargoyles aren't polyamorous like the Fae."

I almost retorted, "Not that you know of," but refrained. I suspected it pained him to be so out of touch with his own home culture. Again, why hadn't his mother reached out to him, at least to invite him for a visit and to introduce him to his younger siblings?

Our massage therapists came in, and while I didn't find the male masseuse's touch to be as calming as Lawrence's, I appreciated his help with the tight muscles in my upper back, shoulders, and neck.

"Goodness, you're tight. Have you been hunching or bracing a lot?"

"Not that I can remember." I spoke into the face cradle, which muffled my words, but he seemed to understand.

"Sometimes we do it without realizing we're doing it, especially when we're really stressed. Have you dealt with a lot lately?"

"You have no idea."

I thought I heard Lawrence grunt in agreement from the other table in the room, but I couldn't be sure.

After ninety minutes of relaxation that I would never have allowed myself to take otherwise, we sat in the innermost part of the spa, a true grotto in a cave. A natural indoor waterfall trickled down the opposite wall from us into a pond lined with crystals and plants that must have gotten enough light from the spotlights in it. The water cast wavering patterns on the walls.

Sir Raleigh, whom I suspected had been hiding in there the whole time, prowled around.

I sipped my detox water, which had mint, cucumber, and ginger slices in it. "Check out the cat."

Lawrence nodded. "Something's got him interested."

Then we both sat upright on our respective lounges, and I said, "It's like the cabin."

This time I knew what I was looking for, so I leaned back and touched the wall behind me. Then I drew on the power from the crystals in the pond, the water, and the stone surrounding us, and sent a vibration through the cave on a molecular level, which most beings didn't know we could do. It wasn't enough for any human or gargoyle to detect, but many magical creatures would.

Indeed, Sir Raleigh jumped straight in the air and glared at me. I laughed. "Sorry, Raleigh."

A white streak darted out from under a stone ledge on the side of the cave opposite us, and as before, Sir Raleigh went in pursuit. I leaned back and sipped my drink, letting Raleigh do the work.

Lawrence watched the white rodent and the grimalkin with a frown. "Shouldn't you help him?"

Both executed impressive leaps over the pond, and Sir Raleigh actually bounced off the surface of the water. There wasn't any doubt of his Fae origins, but that would have confirmed them to anyone who knew to look...

Oh, Hades, had I walked into a trap by showing off my and Raleigh's powers? I sat straight again and cast about with my Fae senses for the presence of another being. The barest wisp of surprise made me walk to the opposite side of the pond, where I found a slab of obsidian embedded into the wall so tightly no one would have seen it if they hadn't been looking. By the time I reached it, it had gone dark, but now I knew how we'd been watched.

A squeak followed by a yowl of triumph made me turn. Sir Raleigh trotted up to me and deposited a white rodent with a broken neck at my feet.

NOTHING BREAKS a relaxing mood like a dead rodent, no matter how proud the cat is of it. Sir Raleigh grabbed it and disappeared, presumably to meet us outside. Lawrence and I finished our water and agreed to cut our spa afternoon short. If the rodent had indeed been sent to spy, its master—or, more likely, mistress—would be missing it soon. We got dressed and said our goodbyes to the confused clerk.

"But what about your facials?" He sounded personally affronted.

"We'll still pay for them," Lawrence assured him, and then did with a new slate-gray credit card I hadn't seen him use before.

"Gift from your mom?" I tried not to allow bitterness to come out. It's not like I'd expected her to give one to me. Plus, I suspected my Fae Amex, or the Faemex as I liked to call it, had a higher limit.

"Minerva slipped it to me earlier. She said to pay for everything with it today, and the city would pick up the tab."

"Hopefully they don't look too closely at us." I patted my cheeks. "Damn, I could've used a facial."

He kissed me on top of my head. "No, you're beautiful, as always."

"Flatterer." But I grinned.

When we reached the lobby, we found that Micah had abandoned his post.

"Probably got bored," was Lawrence's guess.

"You're not super impressed with your younger brother, are you?" I put on my sunglasses when we walked outside, and Sir Raleigh trotted up to me with his present. This time when he dropped it at my feet, it was with an air of, "Don't make me touch that disgusting thing again."

I picked it up and looked at it. It did indeed resemble a white ferret, but with a harder jaw and bigger teeth. Plus its eyes, when I pried one lid open, were an interesting light blue.

"Thoughts?" I asked Lawrence. "You're the animal expert."

"Something from the northern climes. The eyes are interesting."

"Yes, and I've seen some of just that color recently, but I can't remember where." I pulled a brown paper bag from my purse and wrapped the animal in it. "Let's take it to the hospital and see if it's like the ones Barton has been trying to trap."

"All right." But Lawrence's mouth pulled into a resigned line. "All he needed was a supernatural cat."

"To catch a magic rodent? Makes sense."

We took the path from the inn to the Augie statue and crossed the river into the woods. Lawrence looked up when the light disappeared from the sky overhead. "It really is striking.

Why does the spell over the town do that, cause clouds to gather around it?"

"That's a good question. I actually don't know." And I was perturbed that I hadn't thought to ask. But then, I didn't know exactly what kind of spell it was, only what it did and sort of what it cost. Whoever had woven it had been a master spell-caster, like a seamstress who knows just how to hide the seams on a garment so it looks like it appeared magically in one piece.

The clouds broke by the time we reached the hospital. Again, I didn't know why, and I said as much.

Lawrence grinned at me. "This far from the spell? It could be as simple as mundane weather."

"You would go there, to the simplest answer. Like a scientist."

"Madame, you wound me."

We ceased our banter when we walked into the hospital. Today, a few people sat around the waiting room, making for more than I had ever seen in there.

"What's going on?" Lawrence asked the clerk, who gave him the same beaming smile as everyone else had.

She tossed her hair as she answered, "Oh, it's the usual pre-festival injuries. Burns, cuts, nail gun accidents, things like that."

I looked around, noticing gargoyles and other paranormals. "Are the citizens of The Aerie that clumsy?"

"No, but the out-of-towners are."

I could almost sense a thread from the injuries back to the spell, although the Beltane Field sat outside of its border. Perhaps it had enough power to exact payment from afar. If so, that didn't bode well for anyone mortally injured or ill who came to the hospital.

"Is Doctor Lucia in?" Lawrence asked. "I'm a patient, and I have a quick question for him."

She tapped on her computer. "Yes, he's having clinic in the

C-Ward, but that's a restricted area." She frowned. "I'll send him a message." A ding said she'd gotten a reply. "Oh! He says you've already been there, Doctor River, and go on in since you know the way."

"Thanks."

"C-Ward?" Lawrence frowned at the sign in the main hallway. "I don't see it."

"That's because it's a secret. A town with a fertility problem doesn't have much use for a children's ward unless..." Well, I supposed he was going to find out eventually. Barton had apparently discovered my trespassing, and although I had no reason for them, butterflies danced in my stomach. I led Lawrence through the doors, which opened for us without any tricks this time, and into the creepiness of the walls covered with leering characters with giant eyes.

"Good grief." Lawrence muttered. "And this was supposed to be comforting? Ah!"

This time I'd known to expect the small figure who jumped out of the shadows, but Lawrence didn't, and he almost garged out, barely catching himself when Eddie's peals of laughter echoed down the hall.

Lawrence glared at me, and I struggled not to laugh. "Sorry, I should've warned you."

"You're not sorry. Fae aren't supposed to be able to lie."

I patted him on the arm, "No, really, I should've told you to expect that." Then I called down the hallway, "Doctor Barton Lucia, what are you doing, letting your patient scare your other patient like that?"

Barton walked out of the playroom, and his lips twitched in a grin. "It's what he's been trained to do." Then he rubbed Eddie's head. "And he enjoys it too much for me to tell him not to. Plus he confirmed what I'd suspected—that you've already been here."

Eddie looked up at him with a frown. "You didn't 'spect it. I asked when the nice lady with the white hair was going to be back." Then he turned his serious expression on me. "Why do you have white hair? That's something for old people."

I knelt so I could be face-to-face with him. "Well, I am old. Really old."

"But you don't look it, not in your face. You look younger than my mom."

The sound of a throat being cleared made me straighten so I could shrug to Eliza. "Kids."

"They speak the truth," she said with a sigh. "So now that you're here, why have you come? I doubt it's to visit Eddie, as cute as he is." She smiled at her son, the only time the hardness melted from her expression.

"Yes," Barton said. "Why did you decide to find me? Is something wrong with you, Doctor Gordon?"

"No, not at all." Lawrence put his arm around my shoulders. "Reine's cat brought us a present that we thought you might want to look at."

"We got one of the rodents. Well, Sir Raleigh did."

A ball bounced out of the playroom followed by my grimalkin, who pranced after it like a playful kitten. Eddie squealed with delight and went to play with him.

Barton nodded to Raleigh. "That is a very clever animal."

"Yes, he's smart. He's also the one who caught this." I pulled the bag from my purse and handed it to Barton, who motioned for us to follow him into one of the empty rooms. He laid the package on the plastic surface of the naked mattress and unwrapped it. Eliza stood at the door, and she watched where Eddie played fetch with Sir Raleigh. I would not let the grimalkin live that one down, even if he was entertaining a child to keep him distracted.

When the white corpse was laid bare, Barton put on a pair of rubber gloves, and I had to ignore the urge to wash my hands. All right, I didn't ignore it, and so I did wash them in the sink in the bathroom. When I came out, Eliza gave me the first true smile I'd seen on her face when it was directed at anyone but Eddie.

"I know your cat is playing with him for convenience, but it's nice to see him being a kid."

"Of course. I'm glad Sir Raleigh is bringing him some joy."

Her eyes filled with tears, and she nodded.

I walked back to where Barton had flipped the animal over and looked into its mouth and eyelids.

"Do you know what it is?" I asked. "We figured something Scandinavian."

"Definitely, likely Icelandic judging from the build and eye color. There's a kind of witch that lives there who likes to use these critters as her messengers."

Eliza walked over to the side of the bed, and she had the most interesting reaction of all. She covered her mouth to stifle a scream and fainted.

22

LAWRENCE

Barton moved to catch the crumpling Eliza and grabbed her just before she hit her head on the floor.

"Doctor River, help me."

Reine knelt beside him, and they moved the unconscious woman into a side-lying position. I stepped back and found myself looking at a very concerned Eddie. I hadn't had much contact with children since Kestrel's childhood a decade before, so we gazed at each other for a very long moment. Eddie seemed to search my face for something, and then nodded, which prompted a small spark of relief in my chest, although I didn't know why.

"What's wrong with my mom?" he asked.

"She saw something that scared her, and she fainted." I'd never been good at making stuff up or softening it for anyone, least of all with kids.

Eddie nodded again. "It's one of the animals from the witch lady."

And of course the child, whom everyone had been trying to protect, had the answer. "What witch lady?"

"The one with two faces."

Now that struck me as intriguing. "What do you mean?"

Eliza stirred and called out, "Eddie?"

He ran to her, and Barton helped her to sit. She waved him off. "I'm fine. Sorry, I haven't eaten today. Seeing the dead animal shocked me." Although she'd known it was there, and she worked in a hospital, so she must have seen worse.

Reine and I locked gazes, and we both felt the lie in Eliza's words.

"Tell you later," I mouthed.

Reine's frown line reappeared, and she took a breath. Barton put a hand on her arm. "Later."

She exhaled. "All right."

We said good bye to Barton, Eliza, and Eddie, and walked into the balmy afternoon.

"What do you think?" Reine asked. We took the path away from the hospital the other way, and she tensed when we emerged from the woods into a clearing by a hill. There was something strange about the place, but I couldn't quite figure out what.

"I think there's something off here."

She looked around with a slight smile. "You're right. This is where we found the murdered deputy."

"And what's wrong with the hill?"

She touched my wrist, her fingers cool against my skin, and I saw the caves, about a dozen in all. Then when she let me go, they disappeared.

"So the caves are hidden."

"Yes. Another strange piece of the puzzle that is The Aerie."

I started toward the hill. "Should we explore one?"

Sir Raleigh, who had of course accompanied us, arched his back, hissed, and disappeared. Reine frowned for a second, then grabbed me again, this time with urgency. "Not now. Raleigh says someone is snooping through the cabin."

WE WERE breathless by the time we arrived at the cabin, which turned out to be a good two miles away. We didn't have a vehicle, so it was faster to hoof it. I couldn't help a stab of pride at how well I managed our run/jog through the woods.

When we got there, we found three police cars and a dark sedan in front of the cottage. Minerva stood with arms folded about ten feet away from a lanky, dark-haired man in a tan uniform and sheriff's badge. He barely acknowledged us.

Minerva turned to us. "She gave the sheriff permission to search it," she snapped.

There went the frown line again. "Why wouldn't I? I have nothing to hide."

I almost laughed. Fae always had something to hide, but I could see Reine's reasoning. She'd probably felt that allowing a search would be the best way to prove her innocence of...what? The murder?

Minerva gave us an honest-to-gods eye roll. "Yet you've met our sheriff. You should've at least told him to get a warrant." With that, she turned back to the cabin in time to see the front door open. A deputy walked out carrying a plastic evidence bag with another bag inside.

She held it up. "Found something. In the kitchen in the back of a cupboard."

I couldn't see what was in it, but the sheriff's mouth split into a feral grin. "Bring it here."

He examined it, then opened it. I almost objected that he could be tainting it, but Minerva's eye narrowing and a slight shake of her head stopped me. Message received—this was all an elaborate staging for...

"Well, well, Doctor River. It looks like you came to The Aerie to practice more than medicine."

Reine's expression hardened into classic, cool, disdainful

Fae that would make most men quake in their boots. "I assure you, I don't know what you mean. I haven't seen that before in my life."

"So you don't know what it is?" He held it out to her.

She stepped back and put her hands in her pockets, refusing to touch it. "Nope. And you won't find my prints on it, either."

"You're right, there aren't any prints. Because you wiped them off?"

"Because they were never there."

He took a wide-legged stance that Beverly Graves used to call the "foot planted, balls out, male condescension pose." Gods, I missed her and John. They would have been such good supports for me and Reine in this situation.

Kestrel. I needed to call Kestrel. The thought hit me so hard I almost missed what the sheriff drawled.

"Well, let me educate you. This here is meth, crystal meth." He paused, possibly expecting some reaction from Reine. She gave him none, and he continued, "And it so happens that Deputy Sturgeon was in charge of our drug division. He was making great progress eradicating this scourge from our mountains. Think that gives you a motive now?"

"Not at all. As I said, I've never seen that before."

"And how do you think it got in the cabin if you didn't put it there?"

She shrugged. "I only got here a couple of days ago and didn't look through all the cabinets. It could've been there already." Then she narrowed her eyes, and I wanted to jump in and stop her before she dug herself into a hole, but it was like watching an impending car crash and being perilous to stop it.

Reine continued, her tone slow and even, but also managing to convey utter disdain. "Or maybe you planted it, Sheriff. If as you said, the deputy has been making progress on getting rid of it, you'd have some of it on hand in your evidence locker, just waiting to be planted so you can pin a crime on an innocent woman."

I almost laughed again at her calling herself an innocent woman, but I bit it back. The color drained from the sheriff's face—a sign of guilt? Or had he reached his own point of cold fury? Did he not realize who he was dealing with?

No, he didn't. He threw the bag at the deputy, who caught it and watched the whole thing with wide eyes, and turned back to Reine. "You think you're so clever, but I'm putting you under house arrest."

"Under what authority?"

"That of the Mayor." He nodded to Minerva. "That's why she's here. Mayor Agnes said that if we found anything, you're to be detained, and Agent Gordon will guard you. She said no jail could hold you."

Great, my mother had essentially called Reine a criminal on the run. Why did she and the sheriff hate Reine so much that they wanted to pin the murder on her? Or was someone else behind it all pulling the strings, including my mother's?

Minerva might have had the same thought because she and I exchanged concerned looks before she said, "The evidence is circumstantial, Sheriff. It's possible she didn't know it was in there, and I can corroborate that she's left the place for long periods of time."

"And how many keys are there?"

"You'll have to ask Astrid, but at least two sets. One for guests, one for housekeepers."

"Fine. But don't let her go anywhere. Remember, this is a murder investigation."

We watched without saying anything as he got in his respective car and drove off.

Minerva wheeled around and glared at Reine. "What were you thinking? You could've just kept your mouth shut and let him hang himself with his words."

Reine's cheeks turned pink, but, uncharacteristically, she lowered her eyelids and admitted, "You're right. Something about the man infuriates me. What do we do now?"

I tried to puzzle things through, which led to a clenched jaw and only one decision. "I'm going to talk to our mother."

The deputy closed the trunk of her car and smiled at me with the same cloying admiration the rest of the townspeople had directed at me all day. "I can take you, Doctor Gordon."

"All right, thanks." I turned to Reine. "Please try not to get into any trouble while I'm gone. Eddie said something about a witch with two faces. Do you know what that means?"

She frowned. "It could mean a number of things but it does narrow the field. And I'll do my best to stay out of trouble, but you know me."

"Unfortunately, I do." I kissed her and leaned down to whisper in her ear. "And you may be afraid to say it, but I'm not... And that's why I love you. Please don't endanger yourself unnecessarily."

23

REINE

My ear warmed from Lawrence's whisper, both his words and the warmth of his breath. Then I watched him get in the car with the deputy, who drove them off. A sudden chill in the air made me rub my arms.

"He does love you, you know." Minerva turned from the gap in the trees the car had gone through. "That's why Mother can't bear you being here."

"Are you sure it's just your mother?"

Minerva might have misunderstood my question, or maybe she deflected it with, "Well, yes, at least now. I have no problem with you, haven't since I've seen you taking care of Lawrence. Neither does Micah as far as I can tell, or anyone else besides the sheriff." She closed her eyes in a long blink, then opened them. "Believe me, you're not the only one who's had trouble with him."

I walked up the steps to the cabin, the door of which hadn't completely closed. I nudged it open with my boot. My magical wards were still in place. But I'd given the sheriff permission to search it, which had negated my supernatural and legal security.

"Rookie mistake," Minerva told me again.

I pivoted to face her and found we stood almost eye-to-eye since she had reached the next to the top step. "Look, I don't know what you're trying to do, but you're not helping. You call yourself a gargoyle, but you're acting like the most condescending Fae."

That got her attention, and her eyes turned dark. I stepped back, half-hoping she'd transform. I'd never seen a female gargoyle in shifter form. Alas, she got herself under control before she could.

"You're right, I'm sorry. I forget you're not familiar with either gargoyle or American culture."

I declined to argue with her because she was at least half-right. I didn't have much of a clue about gargoyles, and while I'd spent some time in the States earlier in my long life, it had been a while. The current times reminded me of the Victorian era, with society and its expectations changing swiftly and becoming more restrictive as communications sped up. Thank the gods the Fae didn't have Internet...yet.

"Does anyone understand American culture?"

Her lips lifted into the barest of grins. "Probably not, not even us Americans. May I enter?"

"Yes, thank you for asking." Part of the defensive armor I'd put up against her softened at her indirect acknowledgment of my feelings of violation at someone coming into my space, albeit a temporary one, and planting something to incriminate me.

We walked inside, and I touched the top of the door frame, whispering a spell to strengthen the wards against both unwelcome humans and nonhumans. Minerva wandered around, and Sir Raleigh curled up on the cushion of the plush armchair before she could sit on it.

"Raleigh, don't be rude."

Minerva surprised me with a laugh. "It's all right. I actually really like cats, although Mother would never let us have one. She said they were the pets of witches and Fae." She frowned. "And she used the same disgusted tone for both." She held out her hand, and Raleigh sniffed it, then pushed his head under it for a caress. Afterward, though, he shot me a look that seemed to say, *"Tread carefully with this one."*

"Message received," I replied in secret conversation.

The light outside took on the golden tint of late afternoon, and a rush of magic through the Earth made my body tingle.

"What's that?" Minerva looked around, her eyes wide. "What did we just feel?"

"It's the Beltane magic, sort of like a flower opening up. That was a loosening of a petal." I took a deep breath, although I couldn't necessarily inhale the power. Still, it flowed through me, and I knew one thing... "I need to get to the Beltane field, participate in the celebration."

Minerva grinned, wider this time. "Then it's a good thing the sheriff didn't say you had to stay here, only that I had to guard you."

I couldn't remember exactly what he'd said, but he'd certainly intended for me to stay in the cottage. "If you say so, I believe you. Will you help me get ready?"

Now her brows lifted in surprise. "How?"

"Please make me some tea. I need to shower and change. I still smell like a spa, and the bugs are going to love me. I'd rather not have to zap them away."

"Don't Fae have a bug-repellant spell?"

"Yes, but I'm also trying to conserve my magic. I don't know what else is going to happen tonight."

With the caffeination supplied by the beverage Minerva made for me, a shower, and a new sky-blue T-shirt under my faux leather jacket, I felt like a new Fae. I wore my usual jeans.

Minerva took a road that led east, but instead of driving all the way to the mountain, she parked in a large, half-full dirt lot.

"What is this?"

"It's the River Pub. It's also where people park and walk to the fairgrounds. They won't be open yet for revelers, so let's have a drink." She gestured to the white building on the river. Music poured out of it, and it appeared to already be crowded.

"I don't know... There are a lot of people in there."

"Are you scared?"

I could imagine her and Micah daring each other with that question. "You weren't the town pariah yesterday."

"True, but no one will mess with you while I'm here. Plus, some of the hospital staff stop by there for a drink after work."

I doubted the one I really wanted to talk to, Eliza, would be there, but Minerva seemed to really want to stop in, so I acquiesced. I figured it wouldn't hurt to make nice with Lawrence's sister. I hadn't thought through him saying he loved me, choosing instead to hold the memory of the words in my mental space like a treasure to be examined when I had more time. But would I ever? And even if he did, how could we ever be together? Our feelings didn't matter with circumstances as they were.

Perhaps my own lovesick heart made me order a margarita when we got seated, thankfully outside and away from the worst of the crowd, with a view of the river. The hostess had done much scraping and bowing, as we used to say, at Minerva, who looked as comfortable with it as Lawrence would have.

Minerva studied me over the menu, and I couldn't read the expression in her slate eyes.

"What?"

"I'm trying to figure out what to do with you. About you.

Make no mistake, I'm not comfortable with this situation between you and my brother."

I glared at her. "Well, I'm not comfortable with the fact we're still here after having been dragged several thousand miles to land in your hospital. How did you do that?"

"Gargoyle secret."

The server brought my drink and water for Minerva. Again, I wondered if she ever had any fun. She ordered some chips, salsa, and guacamole for us to share.

Minerva assured before I could ask, "Don't worry, it's all organic and locally sourced except the corn." So she'd studied up on what Fae prefer to eat. What else did she know about us?

That old familiar fear that humans or others in the Earth realm would discover the extent to which Fae could manipulate matter raised chill bumps on my skin. Thankfully I hadn't taken my jacket off, so she couldn't see my arms.

The frozen margarita didn't seem so appealing, but I sipped it and found it to be strong.

"All righty. I'll be taking that one slowly." Not that I should have ordered it. I needed my wits about me and magic under control for later. What had Barton said, the Beltane Field was where we'd wage our battle for the hearts and minds of the people? Was he being dramatic, or did he know something I didn't?

I knew I hadn't summoned him, but he walked through the restaurant carrying a beer. When he saw us, he raised his eyebrows and approached.

He had changed from his scrubs into dark jeans and a long-sleeved cream-colored T-shirt with a half-opened buttoned slit from his throat to mid-chest. The color set off his olive skin tone, and the ensemble gave him the appearance of a modern knight. The comparison both made no sense to me and made something click in my brain. He'd hinted he'd come on his own authority, but what if...?

Minerva stood and gestured for him to take her seat. "Here, you both have a lot to talk about."

I almost objected, but I needed to see if my suspicions held true.

A different server put down the appetizers Minerva had ordered plus a dish of cheese sauce. "Compliments of the house."

"Thank you." I nibbled the edge of a chip and waited for Barton to make the first move.

"So tonight's the night." He tapped his glass to mine, which I hadn't touched after that first strong sip. "Cheers. Glad to see you're fortifying yourself. Best thing for going up against the kind of foe we have."

"And that would be...?"

He looked around, and I snapped my fingers. No one could see the bubble of silence I'd erected around us if they looked at it directly, but it would cause a distortion in peripheral visions.

"Nicely done. I'm curious, though, why the extra security? Fae are good at talking around the truth."

I pointed at him. "You're not just Benandanti, you're a Truth Seeker." I didn't hide my disdain for Merlin's band of vigilantes who'd set themselves the task of keeping paranormal creatures like myself from interfering with humans.

"I wasn't going to tell you, but since you figured it out..." He sighed. "Look, it's no secret that the Fae dislike us, and I need you to trust me so we can work together. Your being here is the break I needed to draw the creature out."

I shook my head. "Why should I trust you? You're a representative of an organization with no true authority. What were you going to do when you found it? Try to charm it into cooperating?"

Barton laughed even though I'd meant my questions as insults, not jokes. "And what about you? We both know you're powerful, but you don't have access to your full range of abilities here."

"I should be powerful enough."

He must've heard the doubt in my tone because he shot me a triumphant glance and dipped a chip into the salsa. Then he ate and chewed it before saying, "You don't sound so sure. And I'm not, either. Remember, she managed to turn the town against you with hardly any effort on her part."

I shivered again, this time at the thought of the hostility and the more subtle negative emotions that had flowed through me. Then I clenched my teeth—why should I care what a bunch of gargoyles thought about me? Only the opinion of one mattered, and the awareness of the physical distance between us, although it was only a few miles, made my chest ache.

I grabbed a chip, broke it in half, dipped one piece into the salsa and the other into the cheese, and then stacked and ate them. "That makes me wonder... With a force this powerful, why send a Benandanti? Why not Margaret or one of the other old guard like Tristan?"

"They needed someone with patience and medical experience to slot into the hospital here. I may be young, but I'm not useless."

"And how old are you?"

"Old enough. Look, are we on the same side or what?"

"I grow tired of these games. You've deceived me. Why didn't you tell me right away who and what you are?"

"Because I needed you to experience the truth of the town for yourself so you could see how serious the threat is. Otherwise, you'd bail once you knew Doctor Gordon was stable."

It both intrigued and saddened me that he didn't recognize how close Lawrence and I were. He'd offered to dissolve our bond, so he knew that much, but what did he understand of true emotional connection? The realization hit me. "And what do you think keeps me here now?"

"You want the approval of Mummy Gargoyle, although I'm not sure why."

That particular truth slammed into me, although I wouldn't tell him what it was. Had I been trying to earn Agnes's approval because my own mother hated me and had tried to kill me? Did I have some weird Fae Freudian stuff going on?

"I'm over that now. Perhaps I'll go, leave you to your attempts to be the knight and savior of The Aerie." I sipped my drink, which had melted slightly and made the tequila taste that much stronger.

He took another chip and attacked the guacamole this time. "You can't, for two reasons. First, the sheriff will take your leaving as a sign of guilt. Second, you're leaving Eliza and Eddie in the lurch."

"What do they have to do with it?"

"Eliza told me after you left that she'd seen a rodent like that before."

"When? And when were you going to tell me this?"

"I'm telling you now. She and the deputy went to see the witch in the caves, who told her that if she stopped objecting to his affair, she'd be able to have a baby."

Lawrence's warning came back to me. "Do you know if the witch shapeshifts or otherwise could have two faces?"

Barton swiped another chip through the guacamole. "I don't. I've heard Eddie say that before, but he struggled to explain it." He bit off half of it with a crunch and swallowed. "Guess we'll have to find out."

24

LAWRENCE

The deputy dropped me off at the town's administrative complex, a large Alpine-style building complete with dark wood accents over whitewashed walls. In spite of its attempts to be charming, it had a sinister air.

The thought crossed my mind; *This must be how Hansel and Gretel felt.* Except my mother wasn't a witch. Granted, no one was lining up to canonize her as a saint, either. Still, I had no basis for the feelings of trepidation that filled me when I crossed the threshold into the lobby, which had a decidedly less rustic and more municipal air.

This time of day, only a clerk sat behind the counter, which had a veneer over it to make it look like marble, but any gargoyle would recognize the ruse and sense the lack of stone beneath. I suspected particleboard.

The clerk barely looked up from his number puzzle. "C'help you?"

"Yes, I'm here to see Mayor Agnes Gordon."

"Offices are closed."

I leaned over and plucked the puzzle book from his hand.

He looked up at me with a snarl that turned to wide-eyed fear when he saw who I was. I don't know how he recognized me, but he said, "Oh, I'm terribly sorry, Doctor Gordon. I'll let her know you're here."

"Thanks." I wanted to toss the book at him, but I set it gently down on the counter and marked his place with a general precinct business card from the holder.

I supposed I should have been relieved that someone hadn't immediately fawned all over me, but there was never a good fawning over when one actually needed it. Or was that something only a person who expected it would think?

What was this place turning me into?

"She'll see you now. Fifth floor. Can't miss it."

I took the elevator to the top floor and followed the signs to, "Offices of the Regent." My mother's personal secretary, whom I identified from her name badge, which said, "Maria Counter, Personal Secretary to the Mayor," was just leaving when I walked in.

"Is Mayor Gordon still here?"

She jumped and almost dropped her briefcase. "Y-yes, of course. I'll tell her you're here." She scurried back into the office, and this time I frowned. One fear reaction could be excused. Two meant that the energy in the place had shifted. I wished I had Reine with me to confirm my suspicions. I hoped she'd stayed safe in the cottage with Minerva guarding her, but I knew better. The sun hadn't set yet, but it was close, and when it did, the Beltane bonfires would be lit, and my Fae would be on the hunt.

I allowed myself a slight grin at thinking the words *my Fae*. No one had ever accused me of being an optimist, but I had faith—another new thing—we'd figure out a way to be together. Or maybe have conjugal visits.

Maria emerged from my mother's office and interrupted a train of thought that probably needed to be stopped. "Please have a seat. She'll be out momentarily." Then she left, and the rapid tapping of her shoes on the wood floors gave away the fact she almost ran.

I checked my phone. I hoped this wouldn't take long, and I half-considered leaving the conversation for another day, but Reine couldn't be arrested for murder. I understood—sort of—the issue with loose ends she tried to avoid. Apparently, Fae could be entangled in them. A murder charge would be a big loose end, and it would keep us from ever being able to go out in public should she become a fugitive.

And there I went thinking like a celebrity again. I either needed to get out of this place or start an Instagram account.

Another glance at my phone told me it had been ten minutes. What was taking my mother so long? Finally, she opened the door and motioned me in.

Whenever I'd seen her previously on this trip, she'd been put together so tightly I thought her clothes would choke her. Now the collar of her blouse lay unbuttoned, and she wobbled on her high heels as she walked to the table full of liquor bottles.

"Hello, son. I'm glad you came to visit. Would you like a drink?"

What in Hades, as Reine would say, was going on? "What is this, the sixties? No, thank you. I need to talk to you about something. Something serious."

"Which sixties do you mean?" She shot me a shrewd glance over her shoulder. "Seventeen-sixties? The colonies were getting restless. Eighteen-sixties? The not-so-Civil War almost tore this baby country apart. Nineteen-sixties? All tumultuous times, Lawrence, and worthy of a drink. Don't you remember?"

"I try not to think too much about the past." I accepted the bottle of water she held out, and my instincts had me check the top to make sure it hadn't been opened. What was wrong with her?

She poured something amber-colored and smoky-smelling in a glass. I recognized an expensive brand of whiskey.

"What's the occasion?"

She raised the glass to me. "My prodigal son has returned home. You say you try not to think about the past, yet I'm aware of how long you searched for your father's killer."

Ouch, why did she have to bring that up? "Yes."

"Did you ever find him?"

I decided to give a Fae-style evasive answer. "It's not who I expected, and the situation is more complicated than I thought."

She narrowed her eyes. "You sound like one of them, like one of those pointed-ear bastards that killed your dad. Has your girlfriend been rubbing off on you?"

My inner mischievous side flashed some of the rubbing we'd done earlier that day through my brain, and I shook my head to dislodge the naughty vision. Perhaps my inner gargoyle hadn't integrated with me as thoroughly as I'd thought.

"Actually, she's who I'm here to talk to you about."

She put the glass down on a coaster on the table. "Oh? Please don't tell me you want to propose to her."

"I..." I couldn't lie in the face of such a question. Did I want to propose to Reine? I'd been fantasizing about couples' trips and domestic scenes, not just sexual encounters. "I can't. There are too many complications."

A sharp dip of her head preceded, "You keep using that word, or variations of it. And that's the situation here as well."

Aha, an opening. "What, you mean with Sheriff Jones? Why does he have it out for Reine, and what's with him?"

"She challenges his preconceptions and pushes the boundaries he's set on his reality. She's the most open paranormal creature he's encountered."

"How? This place is gargoyle central." Then it hit me, what I hadn't seen yet. "But no one here changes, do they? And it's more than the threat of what happened to Augie. Everyone pretends to be human even though no humans ever come here."

"As I said, or you keep saying, it's complicated." She grabbed her glass again, but instead of sipping from it, she looked into its clear, dark-amber depths. "Have you ever made a bargain that you thought was simple, but kept having conditions added to it until you regretted ever laying eyes on the person?"

"No, but I don't make com-complex bargains." So much for trying not to say *complicated* again. I ended up with a close synonym instead. "What do you mean?"

She leaned back and stared into middle distance. "I did it all to keep us safe. Well, your brother and sister, after their father was killed. They were just babies, and I didn't know what to do." She blinked, and a tear raced down each cheek. "I wanted so badly to call you back, but I knew you were searching for your father's murderer, and I couldn't bear to bring that part of the past into my present, not with the new grief so raw."

It had been many decades since I'd seen her, and yet I still knew enough to hear the half-truth. She'd had other reasons for keeping me away. "What did you do?"

The ice clinked when she took a long swallow and set the glass back down. "A nature witch approached me. A very old, very powerful ice witch who had managed to break away from her land, which should have been a red flag. She wanted someplace to hide and work her magic, and our mountains suited her needs, specifically the caves."

"What kind of magic?"

"Regeneration magic. She didn't give me any more details than that, but I thought..." She swallowed. "If she'd come earlier, she could've saved my second husband, my beloved Peter."

"The twins' father."

"Yes. He was a good sort. He didn't ask questions when I wanted to keep my last name as a tribute to your father and when I wanted to give it to the twins."

In other words, she'd found a man who wouldn't argue with her. Was that what females wanted? No, Reine wouldn't go for someone who didn't challenge her.

"Right, so you made a bargain with a witch you didn't know in exchange for what? What did she promise you, Mother, and what was the price?" Because that's what it came down to with magical beings—Faustian bargains—and sometimes the price was greater than a soul.

A sigh. "She promised that she would keep me and our kind safe from those who would want to harm us."

"Like the Fae."

"Yes, like humans...and the Fae. She knew the old tales, and somehow, she had become aware of my personal history. I suppose I made no secret of it."

"How did she say she'd do this?"

"With a magical bubble over the town that would repel them."

"And in exchange...?"

She lifted her gaze to meet mine, our eyes the exact shade of slate. "I would allow her to practice her magic."

"And did you ask what side effects the spell would have? Unintended consequences? Mother, you know nothing is ever that straightforward."

She nodded and looked down again. "I came to find that out, and I've regretted every minute since. If you want to know why I never called you back, called you to return, it's because I first wanted to make my own life without the shadows of the past. Then, after I realized the protection spell kept us from procreating, I hoped you'd find someone in the mundane world and start your own family." She frowned at me. "I never thought you'd end up with one of *them*."

I sipped my water and thought through what she'd told me. I sensed the story hadn't ended, so I asked, in the most deadly serious way possible, "And what have you promised her since? I remember something from when I was waking up, but I didn't know if it was a dream."

She sighed. "I heard you were sick, so I struck one more bargain. The witch would allow Micah and Minerva to bring you here with a powerful transportation spell. In exchange, she would take a sacrifice when the time was right. She assured me it wouldn't be one of us."

"Then who?" Although my drink didn't have ice in it, my hands went cold.

"The next Fae who came to The Aerie."

25

REINE

My mind flitted like a caffeinated butterfly, and I wished I could swat it so it would settle on a thought.

The two-faced witch in the caves... The town's infertility problem... The spell that could turn the hearts of the people against me... The love spell on Deputy Sturgeon...

Hades, whoever she was, she had power, and Barton was right—I doubted I had enough of my own to go up against her. Had she been in Faerie, that would be different.

What was I missing? The witch's motivation. She needed all that energy for something beyond *protecting* the town by messing with a visiting Fae, any visiting Fae. No one who was willing to mess with the natural birth cycle of what amounted to an endangered paranormal species only had good intentions.

I needed to open a portal and get help and information, and the best place and time would be at the edge of the Beltane Festival. I'd done something like that before at an Equinox celebration. The celebrants hadn't minded a small siphoning of their power, and I was doing this for them, anyway.

Minerva had paid the bill before disappearing to wherever she'd gone, and so Barton and I headed out together. I straightened my shoulders against the curious looks and occasional leer or suggestive eyebrow twitch. The emotional air of the place stank of lascivious curiosity, although I couldn't imagine why. No, I could. Barton and I hadn't acted inappropriately, hadn't touched, but I knew by now that the gargoyles in this town could have their emotions pushed. Did they think Barton and I had something going on?

Hades, had this been another trap, this time aided by Minerva?

Sir Raleigh joined us outside the restaurant and rubbed against my leg. I leaned down to give him a quick scratch behind the ears, and as always, touching his soft fur balanced me. Although Ellerin had had his own motivation for sending the grimalkin to me, I appreciated the creature's guidance and comfort.

Smoke tinged the air, and I inhaled the scent of the Beltane bonfire to clear the disturbing emotional residue. Barton and I threaded between cars in the large lot to head to the path and follow the other clumps of people to the field.

One point of curiosity hadn't been satisfied yet. "What do the townspeople think of you?"

He held out his hands, palm-up. "Most of the time they don't unless someone is hurt and needs me. I live outside the spell, and I don't go into town unless I have to."

Being the somewhat bitchy Fae I am, I couldn't resist poking him. "Smart, although that's not going to help you observe anyone."

He surprised me with a lopsided smile. "True. But it's also how I've not been influenced and how I'm available to help you now."

"Touché." I could see how he'd lasted as a TS—the non-Originals needed to have a certain amount of charm and patience with the whims and vagaries of the centuries-old. Somehow that made me feel worse...and old.

We continued our walk in silence. I suspected that like me, he shifted his effort from talking to extending his extra senses to determine whether our foe was present. Not that she'd allow herself to be detected so easily, but we could try. Had I already encountered her without realizing? Probably. I hated not knowing, and it irked me to fly blind.

The trail ended with a steep set of stone stairs cut into the side of the hill. We crested the path to find a large clearing. Two women in white robes tended a giant bonfire in the middle. They wore crowns of leaves and exchanged cheerful words with the people who walked around and laughed with each other. I studied faces, both for the familiar and for anything amiss, but mostly I drank in the bright, green energy of the evening. The shadows of the woods surrounding the clearing darkened in the dusk, reminding me that something sinister lurked at the edges of the celebration.

"What do you feel?" Barton asked, and irritation flashed through me that he, not Lawrence, stood there. I hoped Lawrence was having luck with his mother, and I had faith he'd come to me when he could. When I needed him.

That was an odd feeling, trusting in another being.

I searched for feelings I could share with Barton. I'd instinctively shielded when we reached the area with more people, and so I released the barriers and what I found made sense. "I feel the anticipation of the evening, a desperate hope that this year, this fertility festival will work to bring babies back to The Aerie."

He nodded, his arms crossed. "I sense the same. Also suspicion of the outsiders."

I flinched when one man glanced over at me and scowled. "Yes, although it makes sense. When a community is in distress, they turn on those who are different. I saw it in the witch hunts and other persecutions."

He gave me a startled look. "Witch hunts? You're that old?"

All right, I felt less old now in spite of having revealed my age. "Thanks for being surprised. Yes, I've been around for a while."

"Okay, I'm sorry for underestimating you. I now feel more confident in our ability to handle this. Where's your boyfriend?"

I declined to tell him our foe likely had a few centuries on me and how much that worried me. "He's talking to his mum."

More and more people entered the clearing, and a group of male and female gargoyles played a complicated rhythm on the drums that started with what sounded like a crescendoing heartbeat.

The other gargoyles circled the bonfire, and when the energy clicked into place for the ritual, I told Barton, "Excuse me. I need to make a call."

HUMAN AND—I suppose, gargoyle—ritual places had commonalities that they might not have been aware of, but we Fae were. One was that they had a spot any Fae could use to open a portal to another ritual site or to Faerie. As I allowed my instincts to help me find the one for the Beltane field, I recalled how Lawrence and I had been brought to The Aerie, yanked through the aether with portal-like magic.

That, if anything, should have clued me in to the connection between Agnes and the witch. I hoped Lawrence could get some useful information out of his mother, something we could use to defeat the witch and wrest The Aerie from her grasp. The question was, now that the witch's power and the place had become so intertwined, would extracting her destroy

The Aerie, like a wall held together by the roots of a parasitic plant?

And why had Agnes asked me to find out the root of the town's problems when she must have known them herself? Her request now felt like another trap, wherein I demonstrated my powers and weaknesses to the witch.

I found the site just to the east of the field, in a clearing where the oak trees stood in a circle of wood, not stone, but which still drew on the power of the Earth herself. A waist-high rectangle of granite, a makeshift altar, stood in the middle.

Whereas the trees in other parts of the area had been silent, these whispered a welcome to me and told me of their growing isolation over the past two decades as others had been turned against the Fae and had their relationship with other earth and water elementals eroded. That explained why the river had lost its Naiad. My heart ached for these trees, which only had each other now, and the others, orphaned and lost.

Yes, more than The Aerie would need healing after the work I had been tasked to do.

I placed my palm on the stone and whispered the portal-opening spell with the intention of calling to my Council of Three. Two of them responded.

The translucent figures of my brother Rhys and the dark Fae prince Troubadour appeared. Unfortunately, the Fae whom I most desired to speak with did not.

"Where's Ellerin?" I asked. I still couldn't refer to him as my father.

Troubadour gave me his classic mischievous grin. "Well, it's good to see you, too, Your Highness." He bowed with a mocking flourish.

"You're right, and I apologize. I'm happy to see you both, but the problem I have is best addressed to an older Fae." Older being relative, of course. "Although..." I turned to Rhys. "I've discovered something very interesting since being here."

"And here is where, exactly?" Rhys scowled at me, the expression less fierce since our grandmother had healed him of his scar. "You disappeared from the Institute, and I had to find out where you went from that trickster witch Kestrel, but she didn't give me useful details."

I put a hand to my heart but didn't say anything. Rhys had grown into his own since we'd returned to Faerie, and it gave me a warm, fuzzy feeling to know he'd been concerned about me. As for Kestrel... Had she been trying to protect me and Lawrence, or had she deliberately kept the other Fae from finding me?

"I'm in The Aerie. Well, the Beltane ritual site outside of it."

Rhys nodded. "I'm familiar with it."

"So I heard. What were you doing here?"

Rhys touched his cheek and flinched. Did the pain still linger, or were his muscles still becoming accustomed to moving without the impediment of the scar? "I went about twenty years ago looking for the gargoyle who'd maimed me."

As I'd suspected. "All right, that makes sense. Did you notice anything while you were here?" I didn't want to ask him about the murder of Lawrence's stepfather outright, possibly because I didn't want to discover he'd murdered Agnes' second husband, too.

Indeed, his expression shuttered. "Notice anything how?"

"The town itself is under a protection spell that's also keeping the gargoyles from reproducing. Whoever is behind it is old and powerful, and that's why I'm calling."

Rhys rubbed his face from forehead to chin. "If I'd known, I'd've told you."

"Told me what?"

He sighed. "When I was there, a redheaded witch approached me. Beautiful lass, but her mood ran hot and cold. She asked if I'd help her with a regeneration spell so she could stay young-looking. Said she'd already lined up a sacrifice."

All the hair on my body stood on end. "Astrid."

"She didn't give me a name. I told her no, that's not why I was there. She got mad and said she'd make it so that the next Fae would help her whether they liked it or not."

"A regeneration spell…"

Troubadour had been listening, and he grabbed a scroll from somewhere nearby. I supposed I'd interrupted him in the library. "I happen to have this one handy. Says a regeneration spell for an elemental witch should take about twenty years."

"And if it started around Beltane…"

Rhys and Troubadour looked at each other, then me, and Rhys said, "You've walked into a trap, sis."

"My path led me here." As had my love for a certain gargoyle. Was that to be how things went—that our love for each other would constantly bring the other into danger? "Seriously, though, where is Ellerin? I need his advice on how to defeat this creature."

Troubadour spoke with gentle tones, which told me more than anything how worried he was. "He disappeared into the Gray Zone to talk to the Winter Goblin King, and we haven't heard from him since."

I took a deep breath. "That's not good, but I can only deal with one emergency at a time."

Rhys held out his hand, and I took it. The Beltane energy flowed through me into him.

I tried to let go, but he held me too tightly. "Wait, what are you doing?"

"Coming through to help." His form turned from transparent to opaque when he stepped from the Fae realm into the Earth realm. The shadow of his scar appeared on his cheek, but wasn't visible when he turned back to Troubadour. "You got the home front, mate?"

Troubadour saluted. "Aye aye, captains. Don't worry, Faerie will be in good hands, and I'll make sure Ellerin is found."

I let go of Rhys and resisted the urge to shove him. "Are you nuts? Lawrence's mum is here, and if she finds out who you are, I can't promise to protect you from her. In fact, I'm pretty sure she's trying to have me killed."

"Seems to be a theme with you. You're on your path, and I'm on mine."

Agnes had said something about the Fae owing her. Perhaps if Rhys could contribute to us freeing The Aerie, even if it wasn't how she envisioned, we could be even. Then my next task would be to figure out how to make Faerie safe for gargoyles again.

"Thank you, Prince Basil." I used Troubadour's real name to remind him that I still had power over him, and he better not think of double-crossing me as the one member of my Council of Three still in the palace in Lorien.

Troubadour winced and said without any mocking or irony. "You're welcome, Your Highness. I promise I will not fail you or Faerie."

I closed the portal and turned to my brother. "Ready to hunt a witch?"

26

LAWRENCE

I leaped to my feet, and I didn't know where to direct the searing rage that rose through me—at her or at myself. Now I remembered what I'd heard at the hospital and what I had dismissed as a dream of a disturbed mind coming back from the brink of death.

"You can't bargain with others' lives like that, Mother."

She didn't move, and she directed her words toward her glass. "Not even if it keeps us safe? Protects your brother and sister?"

"You mean the ones I didn't know about until a few days ago? Tell me the truth—you didn't want me to come home because you'd started a new family and wanted to put the past, including me, behind you."

"If that's what you want to believe..." She rose with the grimace and slow grace of a centuries-old gargoyle, which I was, too, but refused to show it. "Go, Lawrence. If you believe you can stop destiny, you can try." The smile she gave me lacked any mirth. "You always were a stubborn lad, just like your father. And I could always read you. That's how I know you've been keeping the secret of your father's murderer from me. Let me guess—it's a relation of your pretty Fae girlfriend."

"It's—"

She held up a hand. "I know, complicated. That's why I hope you'll find it in your heart to forgive me someday."

The energy of the day shifted, and I knew, perhaps through our bond, that Reine had just stepped into more danger than she realized. I dashed from the office and down the stairs, not wanting to wait for the elevator, but found the lobby deserted.

"Hello?" I called. "Can someone give me a ride?"

"We have wings, idiot." My inner gargoyle spoke as a separate entity for the first time I'd allowed our full integration. Or maybe that was my panic for Reine pushing my brain out of the fog that affected the gargoyles of The Aerie. Either way, it was a good point.

I ran back up the stairs and burst on to the roof. I shed my clothes down to my underwear, bundled the garments as best I could for carrying, and thanked whatever gods had supervised Micah's packing that he'd sent along stretchy boxer-briefs. I recalled my father telling me, "Son, you never know when you're going to need to change, and some humans and other creatures don't want to see you in your full glory, so always have your smallclothes made loose." He would have appreciated the elasticity of modern era clothes.

I turned my face toward the glow on the horizon left from the sunset and reached out my arms and legs. I hadn't changed since being in Faerie had forced me to, and I found myself blocked by fear...and something else. I called upon my inner gargoyle self and for the first time, had the sensation of electricity running along my nerves and massaging me into the change rather than forcing me into it. Even my wings bursting from my upper back felt like a natural extension rather than twin stabbings.

Without thinking, I grabbed my clothes and leaped into the sky, relishing the freedom of the air and the strength each downstroke required to lift me higher. I didn't need directions—I could have found Reine anywhere in the world. Our bond and my desire for her—would she be willing to try flying sex?—drew me to her like a bee to the brightest, most nectar-filled bud in the garden.

Something crashed into me and knocked me off course, and I scrambled for precious seconds to make my wings, arms, and legs all move in the right direction to stop my fall. I regained my flight, and almost lost my clothes, but held on to them, barely brushing them against the tops of the trees.

I searched the sky around me and roared, "Who *dared* interrupt my flight? Show yourself, coward."

Another gargoyle appeared, fully changed, and I recognized Micah, his features squarer and more chiseled like mine when I changed.

"Micah? What is the meaning of this? You could have killed me. Both of us!"

He hovered, his wings working hard to maintain his altitude and position, and he clenched his jaw with the effort. How could he be so out of shape? Right, he'd probably not changed much in his life.

"Let me help you, little brother. It's not right that you've stifled your inner gargoyle for so long. I can tell how hard this is."

His voice came to me on the breeze. "No, it's not right that you're here upending everything. Don't you see? If your Fae kills the witch, it will be the end of us all." With surprising speed, he came at me again, and I had to make a clumsy turn to avoid him. So he was a better flyer than he'd let on. That also meant he was cleverer than I'd given him credit for.

"Is this about the whole prince thing? I don't want Mother's throne or office or position, however you look at it. I want to go home to Atlanta with Reine and know we're both safe."

He'd disappeared into the tree canopy below, and I listened hard for rustling or any signs of where he could be. I rose several yards, looking for him.

I had been looking in the wrong direction. He attacked me from above, his heel landing between my shoulder blades, forcing my wings to fold and knocking the breath from me. My claws punched through the clothing I carried as my hands tightened into fists. This time I couldn't recover, and I braced myself for impact, praying the trees would break my fall and not impale me.

A dark figure rose from the trees and caught me, supporting me with surprising strength and slowing my fall from a plummet into a still-too-fast spiral.

"Hang on," Minerva said. "Take three deep breaths and whisper the flying spell your father taught you."

"The... What...?" But it came back to me. As a last resort, he said, because it could attract the wrong sort of attention, use the Fae flying spell. I dug back through my memory as we spiraled downward, slower but still too fast to prevent injury.

"Wings of bat and spokes of bird, air the lightest element, Goddess grant my spell be heard, and restore me to the firmament."

A golden glow surrounded both of us, and I found use of my wings again. I flapped and pulled away from her, and Micah roared in frustration, then darted into the trees.

Minerva intercepted me before I could chase him. "Don't worry about him, Lawrence. You're needed in the Beltane Field. Would you rather fly or drive? My car is just below."

"Let's fly. It'll be faster. What's going on?"

"Your Fae has brought in another, and the witch is ramping up her powers to capture both of them. Plus, his coming through caused some sort of ripple, and the energy has gone chaotic."

"Another...?" Oh, gods, that could only be Rhys or Troubadour, and I suspected the former, especially if he had that effect. "Let's go."

27

REINE

Along with Sir Raleigh, Rhys and I walked toward the bonfire from the portal site. The atmosphere had gone from hopeful and desperate to electric and frenetic. What had happened?

"What did you do?" Barton stalked up to us, and anger twisted his handsome features. "Who the hell is this?"

I put a hand on his muscular forearm and sent soothing energy to him. He relaxed and took a deep breath. "Something unbalanced the magic here, Reine. And who is...?" He squinted at Rhys, and I suspected he saw the shadow of the scar. "You're the Fae who unbalanced the Beltane celebration twenty years ago, aren't you? You have some nerve showing up here. The Regent doesn't have another husband to kill."

Rhys flinched, and I said quickly, "It wasn't him. It was the witch. Barton, this is my brother Rhys, and while there is some history, it's not what you're thinking. I'll explain later."

Barton didn't appear convinced, but he nodded to Rhys. "Thank you for coming to help, although you may have done more harm than good."

I scanned the air with my extra Fae senses. "Something's

certainly gone off." Then a tingling at the back of my head turned into a stabbing pain that nearly drove me to my knees. It felt like at the park, but worse. "And she's found me." I sent a quick tracking spell after whoever had just magically attacked me. The line it drew for me faded, but at least now I had a direction.

"This way."

Then a spell came at me from another direction. This time it felt like a pinch on the arm that left a stinging sensation. "Or that way."

Barton scowled into the gloom. "She's toying with you, but your brother and I have a taste of her energy signature now, one that's not clouded by the spell over the town."

Rhys also darted glances toward the celebration and the tree line. "Let's split up," he suggested. "Then as soon as one of us gets a good lead, call in the others."

I didn't like the idea of separating, but I also wanted this to be over. I sensed Lawrence was on his way, so I said, "All right, but no heroes, got it? Call in reinforcements the moment you know you've found her trail."

Rhys headed to the left and Barton back toward the trees. I walked in the direction I thought the second attack had come from, and I ignored a poke on the other side, sensing a reach-around strategy. A familiar face caught my attention, and its relative stillness in a dancing group made her body stand out.

"Eliza! Hey, wait up."

Her eyes widened when she saw me, and she darted into the crowd. I pushed through sweaty, gyrating bodies to catch up to her. So intent was I on finding her that I didn't notice until we'd reached it that she'd led me to the entrance of a cave. She turned and grabbed my arm, dragging me into a small copse of pines nearby.

"Eliza, what's all this about? What are you doing?"

"Warning you." Her eyes almost blazed with the intensity of

her message. "Listen to me. She's powerful, more powerful than you're gonna expect. Don't go head-to-head with her. She has one weak spot—she'll make any kind of bargain to get what she wants."

Although Barton had told me, I wanted to hear it from Eliza. "What do you mean?"

"How do you think I got Eddie? She wanted my husband, and she's been draining the place, but she gave me a baby so I'd stop interfering with her plans." She dropped her gaze. "And I'll never live down the guilt of trading one for the other, but I was so hurt he'd fallen for her and made the promise in a moment of anger."

"You did what you had to." I didn't know if it would help her to know her husband had been under a love spell, so I didn't say so. Plus, I didn't know if he'd been bespelled before or after Eddie had been born.

"We could've moved, could've escaped somehow." She blinked, and the tracks of her tears sparkled with the far-away light of the bonfire. "But I was desperate, don't you see? And she'll figure out what you're desperate for, what you want more than anything else, and try to bargain with you. Don't do it. She's like your kind—she'll always take more than she gives."

I ignored the insult. "Thank you for the warning."

She nodded. "And thanks for helping me and Eddie. We're gonna leave tonight. I have to find a different place for us."

"Good luck, although I'm not sure what I did."

"You coming here made her kill him and end both our suffering. Now I'm free..." She took a deep, shaky breath. "Although in the worst way possible."

"When you do make it far away, reach out to Gabriel McCord through the Institute for Lycanthropic Reversal in Scotland. There's a school there for special kids like Eddie. Even if he doesn't go, they can help."

She squeezed my arm again, then darted off. I had to

admire her loyalty in sticking around in case her husband came back to her. And in keeping Eddie's father in his life. No, telling her about the love spell wouldn't have helped. I pulled out my phone and sent a quick text to Selene that I'd met another young medium like the one Gabriel had found in Scotland, and asked what resources were available for him.

Then I turned toward the cave and sent out a message to Rhys and Barton via secret conversation. *"I think I've found the entrance to the witch's lair."*

28

LAWRENCE

inerva filled me in as we flew to the Beltane Field. "She's been working to turn the town against your Fae since the start. You knocked her plans back with your little procession, so she came up with a different strategy—make the others think she was cheating on you with the handsome physician."

"Why is everyone so taken with him?" I grumbled.

"Because he's good-looking, smart, charming, and single." She shot me a glance that plainly said I should've figured that one out on my own.

"So what's happening now? And why are you helping me? I thought you were on Mom's side."

This time she gave me a look that mixed tenderness and pity. "Micah is a playboy, as you can tell. I can't have love, not here, anyway, with who I am and what I do. You're the one who's found it and has it, and I'm going to support you. Plus, I hate that bitch."

That sounded like the more likely reason. "Which bitch, Mother?"

"No, the witch. She's taken much more than she's given our town, and it's time for her to go."

We landed on the outskirts of the clearing. Minerva unslung the sack she'd been carrying and disappeared into the trees. I also found a spot out of sight of the revelry and changed, both back into human form and into my clothing, which had some holes in it. Hopefully no one would look too closely at my ripped jeans and black T-shirt.

We emerged to a curious circle of faces.

"You...changed." A woman said, her voice incredulous. "How did you do it? And how did you change back?"

Minerva and I exchanged glances. She held up her hands. "I know we've all been told the legend of Augie, but I can confirm it's a fairy tale told to gargoyle children all over the world and for centuries."

"But we can't change. We'll never transform back and be turned to stone."

Minerva frowned at the man who'd spoken. "I just said—"

"You lied. That's what they'll tell us to make us all into statues."

They closed in on us.

"Stand back," Minerva commanded. "I am Agent Gordon, representative of Regent Agnes Gordon, and I command you to step away."

"You don't have a weapon, do you?" I murmured to her. We stood shoulder to shoulder as the angry crowd advanced on us.

"No, and even if I did, I wouldn't use it on them. These are my people, and they're under the influence of the witch. If something's gonna happen, it's going to be through you, big brother and crown prince."

"Right." I sighed, not knowing what my actions would result in, but I stepped away from her and pointed at the nearest gargoyle, who now stood just out of arm's reach. "I am Prince Lawrence Gordon, and I command you to step back."

The man stopped and blinked. "Prince Lawrence? Our crown prince?"

Ugh, it pained me to say it, but I choked out, "Yes."

The edges of the crowd rippled, and Rhys came running from one direction and Barton the other. "Where's Reine?" Rhys asked.

"I thought she was with you." Fear shot through me, and I almost changed again, but I held myself together.

Barton muscled his way through to us. "She sent us a message that she'd found the witch's lair, but the direction got muddled with all this." He waved a hand.

"At least they're not singing," I said.

Minerva frowned. "What?"

"Nothing." I held my hands up and addressed the crowd. "People and gargoyles of The Aerie, the time is ripe to claim your heritage, to become your true selves. I will help you, but I need to find my friend first. Do any of you know where the witch's cave is?"

"I do!" A small figure broke through the crowd, and when it pushed the dark hood of its sweatshirt back, I recognized Eddie. Indeed, the gargoyles looked askance and whispered to each other, "It's a child! A child in The Aerie."

They moved forward to touch him, so I picked him up. "Yes, and he is under my protection. He is the one the witch has allowed to be born, for her own selfish ends, but it's not his fault, or his mother's."

"Go back to your festival," Minerva told them. "All will be explained in time. Let this child be a symbol of hope for you."

Relief tinged the air in waves I could almost see, and the crowd dispersed. I put Eddie down. "Now where is the witch's cave?"

29

REINE

"Lawrence, Barton, and Rhys, where are you?" I whispered into the dark from where I crouched in the stand of immature pine trees. Eliza had disappeared ten minutes previously. I dared not send another message for fear of alerting the witch to where I was. The notion that a Fae queen didn't crouch in the dark, but rather marched forth to face her enemy played in my brain. But there in the dark, waiting on the edge of triumph and doom, I had to admit—I didn't feel like a Fae queen. Somehow the task of solving The Aerie's problems, as weird and complicated as they'd become, felt less intimidating than facing my responsibilities, especially if I couldn't have my consort by my side.

"Well, I've made a right mess of things."

Sir Raleigh hissed, and I barely had time to scramble out of the way before he turned into his full-on bat-winged panther grimalkin self.

"Thanks for the warning." I stood and brushed off the seat of my pants. Sir Raleigh continued to growl in a low rumble that brought to mind the rolling thunder of battle drums. "Well, then, I suppose this is it."

With my grimalkin guardian by my side, I stepped from the shelter of the trees into the dim night. The ever-present clouds that ringed the edges of the spell over the town obscured the moon, and now I understood why—they provided cover for the creature that lurked outside of gargoyle society.

I assumed my most confident stance and glared into the gloom of the cave entrance. The shadows lay so thickly there that even my superior Fae eyesight couldn't penetrate them beyond being able to make out a figure standing there, watching me with sparks in her eyes.

"Show yourself, witch."

"Big words from a Fae who hides behind a title she doesn't want." The voice, familiar and mocking, floated through the night, but with a new, or should I say old, edge to it.

"Greetings, Astrid. But that's not your real name, is it? I should've realized—Astrid means beautiful in your language. So who are you, really?"

The clouds broke, and a gnarled old woman strode into the moonlit strip between us. She walked with a staff much like Ellerin had used, and I could tell that, like him, she didn't need its support, but it could instead serve as a conduit.

Her power wafted toward me like a blast of Arctic wind. I struggled not to shiver. Sir Raleigh rumbled again, and I put my hand on his head.

"You are a powerful Fae who comes with a guardian. Do you not have confidence in your abilities?"

She hadn't given me her name, so I searched through my old lessons with poor old Larry Leafmore, one of my former teachers. He'd insisted we memorize the names of the Old Elementals, as he called them, in case we were ever to encounter them.

There was one, an ice witch so old no one knew if she'd even had human parents or had sprung from the glaciers themselves. "You're Grylja, the original Witch of the Northern Ice."

She inclined her head. "I have been known by many names, and yet you hold just the one, Princess Reine. Come, I'd like to have a chat with you." She beckoned for me to follow her into the cave.

"I'd rather talk out here, thanks."

She shook her head, and her gray curls bounced with her laughter. "Oh, no, Princess. You know where your path leads. If you want to free this town, you'll have to do it at the source of the spell, which is through here."

I looked down at Sir Raleigh, who, although he lacked the full range of human expression, appeared resigned. *"There is danger in following her, but she speaks the truth."*

"Thanks." I told him and turned to her. "Fine, I'll come, and I invoke the codes of hospitality. You may not harm me as your guest."

"And you may not harm me as your host."

Hmmm, I'd walked into that one. I'd have to see what she had in that cave of hers and what loopholes I could find. The good news was that Fae were expert loophole-finders, and while we'd promised not to attack the other directly, the situation still had room for many possibilities.

Sir Raleigh and I followed her into the cave, and once inside, I lit a Fae-light on the palm of my hand so I could see where I was going. The soft, red dirt beneath my boots gave way to granite walls that curved over us. The hush in the air told me she'd found a sacred space to set up in.

The downward slope of the path angled upward, and we walked into a large cavern with stalactites clinging to the ceiling like large teeth. Cliché, I know, but the whole place appeared ready to devour whoever may enter.

The most disturbing feature of the place stood in the center. A large iron cauldron emanated a shrill, discordant energy that made me want to plug my ears, although it wouldn't do me any good. The real Astrid floated above it, and the blue light from the cauldron made the planes of her face harsher and more accentuated the emptiness of her eye sockets. Grylja turned to me, and I saw she had the ice blue eyes that made Astrid that much more striking.

The witch with two faces. Not a shapeshifter, but a parasite.

"That explains a lot, like why she had to keep disappearing and closing the shop. You could only wear her for so long."

The witch nodded. "Very good, Princess. As you can see, she takes much energy."

"So you stole it from the town with your spell."

She held up a finger. "Ah, ah, no stealing. I traded protection for their ability to regenerate their kind."

"And yet I'm here."

"Because I allowed you to be."

I couldn't argue, so I folded my arms and returned to the deal she'd struck. "There's no way Agnes would have agreed to it if you'd put it that way. What terms did you give her?"

Grylja laughed. "I am not at liberty to say. I made a, how do you say, non-disclosure agreement with Mayor Agnes."

"Where's the source of the spell?"

She cocked her head. "Why would I tell you all my secrets? I brought you here to make a bargain. You see, I need you."

One of the white rodents ran up to her, climbed up her clothing, and whispered in her ear. A grimace of displeasure crossed her face so quickly anyone else wouldn't have caught it. I hoped that the bad news for her meant good news for me.

I walked toward the cauldron over which Astrid was suspended, but between the iron and the stench of the stolen regeneration magic, I couldn't get close to it.

Grylja walked past me and stood in front of it. I recognized the show of power, but I didn't react. "What do you need me for?"

"I need your power, your vitality. If you give it to me, I will no longer need the town's energy. I can have what I want, and you will get what you wish."

"And what do you think I wish for?"

She laughed again. "You wish to be ordinary, like the humans you've lived among for so long. You want to settle down with Agnes' handsome older son, which you cannot do with your responsibilities. I call you Princess because while you have been given the throne of the light Fae, you have not claimed it. Instead, you left your no-good brother, a dark Fae, and the father who abandoned you in charge."

Behind her, Astrid lifted her head and blinked. I couldn't tell—were Astrid's actions due to the fact the spell had almost reached completion, or something else?

I slow-clapped to cover the terror that washed over me at the possibility of the *something else*. "Bravo, you've done a brilliant job of observing me. Do your little minks, or whatever they are, go into Faerie? If so, I'll have to do something about that."

"I have my sources." She certainly looked pleased with herself. Astrid smiled. Similarly thrilled, or another reason?

My moment of honesty in the dark made me aware of the partial truth she spoke. But she was wrong about one thing. "I never desired to be ordinary. No, the only thing I've ever wanted was to help others, which isn't looked kindly upon in Faerie. The irony is that my failure to do so got me exiled. And now let me tell you how I can help you." For I'd figured out the loophole.

"I've already told you how you can help me. Give me your power. Your Fae-ness."

"Why? Why do you want to be Astrid? Isn't being the most powerful of the ice witches enough?"

She laughed, and this time Astrid silently laughed. Oh, gods, this had gone beyond creepy. "You see me, do you not? You know how society views us females. We can have all the power in the world, but if we're not physically attractive, neither men nor women will take us seriously. That's the power I miss. You, ruler of the paranormal race that prizes perfection above all else, know this."

"But you can cast love spells like over Deputy Sturgeon." And, the insight hit me, over Micah, although I didn't know how I knew. Now my shiver came from concern for Lawrence. He wouldn't look for a threat from his little brother.

"You have to get close enough to a target to cast a love spell. It's not as simple as waving your wand and wishing." She waved her hand, and Astrid mimicked her, then put a finger over her lips.

Hades, Astrid's actions came from *something else*. And time for me to leave since the situation had just reached a level of complication I had no desire to participate in.

"And do you know why the Fae prize perfection?" I asked, edging backward toward the tunnel out of the cave.

"Why?" She pointed her staff at the entrance, and a boulder rolled in front of it, blocking me in.

"Because when it comes to certain spells, especially the complex ones that take years, even the smallest misstep can result in unintended consequences."

For the first time, uncertainty flickered over her gnome-like features. "What do you mean?"

"In a regeneration spell involving a proxy body, if you don't allow the body enough rest between wearings or make sure to fully eradicate the spirit, it can become aware and decide to divorce the author of its spell."

"That's not possible. I chose a being who lived in fluidity so I would encounter less resistance."

The meaning of the warning and plea I'd received at the river came clear, and sorrow for the naiad nearly buckled my knees. "Where did you find Astrid?"

Grylja wheeled around and found herself facing the proxy

in question, who now stood in front of the cauldron. She folded her arms and spoke in an echo of what must have been her voice. "I was the town's water nymph. She stole my body, but thanks to you, Fae, I found her again. And…" She wriggled her fingers as small lightning bolts played between them. "I've been siphoning her powers for years."

Ah, I'd suspected her personality might not entirely reflect Grylja's influence.

"No!" Grylja pointed her staff at Astrid. "Go back to your stasis. You are not ready, not yet."

Oh, Hades. This was going to get ugly. "She's been watching you, witch. She's seen how you take and take, and even when you give, it's strategic."

"This town wouldn't have survived without the spell. Others would have moved in and ruined its gargoyle-ness, its charm."

"Sorry, but xenophobia isn't a noble motive, and I know what you did to start the spell. You sacrificed Agnes' husband and blamed a Fae. That Fae happened to be my brother, and so you owe me a debt."

Grylja kept her staff pointed at Astrid, but backed up as Astrid advanced. "Back! Get back to your cauldron! I'll start you over if I have to."

Astrid laughed, and as she did, her jaw elongated, and she lunged at Grylja, barely missing her. "I will devour you like you wanted to steal my body and banish my soul to Hades."

A stream of white light shot out of the staff, and Astrid was blasted back to the cauldron, but she dropped out of the light stream before Grylja could deposit her back in it. This time she launched a red bolt at the witch, who deflected it with her staff, but with a grunt of effort.

"You have a choice, Grylja." I tried to sound calm and channel my Fae bargain charm. "I can help you."

"How?" She dodged another red bolt from Astrid.

"I can give you the keys to defeating her, but you need to do a few things for me."

This time I had to dodge a red ball of flame. Noted—don't piss off a redhead.

"What?"

"First, end the spell over the town and aid them with fertility. There's a lot of making up to do. Second, help me to make Faerie hospitable to gargoyles again so they can eat our food and breathe our air without getting ill. Third, end any and all love spells you've cast and embrace who and what you are."

With a speed that belied her age, Grylja ducked out of the way of another glowing red bolt, which singed the edge of her robe. She ran over to me and scowled. "Those are harsh terms."

Another fireball came our way, and I deflected it, but with effort. With my powers as attenuated as this place made them, I didn't know how long I could continue the battle alone.

The fireball caught the end of Sir Raleigh's tail, and he yowled and disappeared. I hoped he was going to douse it somewhere close by. "Bitch! I love that cat. He better not be hurt." I turned to Grylja. "She's getting stronger as she turns the flow of the spell to her own ends. I'm your only chance."

"You're forgetting one thing."

"What's that?"

"You're stuck in here with me. You can't get past that boulder."

I placed my hand on it and attempted to teleport out of there, but she was right. I was trapped.

30

LAWRENCE

We met Eliza, who'd been looking for Eddie. Together they led us to the cave, and I sensed Reine had just recently been there. I stifled a growl so I wouldn't frighten Eddie, but every heartbeat increased my need to find her.

Barton looked around with a frown. "Where is she? She wouldn't have gone in without us, would she?"

Eliza held Eddie close. "The witch is clever. She could have tricked the Fae."

"Not as clever as Reine." But I also knew Reine wouldn't back down from a challenge. If she had gone in, it would have been with good reason. The sense of her being in danger increased to the tipping point of bringing out my inner gargoyle, and I darted into the nearby group of trees for some privacy. I'd just barely stripped out of my clothes when I changed again.

I walked out to find the others staring at me wide-eyed. Well, except for Eddie, who clapped. "That was awesome!"

Apparently, those trees hadn't been as close together as I'd thought. Thankfully I'd had my back to them, and my pants stretched to fit.

When I spoke, my growl came through. "Thanks. I'm going in after her."

Sir Raleigh, in his bat-winged panther form, appeared, the end of his tail on fire. "What the hell?" I grabbed it and doused the flame, and Sir Raleigh rubbed against me in thanks.

Barton blinked and shook his head. "So that's his grimalkin shape. Impressive. Looks like things have gotten intense in there. Let's go."

I refrained from commenting on his statement of the obvious. In truth, I'd have only been redirecting the irritation I felt at Reine facing the witch on her own. I reminded myself I had to trust her to know her own limitations.

But did anyone really know what they could and couldn't do until something tested them?

Five of us—me, Barton, Rhys, Minerva, and Sir Raleigh—descended into the cave and came to a wall of stone.

Minerva and I put our hands on it and attempted to speak to it, but it remained silent. Rhys touched it with a fingertip and announced, "Enchanted. It can't hear you."

A blast from beyond the stone shook the cave, and I closed my eyes against the shower of dust and spike of alarm. "We have to get in there."

Minerva stood back and scowled at it so fiercely I thought it would obey her, but it stayed stuck. "It's going to take brute strength to move."

Another tremor shook us, and all of us used the rocking to get the stone to budge. It moved slightly, but not nearly enough.

I did the last thing I'd ever want—ask my father's murderer for help, but I had no choice. "Rhys, can't you do something to it? Make it disintegrate or something?"

He shook his head. "Sorry, mate. The spell on it is too strong for just one of me, and I can't reach Reine."

A familiar and unexpected voice said, "Let me help."

We turned back to see the last thing I expected—my mother, fully garged out, with a sheepish Micah in tow. I'd rarely seen her in her true form when I was a child, and gods, she appeared more intimidating now than she had then. As for Micah, I balled a fist, and it was only with a surge of self-control that I kept myself from hitting him. If he hadn't delayed me, I could have reached Reine faster, gone in with her...

"What are you doing here?" I pointed at Micah with my other hand, and my exasperation with everything came out with a pouty-sounding. "He tried to kill me!"

"Yes, and he's very sorry. Whatever your friend is doing in there cleared his head, and he's come to apologize."

Micah sighed and said, "Sorry, Lawrence. I was under a love spell."

He didn't sound sorry enough, but I let it slide. "From whom?"

"Astrid."

So there were two witches? What was going on?

Sir Raleigh nudged me, and when our eyes met, he sent me an image of Astrid, but with blank eyes, and an old witch superimposed on her.

"That's interesting." I looked at Minerva as I made the connection that the witch had somehow been controlling Astrid, perhaps possessed her. Both were illegal and showed potential desperation. "Think that four gargoyles plus a Fae could move this thing?"

Minerva nodded and pushed past my mother and Micah, then reappeared in her gargoyle form complete with black leather clothing to cover her intimate parts. "Let's do it."

The four of us gargoyles, Barton, and Rhys all gripped the stone where we could, and I instructed them to lean right, then left, then right, then left again. At first, the boulder didn't seem to want to move, but I could feel it loosen more each time.

Finally, we got the stone to move enough that it destabilized and rolled sideways to show us the scene in the cave.

A pissed off Astrid the bakery owner launched fireballs at Reine and an old witch. My protective urge kicked in, but I couldn't tell who was supposed to be the enemy. At least my logical side kicked in with my default strategy—get information.

"Reine! What's going on?"

She tossed a strained grin at me, and I went to her side, although I couldn't do much against flame. She answered through a tight jaw. "Negotiations. Meet Grylja the ice witch and Astrid, the former river nymph that Grylja tried to take over and has instead been fighting her."

My mother walked into the cave, and Reine's surprise came out with a squeaked, "Oh!"

"Yes, I came to help my son." She huffed. "And you, I suppose."

Astrid launched fireballs with both hands. My mother and Reine stood shoulder to shoulder, and Reine deflected one with her magic while Mum caught a fireball, then threw it back at Astrid, who ducked out of the way. I pumped my fist.

Micah's grin looked boyish even on his gargoyle face. "Way to go, Mom." Then his face crumpled into confusion. "And I don't know who to fight."

"The redhead for now." Reine shot me a worried look, and I caught on to her concern—if the witch and the nymph teamed up, it would spell trouble for the rest of us.

I looked around for some way to get behind Astrid, but the cave's layout didn't allow for sneaking. I growled again, this time in frustration at the helplessness warring for the need to *do* something.

Mother scowled at both Astrid and Grylja. "It's going to take more than a fireball to stop me. Reine, what's the source of her power?"

Reine released an exasperated sigh. "The cauldron, but I can't get close to it, and my magic can't penetrate the invisible barrier around it to topple it."

Indeed, Sir Raleigh had apparently had the same thought as me—get around it to attack from behind—but appeared to be blocked by something, including when he tried to fly over it.

Rhys sent a lightning bolt toward it and shook his hand when a flash traveled back and burned his finger. "Turn it off, witch."

Grylja shook her head. "I can't. She has control now." She covered her face with her hands. "I can barely wield my own powers."

Mother snarled at her, "Our bargain is over. You betrayed me and violated our terms by taking more than you gave us."

Grylja lowered her hands and opened her mouth like she wanted to argue, but Mother cut her off with, "Now do you want our help or not?"

She narrowed her eyes, but said, "Yes."

"Then agree to what the Fae wants."

"I've already released the love spells! That's how he's here and on your side." She leered at Micah. "He's a handsome one. Hard to let go."

I turned to hide my laugh when Micah's face went light shale pale. "You're the one I...?"

"Later," Reine snapped. "*All* the terms, Grylja. That was the third."

Mother nodded. "And the first two?"

"Release the spell over the town and help them rebuild their fertility and..." She inhaled deeply. "Help me make Faerie hospitable for gargoyles again. We're going to need your help, Agnes."

Grylja studied Agnes for a second, and then glanced at Rhys, who had been deflecting Astrid's attacks. The nymph didn't show any signs of slowing down. Then Grylja grinned.

Again, I made the connections, and when Reine's gaze met mine, I suspected they mirrored my panic.

Grylja spoke with the slow drama of a drawing room detective making her big reveal. "And did you know, Mayor Agnes, that you have your first husband's murderer in your midst?"

My heart sank, and I resisted the urge to punch Rhys. Again. Everyone froze, including Astrid, who crossed her arms and said, "Oh, this just got interesting."

"And your second husband's killer." Rhys pointed at the witch. "He was the sacrifice that started the spell."

Perhaps it was because she had taken on her gargoyle form, but my mother barely flinched. "That's business to be sorted out later. Agree to Reine's terms."

Grylja's face fell. "I agree. I will do what she asked in exchange for help in defeating the nymph."

"Is this agreeable to you, Reine?"

"Yes, I will help her defeat her proxy in exchange for the terms laid out. No more, no less."

They shook hands, and then Reine motioned for Rhys to join them. "Now, Grylja, we're going to augment your ability so you can turn off the spell around the cauldron."

Grylja nodded, and her smile turned from conciliatory to predatory. I barely had time to send a quick warning thought to Reine before everything went dark.

31

REINE

All light disappeared from the cave, and the temperature plummeted. The witch gave a mighty pull on my powers, and Rhys' grip on my other hand tightened. Instead of disabling the spell around the cauldron, I found myself in a tug-of-war for my magic.

My teeth chattered so hard I could barely ground out, "This isn't what we agreed to. No more, no less."

Grylja cackled. "I told you this is what I wanted, your power and your life. Why waste my time trying to finish my project with Astrid when I can have you instead? I've always wanted to be a Fae queen."

"Hospitality."

"But you don't know that this isn't for your good in the end. Remember—you can't handle being queen. I'm not harming, I'm helping you."

As she pulled on me, I examined the strategy she'd used to trap me. First, she'd faked my credit card declining so I'd be in her debt. She'd also tried to get me to invite her in to clean so she could get past my wards. Then, knowing about my sweet tooth, she'd attempted to get me addicted to her baked goods.

She'd taken other actions against me, culminating in putting me in a situation where it would look like I was cheating on Lawrence with Barton. I sensed her frustration that Minerva hadn't cooperated with the plan her mother had given her for that. Not that it would have helped—Lawrence had trusted me, even in spite of everything I'd withheld from him.

"Hang on, sis," Rhys encouraged me through our Fae sibling bond, but he sounded far away, and his words retreated into the barest echo of a whisper.

I wished I could see, but the total darkness frightened me. It beckoned me to become part of it, to disappear and let all my troubles go. It whispered to me with tempting promises as it pushed out everything positive in my life. I could have peace. No worries about the Fae realm. No responsibility I couldn't handle. No broken heart when Lawrence and I couldn't be together, as would inevitably happen. Just deep, dark, velvet sleep.

I'd experienced shades of this during my time in The Aerie, and I hadn't recognized how they'd weakened me. The last time I'd felt a creature trying to take me over, I'd fought with vulnerability. That would kill me now. I had to think fast. What did I have that the witch didn't?

I had discovered the ability to connect with others in a genuine way, which I had lacked until this whole adventure had started. I didn't need a spell to make Lawrence fall in love with me. In fact, I hadn't wanted him to. Neither of us had, and yet we did, and the memories of our times together anchored and strengthened me. Of course I thought about our sexual encounters, but also sitting together, laughing, talking, all those moments that lovers—true lovers—have when they connect more deeply than physically.

The whispers of Rhys' voice, and then Lawrence's, grew louder, and I released a sob when I felt Lawrence's hand rubbing my lower back, which had always calmed and steadied me. Then I became aware of a weight on my shoulder—Minerva's hand. Barton's hand rested on my other one, and Sir Raleigh purred hard against my legs. Even Micah and Agnes chanted something in Celtic, some sort of prayer or spell for strength. The words sounded familiar, and I found myself murmuring along. Anchored by love, support, and hope, I reached for the power of the ley line I'd discovered in my very first moments in Aerie hospital, and something glowed—my own skin.

Now rage flooded through me. How dare she? How. Dare. She?

I released Rhys' hand, and he said, "Stand back, everyone. She's returned to us."

I caught his delighted grin in my peripheral vision as he and the others moved away from me. Although they no longer touched me physically, I felt them and knew the devastation I'd cause, not just to my realm, but to their hearts, especially Lawrence's, should I give into the temptation to fall into the dark.

And she had tried to make that decision for me. Fire, the element I went to when I needed to destroy, flickered through me, and I sent a blast of heat through my palm to hers.

And nothing happened.

"Hospitality, Princess. You can't harm me."

Rhys stepped forward. "No, but I can." He grabbed my hand, and I read his intention.

"Stop! Think of Faerie."

"Think of yourself."

Before I could stop him, he unleashed a torrent of flame at her. Her surprise melted into a spike of rage, but nothing happened.

I became aware of Barton's chanting and recognized the tail end of a stifling spell. The gargoyles growled in unison and lent him strength.

The twin stenches of burning flesh and hair filled the room, and I released the witch's hand as it turned to char and then crumbled to join the rest of her in a pile of ash on the floor.

The torches that had lit the cave flared back on to show us Astrid, who knelt by the cauldron and clutched her chest. When she looked up at me, her eyes had turned normal in appearance and were the dark green color of a forest river on a sunny day.

"What happened?" Her voice had taken on the higher tones of the babbling of water over rocks.

"Long story." Micah gestured to the cauldron. "Do you mind if we take care of that?"

She shook her head and crawled to the side of the cave, where she slumped against the wall. Barton went to examine her, and I almost protested, then remembered he specialized in paranormal medicine. Hopefully he'd studied up on water nymphs.

The gargoyles marched over to the cauldron. It took all four of them, but they managed to tip it over so that the liquid poured into the sand of the cave floor. Then they heaved it against the other side of the cave, where it smashed into a thousand pieces.

Although the air didn't visibly change, the echo of the spell, even here outside its perimeter, disappeared, leaving the atmosphere feeling cleaner and fresher. Rhys and I both inhaled, then exhaled with relief at the cessation of the discordant vibration.

Lawrence walked over to me, and I ran into his arms. He folded me into them, and I allowed myself to cry. He stroked my hair until I finished, and I looked up at him with a tear-stained face. Then I turned to the others. "Thank you."

Everyone gave shaky smiles and nods and murmured some version of, "You're welcome." I knew it would take time before we'd all recovered. No one could step that close to the darkness of despair and be okay, not for a while.

But I knew one thing with certainty—we'd have each other, at least for now.

AFTER THE BATTLE in the cave, Barton had dropped me and Lawrence off at the cottage, where we'd made love and fallen into an exhausted sleep that lasted until noon. Then we awoke to messages from Lawrence's mother and Kestrel. John's and Beverly's funeral would be the following day, and Kestrel wanted Lawrence back for it. She didn't say anything about me.

"Should I go?"

Lawrence squeezed my hand. "I would appreciate if you would be there."

"Then I'll go for you. And for her, even though she doesn't want me."

That evening we met at Agnes' house for a barbecue. I thought the smell of a charcoal grill would make me ill if the smoke of the Beltane fire had become associated with the trauma of what had happened in the cave, but it didn't. I found myself relieved and curious...and less sure of my path than before. Had any Fae queen before me not wanted the title? I doubted it, and I had to suppress the shame at my own desires.

Barton was there, as were the twins and Rhys, whom Agnes had allowed to stay with her. I hoped they'd talked and gotten things straightened out. The tension between them told me there were still some hard feelings.

"How'd it go?" I asked Rhys as soon as I could pull him aside.

"I told her about the mistaken identity." He rubbed his eyes. "And I apologized. She said she understood, and she's grateful I was there to help you and Lawrence yesterday, but..."

I patted his shoulder. "Yes, it'll still take time. These things do."

He glanced over his shoulder, and I saw Astrid had joined the party, or at least the woman we'd known as Astrid. "Hey, Astrid said she couldn't connect with the river anymore. It had been too long, and she doesn't even remember her Naiad name. She wants to know if she can return to Faerie with me."

"Why are you asking me?"

He gave me a strange look. "Because you're the queen, and you can authorize it."

"Oh, right." I didn't feel like I could burden my brother with my doubts. "Yes, that's fine. I'm sure she needs the company of her own kind to recover."

Karen Lovejoy from the visitor's center walked into the back yard carrying a square ceramic dish covered with a towel. She looked around with trepidation. Then she smiled when she saw Minerva, who walked over to her, pecked her on the cheek, and said, "I'm glad you came."

Agnes raised her eyebrows, and Micah said, "Finally. I thought you two would never get together."

Lawrence and I exchanged bemused glances.

"Did you suspect?" he asked.

"No, but I'm glad to know that's why Karen would be so nervous when Minerva and I went into the visitor's center. I thought she was afraid of Minerva, but it was something more."

I wish I could say the evening felt relaxed and easy, but of course tension doesn't magically disappear after a group victory, especially not when everyone still had to adjust to the absence of the spell. Although it was a good change, it was still a big one. They'd need time to figure out their new normal.

"Are you ready for the baby boom that will be here in nine months?" I asked Barton when he came to join me and Lawrence after dessert. We sat in Adirondack chairs beside the firepit, which smoldered with the last of the logs.

He corrected me with, "Gargoyle gestation is closer to eleven."

"Good to know. But... It just occurred to me. Are you going to stay here, or will you get a new assignment?" I didn't mention his organization since Micah had told me from the start that they didn't deal with the TS.

"They want me to stick around for the next two years to monitor the fallout and make sure something more sinister doesn't move in. Plus, I've already met with the sheriff to help him start easing into his life as a shifter. That's not going to be a short process. By the way, he's dropping all charges against you."

"Thanks." The last bit of anxiety I had fell away along with the metaphysical connection that kept me tied to The Aerie.

"And thank you. I couldn't have done this without you."

I squeezed his hand. "Nor I you. All of you. Thank you."

Minerva smirked. "We'll get you to start saying 'all y'all' eventually."

I laughed. "Don't count on that happening for a very long time."

32

REINE

Thankfully Lawrence and I were able to find funeral-appropriate clothes in The Aerie and dress before we left. Atlanta traffic caused us to arrive just in time for the dual Graves funeral in one of the city's older parks. Kestrel met us at the edge of the crowd and hugged Lawrence tightly. She barely nodded at me. I didn't begrudge her coldness. I suspected she still held the fact that John had died against me, both for my role in bringing them into Faerie, and in not allowing her to channel the power of necromancy to bring him back as he lay dying.

She led us to the front row of chairs, and I sat on the other side of Lawrence from her. I don't know if he'd told her he wanted me there to support him, but she didn't object. Corey, the lion shifter, took the empty seat beside her, and members of her parents' coven, including the young witch who'd helped us defeat the soul-eater at the 'Con and Aria, the talented medium who'd also assisted us, filled in the rest. I was glad Kestrel was surrounded by friends, and I didn't resent the time spent at the long reception at the house after. The only problem was that in spite of being on Do Not Disturb, my phone kept buzzing with calls during the last hour.

Finally, after the fifth time, I pulled it out of my purse and saw it was from the Institute for Lycanthropic Reversal. I checked my watch—it should have been after business hours. Who could be calling?

I walked outside and away from the spot on the driveway where Ellerin and I had waited for John and Kestrel before we journeyed to Faerie. Sir Raleigh trotted out after me.

"Hello?"

"Reine! Oh, thank gods. Lonna, I've got her on the line." A click came through, and then Selene's voice, sounding slightly more far away. "You're on speaker."

"What's going on?" I didn't bother to hide my annoyance when I said, "I'm at the reception after the Graves funeral."

I could almost hear Selene grimace as she said, "Ohhh, I'm sorry for interrupting. We wouldn't be calling you if it wasn't urgent."

"There's a problem at the Institute, a big one." That was Lonna, head of the ILR. "And it goes beyond our Lycanthropy work."

"You don't have to convince me it's important. Just tell me what it is."

Selene's voice cracked with anxiety. "Gabriel and Max have gone missing. And there's a note."

"You mean they've been kidnapped?"

"We don't know," Lonna said. "But the note mentions you."

In spite of the warm afternoon, a chill shimmied down my spine. "What does it say? And who's it from?"

Selene answered. "From the Order of the Silver Arrow. They say, 'We have Ellerin the Fae and will have the wizard and the werewolf soon. We have business to discuss with Queen Reine. If she does not respond, we cannot be responsible for their fates.'"

Ugh, the Order of the Silver Arrow. Wolfsheim's group, the one who had assisted the English at the Battle of Culloden and had plagued the lycanthropes since. Although Wolfsheim had been defeated by Gabriel the summer before, his little cult apparently hadn't ended. "Is that it?"

"Yes." Lonna sounded all business, as usual, but I caught her undertone of worry. "How soon can you be here? They want an answer."

"Soon. Tell them within the week. I need to make arrangements. Please let me know if you hear anything else from them."

"We will," Lonna promised and clicked off.

I turned back to the house to see that Lawrence had followed me out and stood a discreet distance away. "What's going on?"

"Trouble in Scotland. I have to go back."

Disappointment flickered over his face, and my heart sank. "To Faerie?"

"No, to Lycan Village and the ILR. Can you come with me?"

He looked over his shoulder. Kestrel waited at the front door. "Let me see what I can do."

I nodded since I couldn't speak around the tears that clogged my throat. I couldn't complain about divided loyalties, could I? The girl had just buried her parents and no doubt had all kinds of legal things she needed help settling. Lawrence, her godfather and parents' best friend, made the most sense to help.

"Hey." He lifted my chin so I had to meet his eyes. "I'll be there as soon as I can. I won't abandon you. I promise."

I nodded and allowed him to pull me into his arms so I could rest my head against his chest. His heart beat a promising, strong rhythm, and I had to believe him, to believe that if we had this strong of a bond, both magical and emotional, we would find some way to be together.

Wouldn't we?

Continue the adventure by grabbing your copy of Shadows of the Past, Fae Files book five.

No good deed goes unpunished. As for Fae deeds, well, those get a bit more complicated...

If you'd like to be added to a special list just for Fae Files updates, please go to https://www.subscribepage.com/faefilesnews

AUTHOR'S NOTE

Here's something you're probably seeing at the end of a lot of books: a plea for reviews. That's because they help our books to be found and helps other readers know they're good. Did you know that some major vendors only start showing books to potential readers when they have a certain number of reviews? I would be so grateful if you'd leave a few words at the site where you bought the book, and, if you're feeling frisky like Sir Raleigh on catnip, other places, too. Thanks so much!

N o good deed goes unpunished. As for Fae deeds, well, those get a bit more complicated...

. . .

I THOUGHT I came to Scotland to rescue friends who disappeared under mysterious circumstances connected to the Fae. However, a deadly attack on the highway drives me and my allies into the woods and straight into my history...

History I've tried to forget. I'd avoided the witch's cottage since the fateful night my brother Rhys and I were exiled from Faerie, and I soon discover the supposed sanctuary hides its own deadly secret.

To escape the trap, I need to confront the deeds of my past, which will require me to risk my own and the others' futures.

Can I figure out the puzzle in time to save us all, or will I have to sacrifice everything, including my gargoyle lover, to make amends for my mistakes?

SHADOWS *of the Past is the fifth book in the Fae Files series. If you like snarky heroines, stories of good intentions gone bad, and second chances with a price, you'll love this penultimate installment in this addictive and magical series.*

BUY *Shadows of the Past* to unlock a treasure hunt through history today! Ask for it at your favorite retailer with ISBN 978-1-945074-71-4

HERE'S **a preview of the first chapter:**

The airplane wheels touching down woke me from a sound slumber and a dream of Lawrence. I started, hoping I hadn't been puckering up at the guy next to me. He'd seemed a nice enough sort, but as the hour had gotten later, and he'd drunk the free first-class booze, his attempts at conversation had turned flirtatious. If I'd given him a little assist to sleep with a minor spell, it had been for his protection, after all. And mine.

My heightened strength as Queen of Faerie had allowed me to not pass out as I typically did inside the horrid flying metal tubes, but grogginess had crept over me the longer we were in the air, especially once we reached open water.

Sir Raleigh grumbled from the pet carrier at my feet, mostly for show. He'd spent most of the night under the blanket on my lap and had teleported into the carrier once I'd woken. That was another reason to make sure my seatmate didn't disturb me—he would have deplaned with a few fingers missing, and that would've been hard to explain to security.

"Just a few more minutes," I promised the grimalkin.

"He's been such a good kitty," the flight attendant cooed and used tongs to hand me a warm washcloth. "Can I get you something to sip on as we taxi to the gate?"

"No thank you." I wiped my face and hands with the warm cloth and tried not to grimace at the deadness of the water. What did they do to it? I sure as Hades didn't want to try any of their coffee or tea. Even a not-so-well-traveled Fae such as me knew better.

I sent a quick text to Lawrence and tried not to fidget. Oh, and I woke my seatmate.

"Wow," he said with a stretch, "I've not slept that well on a plane in a long time."

"Must've been that rum you were drinking. You'll have to keep that in mind for next time."

"Are you sure I can't buy you breakfast? My train to Newcastle isn't for another two hours."

"No, thanks." Newcastle... Lawrence had grown up there. The plane pulled into the gate before I could ask about my seatmate's business. Plus, I couldn't inquire whether any gargoyles remained and if so, were they related to my... boyfriend? Soul-bond mate?

Hades, did we even have a title? And why was I even thinking about it, considering the thing between us, whatever it was, was doomed? I had to return to Faerie to fulfill my duties as queen once I'd tied up all my loose ends in the Earth realm, and the atmosphere in Faerie burned gargoyles' lungs like Fae fire exposure.

Soon we deplaned, and I emerged into the hustle and bustle of the Edinburgh Airport. I toted the overnight bag Lawrence had given me and Sir Raleigh's carrier since I'd brought only my keys, phone, and wallet when I'd traveled to the US the last time. That was another reason to find a powerful Earth and Water elemental—they could make travel portals from one point on the planet to another.

My phone buzzed, and I glanced at it, then smiled when I read Lawrence's message—*"Glad you're safely there. Hope all goes well with L & S."*

I'd confided that I had some trepidation about meeting up with Lonna and Selene since, well, I'd been a Fae bitch. They'd only been in contact because they needed me to help find their kidnapped partners.

I found the exit and emerged into the cool morning, chillier than The Aerie and Atlanta, which had been flirting with summer. I loved May in Scotland with its riot of flowers and continued chill, although sometimes a warm breeze teased the season to come. I pulled on my black faux leather jacket, and the lightening of the carrier preceded Sir Raleigh's appearance on my shoulder. I relished his familiar weight and musky cat-grimalkin scent as we both inhaled the fresh air stained by exhaust fumes.

"Mrrowl?"

I reached up to scratch him behind the ears. "Feels good to be home, doesn't it?" Although it felt less like home since I'd been to Faerie. Plus, my bond to Lawrence ached at the thousands of miles that separated us. I rubbed my chest and wished I could have convinced him to come with us, but he had responsibilities to a young woman who had just been orphaned. And that was partially my fault.

A sky-blue Mercedes driven by a chauffeur pulled up, and the back door opened to reveal Selene and Lonna. Selene wore a denim jacket that set off her red hair, and Lonna had pulled her long, dark curls into a messy bun. Her topaz eyes glinted at me with resignation, not welcome. However, Selene emerged, gave me a brief and thoroughly unexpected hug, and got in the front passenger seat. The driver helped me to stow the now-empty carrier and my bag in the trunk, and I scooted into the back seat.

"Good flight?" Lonna asked. Her worry for Max showed in the dark circles under her eyes and the thinness in her hands, which she continually folded and unfolded. Or perhaps part of that came from me being there, too.

"As good as possible, thank you."

Selene half-turned so she could make eye contact. "Did you sleep the whole time?"

"For a good part of it, yes. Thankfully I'm better able to tolerate flying now."

"Good. How'd the cat do?"

I gestured to Sir Raleigh, who had moved to my lap. "He pretty much spent the flight like this, but under a blanket."

The driver pulled on to the highway, and Selene turned around. "Thank you for picking me up," I finally remembered to say. "I'm wiped and wasn't looking forward to another flight or train ride."

Lonna extended her hand for the grimalkin to sniff, which he did. "Of course. We wanted to see you as soon as possible, and those would have introduced unnecessary delays."

"Has there been any news?" Since Lonna's husband Max and Selene's fiancé Gabriel, both friends of mine, had gone missing, there had been frustratingly little information. I glanced at the driver, who didn't seem to attend to the conversation. He didn't look familiar, and I thought I knew everyone in Lycan Village by sight. I could tell from his aura he was another werewolf, which made three of them in the car. And one Fae. And one grimalkin. Who would've ever thought such a combination would happen?

I blinked. My thoughts had wandered again, and I had to ask Lonna to repeat what she'd said.

"No news," she sighed. "Not even a ransom demand. Did you hear anything from your contacts at home before you left?"

I guessed she meant in Faerie, which indicated she and Selene didn't necessarily trust the werewolf driving the car with all their secrets. Or with mine, which I appreciated.

"No, no one's heard from Ellerin in the same time period, so that part of the story at least seems plausible." The original note had said that Ellerin had been taken, and the others would be soon.

Sir Raleigh huffed, and I could feel his frustration. While he had been sent to be my companion and guardian, Ellerin had been the one to summon him to do so, and so Sir Raleigh had some loyalty to the gray Fae, who also happened to be my father. I still wanted to know how all that had come about.

The honk of a horn and the roar of an engine alerted me to something coming up behind us. A black Mercedes going twice the speed of traffic wove between the other cars.

"Hold on, ladies." The driver tightened his grip on the wheel. I inhaled deeply and felt for any nearby ley lines or bodies of fresh water. Or caves. I could draw strength from any of them, as well as trees, although since those were living beings, I was reluctant to do so unless necessary.

"What is he doing?" Selene asked. "He doesn't seem to see where he's going."

Our driver pulled into the slow lane as the other car approached, still weaving. The whine of a siren followed them, so at least the police knew of the issue. Or was this a high-speed chase? Hades, I thought I'd left such nonsense behind me in the US.

We all held our breath as the black Mercedes pulled next to us and matched our speed. I exhaled with a whoosh and willed for them to keep going, but they didn't. In fact, they stayed beside us no matter what our driver did, and they crept closer like a predator playing with its prey. Sir Raleigh growled, and I ran a hand over his back.

"What do you sense?"

He didn't answer in so many words, but an impression of a thought came through, that the people in the other car had been looking for us. And now they wanted to hurt us.

The black Mercedes jerked to the side and hit us so hard my internal organs sloshed against my ribs. The sound exploded through the car, and our driver slammed on the brakes, jolting me and leaving me nauseated and shaking. The Mercedes must have anticipated our driver's response because they did the same and slammed into us again. Our car scraped the guard rail, and I'm pretty sure we all screamed. One more hit, and the driver's side window shattered. This time there was no guard rail, just empty air.

CONTINUE the adventure in *Shadows of the Past*! Ask for it at your favorite retailer with ISBN 978-1-945074-71-4

ABOUT THE AUTHOR

By day, clinical psychologist Cecilia Dominic helps people cure their insomnia. By night, this USA Today bestselling urban fantasy and steampunk author writes fiction that keeps her readers turning pages past bedtime. She prefers the term "versatile" to "conflicted" and has published both short story and novel-length fiction. She lives in Atlanta, Georgia, with her husband and the world's cutest cat, who may or may not have been the inspiration for Sir Raleigh.

Read more from author Cecilia Dominic at her website:

ceciliadominic.com

~

Sign up for Cecilia's newsletter and get a free story–or even two–at the following link:
https://www.subscribepage.com/CeciliaDominicbackofbook

If you'd like to be added to a special list just for Fae Files updates, please go to https://www.subscribepage.com/faefilesnews

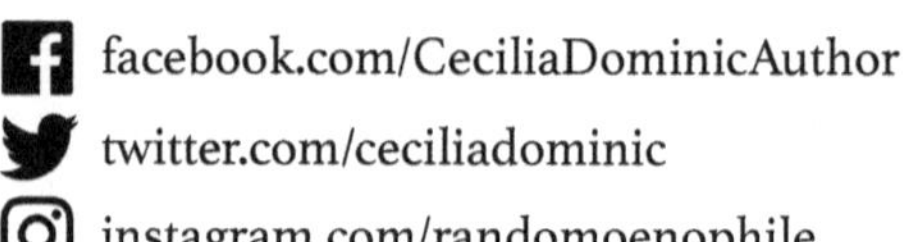

facebook.com/CeciliaDominicAuthor

twitter.com/ceciliadominic

instagram.com/randomoenophile